Eikon

Eikon

The story of a lost miracle

D. Eynon

Authors Choice Press
San Jose New York Lincoln Shanghai

Eikon
The story of a lost miracle

All Rights Reserved © 2000 by D. L. Eynon

No part of this book may be reproduced or transmitted in any form or by any means, graphic, electronic, or mechanical, including photocopying, recording, taping, or by any information storage or retrieval system, without the permission in writing from the publisher.

Authors Choice Press
an imprint of iUniverse.com, Inc.

For information address:
iUniverse.com, Inc.
620 North 48th Street, Suite 201
Lincoln, NE 68504-3467
www.iuniverse.com

ISBN: 0-595-12404-6

Printed in the United States of America

Foreword

❦

"Icon" comes from the Greek word "eikon" meaning "image". The form originated from tomb portraits of Ancient Egypt. Icons were among the first religious objects brought into Russia from Byzantium, at a relatively late date when Christian Art was already highly developed. The technique of the icon—the sacred picture of the Greek Orthodox Church—had apparently reached perfection in the Byzantine world; yet the Russians were able to give it a new, national complexion and produce some of the finest examples of the art.

ICONS—T. Talbot Rice

"The faithful believed that these images, through their likeness to the person represented, became a tangible presence of the Holy and were able to work miracles, deliver oracles, and bring victory on the battlefield...."

Likeness and Presence—Hans Belting

Chapter 1

❁

Novgorod, Spring, 1394

It was the sun he missed the most. Feofan accepted the cold. The barbarous language. The crude brutal way the Boyars exercised their power. But he thirsted for, starved for, the rich sunlight of his Greek island. Even in the city of Constantine, there had been—but never mind what there had been. He was here. Novgorod was now. God had delivered him to this place. God had also provided compensations.

The Russian girl. She must have been a farm girl. Her hands were strong. Rough. Like a man's. A faint smell of cow manure clung to her ragged shawl. But her face was the face of a wingless angel, a moon with eyes, a vessel of innocence. Her face was a flower of desire. Her young body was one of God's softer miracles.

Perhaps the Turks hadn't raped her often. Something had driven her here. Feofan found her in the marketplace. A meeting of eyes. A piece of bread offered. Accepted. She had followed him home, as the last of the sunlight faded early in the afternoon.

"You are Feo…fahn?" The girl's accent was strange. He understood her tone, not her words. She must come from a far region. That would also explain the condition of her feet.

"Feofan." He corrected her.

"Feofan." She stared at the paintings lining the walls. Her head turned slowly, like an owl's. Her look settled on the small panel tilted on the easel. He had finished the Child. The Mother's face was almost done. Except the eyes. He had not yet got Her eyes. Feofan was still struggling with the memory from the city of Constantine. The image of the Virgin painted by St. Luke. St. Luke had painted Her portrait from life, they said. Feofan wanted to catch the feeling seen in those eyes.

"Slawa." The girl crossed herself. She must be Christian.

"Maria." He said. He pointed to the unfinished Virgin. "Maria."

She smiled. Put her finger between her breasts. "Slawa!"

Of course. Her own name. Slawa. The smile brought a different person to her face. The girl…the woman inside, appeared. She pulled off her shawl. Folded the cloth as if it were not a ragged scrap. Placed it on his bed.

Slawa moved to the stove. Began to investigate the pots. He watched her until she appeared content with the pot she found. Then he stepped to the back room for wood. When he returned, she was preparing dinner. The heat from the stove began to fill the room.

They ate together in silence. Slawa dipped her bread into the stew with a delicate motion of roughened fingers. He saw that she had not eaten for a long time. She finished a second bowl. A third. The warmth of the stove on her back, the full belly, made her nod. She fell asleep sitting at the table.

Feofan rose quietly. He lighted a taper. Set the light where it would fall on her face. There was no danger of waking her. She slept as if drugged.

In sleep, her face had relaxed. The caution of the eyes, the pinch of hunger and cold, had faded, as passion fades from a corpse—Feofan had sketched enough corpses to know. But the girl was alive. Her high cheekbones, the full lips. Her hair shining against the rough, threadbare hand-weave of her smock. She still smelled of the outdoors.

Slawa curled herself deeper into the chair. The tiles of the stove were cooling. Soon the room would chill. Feofan banked the fire in the stove. Added three chunks of pine.

He lifted Slawa, at first careful not to awaken her. She slid an arm over his shoulder. Sleepily pressed her face into his neck. Slawa smelled of wet fields and crushed hay. The woman smell of her was strong. Feofan rolled her onto his bed. Threw back the quilts. Made a nest for her against the wall.

Feofan checked the fire. Set the chamberpot within easy reach. He slid into the bed. Drew the quilts over his shoulder. Lay listening to the girl's breathing. The warmth of her body reached him through the darkness like a faintly heard chant. Sleep melted his consciousness of desire. The world went black.

Dawn. It must have been dawn. Or had she got up and lighted a taper? In the light her face looked determined. Resigned. She slid beneath him. Positioned her hips. Took him inside her.

She went through the motions slowly, thrusting her hips as if she were milking a cow. She was practiced. Uninvolved. Doing her chore while she waited for him to finish.

When Feofan didn't finish, she gave up. Her buttocks dropped to the mat. Her thighs relaxed. He continued to probe her. Slowly. Gently persistent. He began to feel changes inside her. Gradually, she turned hot, buttery. Slawa twisted her head to one side. He felt a sudden, short squeeze. Half an instant later she seized him with a swift contraction. Fierce pleasure grew to a furious intensity. Became a painful release. Just as he felt he could not endure another second, she finished.

It was over. Slawa lay with her face still twisted against her right shoulder. After a dozen heartbeats her eyes opened. She turned her face towards him. Her eyes burned with shame, submission, acceptance. Her look flared with the knowledge that she had been taken by something, someone, greater than herself.

"Slawa." He knew she would not understand his words. Feofan put everything into his touch. He felt the tears on her cheek. He kissed her slowly, carefully, pressing his face into her bosom. Gratefully. She had given him the eyes for his picture of Her.

∧ ∧ ∧ ∧ ∧ ∧ ∧ ∧

WASHINGTON, Spring 1990

"You'll need to use some imagination." Morris Reid spoke while he stared out his office windows at the Washington Monument. "Imagination." He swiveled his chair around to face Philip directly. "And you might find it amusing, Phil."

'Imagination.' 'Amusing.' Philip translated the Reid code into plain language. A near-impossible job. A chance to botch his career at State for good and all. Charming, Philip thought, using his own code word. Charming.

"How amusing?" Philip didn't bother to conceal his wariness.

"Middle Europe. Rare art. It's just your line of country." Since he'd moved to Potomac Reid had begun sprinkling his pronouncements with horsey-set clichés. 'Middle Europe.' That was meant to suggest that Philip might get the Austrian desk one day. But what did rare art mean? Reid had already built the trap with Middle Europe. Now it was time for Reid to jiggle the bait.

"If you make a success of this one, Phil...." Reid dropped into a confidential tone, steepled his fingers, impregnated his pause with ineffable promise. "Well, someone will have to run the Austrian desk, when Pete Anderson takes retirement next year."

Success. That was to be the bait. Reid was shrewd enough to know that Philip didn't want for money. His great-grandfather's textile mills had seen to that. Reid was careful to go for the one nerve he knew would make Philip jump. Success. The Austrian desk.

For half a second, success in all it's many-splendored forms flashed through Philip's mind. The success his father had achieved as a soldier and then as a lawyer—just before the old man died so dramatically, leaving Philip a legend with which to compete.

Success. The endless pursuit of matching his father's matchless prominence. While Reid lighted a cigarette Phillip recalled the briefly-enjoyed success of getting into Yale. At Yale, success had shifted; the goal was getting into Alice Wentworth's pants. Alice, armed with the powers of natural selection, had been far more artful than Reid in motivating Philip. The results were named Susan, Elizabeth, and John. Now Morris Reid was dangling the Austrian desk.

"What do you want me to accomplish?" Philip nibbled at the bait, as if he still had a choice. The fumes of Reid's Marlboro drifted across the room. Reid knew exactly how long to pause for effect.

"This comes from the White House." Across the vastness of his mahogany desk Reid opened a folder. A twinge of panic struck Philip. The White House. The White House meant an urgent, probably irrational, demand. Something that could affect even Reid's career at State. Philip had taken the bait too soon. He should have bargained for a promise of the Austrian Desk. A firm promise—as firm as any Reid promise—before he agreed to consider the assignment. Reid had short-changed him again.

"The Hungarians—*our* Hungarians, not the Red ones—are looking for something they think is in this country."

"An art treasure," Philip filled in. I may not be as crafty as you, Mr. Reid, but I can think just as fast.

Reid nodded a *touché*. "Their embassy got to the White House. We're asked to cooperate."

"Why us? Does this involve diplomatic immunity?"

"The CIA can't operate inside the U.S."

"Technically."

"Technically." Reid nodded. "The FBI is…not always adroit."

"And leaks like a sieve."

"There's also the question of legality. Statute of limitations. What all."

"You mean this art treasure wasn't stolen."

"Not recently, at least. It was 'liberated'."

"Liberated?" An image of sexually promiscuous young women winked into Philip's memory. Chieko Willensky in the Department library.

"In World War II. From the Nazis. When American troops invaded Germany." Reid made his voice sound matter-of-fact as he laid out the details. His adroitly casual tone was another danger sign Philip recognized.

You bastard, he thought. You took on this crazy request because it came from the White House. Now you're going to stick me with it. If it goes down the drain, I spend the rest of my career in a windowless office, stamping passports. If it succeeds…if *I* succeed…*you* trot over to the White House and take credit for it. You'll….

"We'll get details when we meet with…" Reid tilted the folder to read, "…Tibor Szilágyi. He's a Third Secretary of their Embassy. Szilágy's coming over for lunch. There isn't a whole lot of time to get this job done." Morris Reid closed the folder and slid it into the center drawer of his desk.

Of course not. There's never time for anything really urgent. Especially to find an art treasure "liberated" in Germany half a century ago. Was Reid crazy? No. Reid was just passing on an absurd assignment. Or perhaps Philip's own mind had finally slipped into his often-feared dementia, that living dream where his constant chase after success ended in his constant disappointment. Or in bed with Alice Newbold Wentworth, now Downs; the only real, renewable success in his life.

Philip realized, with dismay, that he had not even accepted the assignment. Reid had simply assumed his acceptance. And moved ahead, into the details. For Philip to protest now would cause serious embarrassment for both of them.

∧   ∧   ∧   ∧   ∧   ∧   ∧   ∧

Nádudvar, September, 1944

"*Jesus Gott*, why didn't you reserve some tanks?" In the chill of the evening, the *Gauleiter*'s face shone with sweat. He had changed his party uniform for a double-breasted suit. Dark blue. Pin stripe. Very British. Except for the bulging gut and the thick neck that anchored a head like an overblown Edam cheese. The *Gauleiter* stank of raw schnapps and blood sausage.

"There are partisans on every road! You have *failed* in your duty! Your superiors will soon learn of this, Herr Oberst, believe me!"

"Tanks do not have room for baggage, Herr Gauleiter." The *Oberst* looked at the suitcases, boxes, bundles, stacked on both sides of the doorway. On top of the left-hand pile he could see a gold monstrance, some folded vestments, and the gilded edge of a framed icon. "You have been to church, Herr Gauleiter? One last prayer, perhaps—for a safe journey."

"My safety is *your* responsibility! My journey is your responsibility! My *transport* is your responsibility! For failing such responsibility, men have been shot. Even Obersts!"

"One lorry. One staff car. Petrol enough for a hundred kilometers." The *Oberst* listened for a second to the approaching thunder of the Russian heavies. Malinovsky's T-34s were closing on Debrecen. "You might reach Army Group IV."

"Without protection? While every road is crawling with partisans? What are you *doing* to me!"

"Already, Herr Gruber, German soldiers are dying for want of the truck and the petrol you are using to remove your booty. Every minute you stand here whining, you decrease your chances of surviving even this one night. I suggest you stop your sniveling. Squeeze your fat ass into that staff car. And flee for your miserable life—while you still have it!"

"Be *careful* of those—those are valuable cultural artifacts!" The *Gauleiter* burst his fury at the *Landser* who picked up the monstrance and the icon. He stamped out behind the soldier. From the darkness, his voice reached the *Oberst* like the bloated scream of a pig being butchered. "You have not heard the last of this, Herr Oberst! I *promise* you!"

∧ ∧ ∧ ∧ ∧ ∧ ∧ ∧

WASHINGTON, D.C. Spring 1990

The food in the Executive dining-room was institutional elegant. High on presentation. Less on actual nourishment. The idea was to confer status, to provide privacy for discussion. And, for visitors, to impress.

Tibor Szilágyi was careful to be impressed. His elaborate Middle European manners were countered by a frankness in his voice. Gold was a prominent feature of his dental work. You would never buy a used car from Tibor. You might well accept his advice on women.

"Of course, World War II. Such a long, long time ago, yes?" Tibor agreed to Reid's point with a disarming chuckle. "We do not make little of the difficulties. But you people have such...." his eyebrow formed a sensuous curve as he glanced around the dining-room, "...such wonderful resources. Yes?"

"But how can you possibly *know*? That the icon came to this country?" Philip turned from Reid to Tibor, trying not to slip into the "good cop -bad cop" routine.

"Ah. Just so. Yes." Tibor smiled, pressed the air with his palms. "We know the painting is no longer in Europe." He shrugged a concession that his statement sounded absurd. The Hungarian's face, tired but agile, shifted from apology to resignation. Philip sensed it would be possible to like this man. He reminded himself of the danger that personal feeling always carried.

"You've scoured the Continent, as it were." Morris Reid was helping Szilágy along. And why not? It wouldn't be Morris who would have to take the hit for this bizarre nonsense.

"We have had forty-five years. Yes?"

"Then why come to us now?" Philip asked.

Tibor paused. He studied Reid for a few seconds. He appraised Philip. He adjusted himself in his chair and moved his coffee cup aside.

"Might either of you gentlemen be…what one would say is…'religious'? Or is that a subject one does not discuss at lunch?—you must forgive me if I make a personal intrusion. Yes?" Szilágy's smile worked hard to disarm the question.

Philip waited. Morris Reid could field this question.

"Well, technically I suppose. I'm Episcopalian. Phil?" Morris gave Philip a look of stage inquiry.

"Presbyterian. With a Quaker wife."

"Ah. Technically, you *are* religious. Yes. But do you…." Tibor sucked his lower lip in concentration,"…do you accept, for instance, miracles?" His look moved from Reid to Philip and back.

"Not in the State Department, we don't." Philip spoke too soon. It had gotten him into trouble before. But Tibor smiled.

"You would not be inclined, I think, to see God's hand in the outcome of an election, for example. Yes? Your American people would not, that is. Your ordinary citizens."

"As a *political* issue, religion's always tricky," Reid said. "Religion cost Al Smith the Presidential election in 1928." Reid was a master of the precise historical reference that revealed no personal position, made no official commitment.

"How so, please?"

"Smith was a Roman Catholic. He made no bones about it."

"But surely...your President Kennedy?" Tibor looked puzzled.

"Two wars and thirty years later."

"Ah. Just so. But in my country, God, the church, politics...these remain strongly together."

"And the communists?" Reid asked.

"Godless, of course. Yes? But also *departed*. For the moment. God willing, forever. Perhaps. If only there were a sign from God that...." Tibor looked to each of them, searching their eyes for comprehension.

The Hungarian suddenly put the tip of his index finger on the tablecloth and drew a wide circle arounfd his cup and saucer. "Once you are out of the cities...Once you are in the agricultural regions...you have gone back many, *many* centuries. Away from electric music. Television. Drugs. Yes? The people have simple lives. They do not afford television. They have no money for drugs. In the middle of their lives is only the church. Their belief in God. Yes?"

The Hungarian's eyes appraised his audience. Reid's face remained politely attentive. Philip leaned forward in his chair, a trick of body language he had learned while on a Transactional Management course at Georgetown University.

"The Mother of God from St. Emeric's has made miracles. In the 15th Century, the presence of Her image turned back the soldiers of the Sultan. She rallied our warriors. She put fear in the hearts of our enemies. She saved the town of Nádudvar from devastation."

Tibor smiled and pressed the air with his palms, in case he had not been believed. "Here in your so pleasant dining-room, such an idea may appear...unbelievable. Yes? In the Debrecen region, however, this belief lingers strong."

The Hungarian paused. Smiled a calculated smile. Tilted his head. "For you...perhaps for me, also...this icon is no more than a painting. Exquisitely beautiful. Yes? *Valuable*. Yes? But no more than a treasured portrait of the Virgin. Yes?"

Szilágyi looked across the dining room, focusing on some point beyond infinity. "For the simple people of Nádudvar region, this icon *is* the Virgin. *Their* Virgin." He shifted his look quickly, to see if Reid and Philip understood. Believed. "And do not forget. When She disappeared, when She was taken off by the Nazis…" Tibor shrugged his Q.E.D., "…darkness followed. Yes? Forty-five years of darkness." Szilágy's voice changed into that of another man, in a time far distant from the warm atmosphere of the Executive Dining room. "Darkness black as the anger of God."

There was a long pause. Szilágyi waited for one of them to speak. Reid looked at Philip. Philip reluctantly took the cue.

"So if your Mother of God were to reappear at this point…." Philip leaned back in his chair. The Hungarian's story was intriguing, but Philip was determined to divorce himself from any responsibility for bringing this miracle about.

"Ah! If She were to come back…." the Hungarian's voice went inward, the muscles around his eyes moved,"…the simple peasants of that Eastern district, they would see Her return as a sign from God. Yes? A promise that the darkness was lifted for good. These simple people…they would be given heart to support a Democratic government. Yes?" He looked at Reid, as the clear source of power in this situation, the one to be persuaded. "And your people at the White House. They would like this, I think. Yes? What do *you* think?"

That evening Philip was still thinking of the Hungarian's words, when he and his wife left the Georgetown Theater. Leecie tugged at his sleeve to get his attention.

"I said, 'Isn't it wonderful the way Meryl Streep managed a Polish accent?'"

"Accent? Yes, I suppose…" he had missed much of the picture's dialogue, instead ruminating about Tibor Szilágy's story. "Accents are probably easier to acquire than to lose." He smiled, recalling the splatter of "yeses" in Szilágy's speech. "For an actress, anyway." They turned up N street towards the car.

"My God!" Leecie's awed tone shocked Philip from his ruminations. "The car's been broken into!"

Philip strode ahead, careful to wave Leecie away from the pulverized window glass. Inside, the contents of the glove compartment were scattered on the seat and floor. The parking dimes and quarters had been scooped from the compartment between the front seats.

Philip got the snow brush from the trunk and swept the glass fragments into the gutter. It was a standard urban encounter. Only later, after Tibor was in the hospital, did he connect it with the Hungarian and the Eikon.

∧ ∧ ∧ ∧ ∧ ∧ ∧ ∧

PASSAU, Winter, 1945

The fresh snow had thrown a blanket of silence over which distant sounds floated. The bleak murmur of the *Donau* rose from below the house. In the dead black he could hear the American's breathing. Slow. Deep. The contented oblivion of a man who has screwed and drunk far too well. He listened for another minute, careful in case there was a girl in the bed. From across the river the bell in *St. Stephan's Kirche* struck the hour. 2 AM. The last echo of the bell died in the darkness. He gripped the hatchet in both hands.

The American stirred. The rustle of sheets, the muffled breathing were like eyesight for the man poised in the darkness. He could smell the Lucky Strikes the American had been smoking. He raised on the balls of his feet and brought the hatchet down, all his weight behind the blow. He felt the blade wedge into the man's skull. Wrenched the hatchet loose. Struck again. The pillow cushioned the impact, but the hatchet was sharp. After the third blow, he waited. There was no sound of breathing. The damp warm odor of blood rose to his nostrils. Sweat trickled down the back of his neck.

Had anyone else in the house heard? He held his breath. In the deep darkness, the slightest sound struck like a blazing light. He suddenly had the sixth sense that the blind develop. Carefully, counting his heartbeats to measure the time, he waited long enough to be sure the other two Americans had not been awakened. Seventy five heartbeats. One hundred. One hundred fifty. All was silent. He shifted the hatchet to his left hand. Slowly, placing each foot with practiced care, he turned to go to the next bedroom.

∧ ∧ ∧ ∧ ∧ ∧ ∧ ∧

WASHINGTON, Spring 1990

Philip called his insurance agent and reported the damage to the VW. Then he buzzed his secretary.

"Would you send Mr. Szilágy in, please, Kathie?"

Tibor was wearing the same tired brown suit. His necktie matched the odor of tobacco he brought with him. His briefcase looked like a road kill.

The Hungarian accepted the chair Philip offered. Settled his briefcase on the floor, looked around for an ashtray. He turned to Philip, raising a hand to forestall any comment. Tibor balanced his half-finished Gauloise on the edge of a pool-sized ashtray.

"Mr. Downs, before you begin to ask your questions. Please, permit me to assure you that I quite understand. Yes? Many, many hesitations you must have about what I have told you. Yes?" He flicked his head towards the door through which Reid had just departed. "It is easy for your superiors to accept our request. Yes? Especially, I think, when such a request comes from your people at the White House. Yes?

"But I am not just some crazy foreigner who makes this absurd request. I understand something else, yes? It is *you* who will do the actual work. Not your superiors. Not the White House. Yes?"

The Hungarian's manner weakened Philip's reserve. He had always felt a dim sense of inferiority, dealing with a anyone who had learned to speak English much better than Philip could ever have spoken the other person's language.

"So it is *you* I must convince. Yes? Therefore I ask you. Express for me now whatever doubts you have—and you must have *many*, I think? Yes?" Tibor's hands massaged the air in front of him. "Have no fear that I will find you…impolite? Yes? Am I being clear, I hope?"

"Perfectly clear." Philip smiled at his unintended Nixonism.

"So you will tell me now, please, all your doubts. Yes? I shall be very grateful. Yes? It also may be that I can help you succeed. And impress your Mr. Reid. Yes?"

Philip leaned forward, carefully shifting his position in the leather chair to give himself time to think. Candor was not his daily bread in the Department. Mr. Tibor Szilágyi was neither boy scout, fellow Ivy-leaguer, nor English gentleman. Caution was advised. Finally Philip decided he might with prudence advance one unobjectionable misgiving.

"It seems remarkable to me, Mr. Szilágy, that you could be so certain. So sure your icon was taken by two American soldiers. Two *specific* soldiers, that is. Yet not know their identities."

"Ah! You are right. How could we know the one fact, and not know the other. Yes?"

"How, indeed."

"I will tell you. It is because we have been working slowly. Very slowly, yes? We had no choice. Once the Red Army came to Hungary, people who cared about such things as God and holy icons were scattered. Disorganized. Struggling for our lives. Yes? We could not even begin our search until…" his eyes went back in time and searched some interior place, clearly an unpleasant region,"…until years after the war." Tibor gave a professional shrug.

"And 'years after the war', you were still able to establish that your icon was taken by American soldiers."

Szilágyi paused to offer a Gauloise from his pack, accepted Philip's refusal, then lit his own. He drew deeply. Exhaled a cloud that made Philip's office smell like the Paris Metro at rush hour. He poised his Gauloise with care on the rim of the ashtray.

"You have read Sherlock Holmes, yes? 'When one eliminates all other possibilities, the one possibility left—no matter how strange this may appear to you—this *must* be the one.' Yes?" Tibor looked carefully at Philip, head tilted, the skin crinkling around his eyes. "We worked as your Mr. Sherlock Holmes worked. Yes? It took us many years. We had no money. Yes? We had no official…standing, no status. But in the end, a *single* possibility *was* left. Two soldiers. Two *American* soldiers."

Tibor retrieved his Gauloise from the rim of the ashtray. "By that time, it was the nineteen fifties." He inhaled deeply, like a man who remembers when cigarettes were as scarce and costly as gold.

"The two soldiers—whoever they were—they had long since gone back to America. You remember 1956? Probably you are too young. We had other things to occupy us, in 1956. Yes? Unfortunately, the Communists remained in power. Despite everything. They had the tanks, yes? In those terrible years there was no point in seeking the return of a religious relic. Also, we still had no standing. We were not the government. Yes?"

"I can understand that, Mr. Szilágyi. But *two* soldiers? Out of the whole United States Army?"

"You doubt. Yes?" Tibor's chuckle, soft as a cat's purr, teased at Philip. He broke it off, sucked at the cigarette, and blew out a gust of smoke. "But I play with you. I should not play with you. You are not a fool. Yes? Of *course*, we know more about these soldiers. Much more. We know they were in a particular place. Yes? At an exact time. Yes? We know also their military unit. More than that, we do not know." He carefully stubbed out his Gauloise, now burned so short that Philip wondered how the man could hold it without scorching his fingertips.

"But *I'm* supposed to find out."

"God willing."

"And then, if they're still alive...and if they still have your icon..."

"Oh, they have it. I assure you, Mr. Downs. These men have it. There is no other possibility."

"As in Sherlock Holmes."

"Sherlock Holmes. Yes." Tibor's chuckle purred again in the tranquil elegance of Reid's walnut paneling and leather furniture. "Yes, Mr. Downs, as in Sherlock Holmes. *They have it.*"

"And where am I suppose to start, then, Mr. Szilágy?"

"You will begin," said the Hungarian, as he unlatched his wearied briefcase, "with a triple murder. Yes?"

Tibor pulled out a wad of notes as tattered as his briefcase. He slid his chair nearer to Philip, lighted another Gauloise, started his story.

When Tibor finally departed Philip emptied the ashtray into his wastebasket and sat in silent contemplation. He searched his mind for a way out. A sudden illness? Resignation? A career change? Back to school for a Ph.D.? He was kidding himself. There was no escape.

So then, where did he start? A maxim oft quoted by Downs *Pere* popped up, like a help window in WordPerfect: when in doubt, collect information. Right. Information, then. Which meant research. Which meant the Department Library. And that meant Chieko Willensky. Philip opened the Department phone directory and found her extension.

"Ms. Willensky? Philip Downs."

"Yes, Mr. Downs." Chieko's voice was pleasantly businesslike. She had the clear, soft, Southern California accent of a Sansei. Nothing in her manner suggested that she and Philip were more than casually acquainted. Yet a summer ago, when Leesie had taken the children to Rehobeth to stay with her parents for August, Chieko and Philip had met inadvertently when he stopped for a hamburger at the Third Edition on Pennsylvania Avenue.

They had recognized each other as being from the Department, shared a table, and through a chain of signals Philip still didn't understand, found themselves back at Chieko's studio in the Watergate, making the beast with two backs. All he learned about her was her B.Sci from UCLA, her divorce from Willensky, and her prudence about precautions. This was the first time since that he had spoken with her.

"Chieko, I need some information."

"What may I help you with, Mr. Downs?"

"World War II."

"The Japanese lost, Mr. Downs."

"I'm concerned with the war in Europe, Ms. Willensky."

"Then the Germans lost."

"Yes. I understand, Ms. Willensky." Philip paused for an angle of attack that wouldn't get him deep into innuendo. "What I'm concerned with is locating two veterans. Of the war in Europe."

"You're a bit late. There's no directory."

"I thought you might have…sources."

"I do. Can you give me names?"

"Not yet."

"Social security numbers? *Anything*?"

"Soon, I think."

"So your question now is both exploratory and hypothetical."

"That puts it precisely, Ms. Willensky."

"I could make inquiries."

"I'd be obliged, Chieko." He dropped the pretense of formality, tried to sound both serious and sincere.

"You will be," Chieko said. "You surely will be obliged, Mr. Downs. I'll call you."

∧   ∧   ∧   ∧   ∧   ∧   ∧   ∧

PASSAU December 1945

The killer would soon be back. She knew he would be back. Despite the Americans. Even after the murders. He would be back to look for the painting. And if he found the painting, found it with her, he would surely kill her. Exactly as he killed the Major and the other American officers. If an American officer could not be safe from him—*Lieber Gott!*—what chance had a defenseless old woman? Her hands began to shake. To die like *that*!

Should she tell the Americans? Give them the Holy Mother? But then, whoever had come in the night would *know* she was the one. He would surely kill her, without mercy.

The old woman left the lights off and stepped carefully into the bedroom where the Major used to sleep. Before he moved across the road, to the villa. Before he was hacked to death in the darkness. The bedroom still smelled of American cigarettes. That girl's perfume. The girl would never talk. Now that the Major was dead, the girl would never be seen here again.

The old woman found the footstool in the darkness. Slowly—her aged knees no longer bent easily—she raised herself on the footstool until she was high enough to feel blindly above the clothes press for the painting, still wrapped in a Wehrmacht blanket.

The old woman stopped, listening to the grind of an engine as it drew closer. Brakes squeaked softly from the darkened street. A jeep. More Americans. About the murders. But soon, the Americans would go away. Then *he* would return. To look for what the Major had hidden. When he found nothing across the street, he would come to this house.

She clutched the bundle, remembering this morning as she watched the Major's body being carried out of the Villa Kohler. Tonight. Tomorrow morning. It could be her corpse on the stretcher.

The thought of her lying on a stretcher, her head smashed by a hatchet, put new strength into her protesting legs. She headed for the cellar. She needed no light to find her way out the back cellar door. Night air struck her face. She listened. Nothing. Started across the yard, her footsteps silenced by the fresh-fallen snow. At the gate she stopped again, already frozen with terror. The alley was empty. The Americans had parked their jeep in the side street. The only sound was metallic gurgles from the cooling engine.

Was there an American soldier waiting in the jeep? She looked for the glow of a cigarette, listened for the creak of seat springs. She sniffed. An American would always be smoking a cigarette. There was nothing. Only the gasoline smell. The jeep was empty.

The old woman started out into the street. She was almost at the end of the alley when she saw it. Far ahead. At the end of the street and just beyond. A shadow moved, inside the shadows.

The old woman hugged the Lady within the blanket and begged. Pleaded. Holy Mother! Not *now*! Not me! Not after the bombings and the Russian soldiers and all the terrible losses of all the frightful years! Blessed Lady! Leave me my life! Mother of God, only my life!

Stiff with terror, the old woman recited the prayers of her childhood. *Gegrusst seist du, Maria, voll der Gnade…*

No more shadows moved. Across the Danube, somewhere in the town, a truck engine growled. The bells of St. Stephan's sounded the quarter hour. The old woman's panic subsided to terror. The sweat turned cold on her face.

The Americans had parked their jeep against the curb, the door loosely latched. She fumbled with the door latch, cold metal against her fingertips. The door swung out. She caught a smell of male sweat, gasoline, cigarette smoke. The back of the jeep was empty, except for a gas can and a folded tarpaulin. She lifted the tarpaulin and slid her bundle underneath. Closed the door. Fled.

Back in her house, the old woman began. Over and over. *Heilige Maria Mutter Gottes…* Her knees went dead. *…bitte fur uns Sunder….* She heard the jeep's engine rasp into life. *…jezt und in der Stunde* *unseres Todes*…. The gears meshed. The sound of the jeep slid off into the snowy silence. *Gegrusst seist du, Maria*….

∧ ∧ ∧ ∧ ∧ ∧ ∧ ∧

WASHINGTON, Spring 1990

"I've made a start on your search, Mr. Downs." Chieko's voice on the phone was mock-businesslike. "When would you like to see the prelims?"

"Now." Philip felt a surge of elation, tinged with caution.

"I'll be free at lunchtime, Mr. Downs."

"This is going to cost me?"

"Your virginity." She said the words with whispered precision.

"But I'm not—"

"An illusion soon shattered. Lunch is off, Mr. Downs? Or is it on?" She used the disinterested voice of a ticket broker.

"The Third Edition?"

"*My* place. Twelve-fifteen."

"Uh…."

"Be there."

The phone went dead.

At the Watergate lobby Philip realized that he had forgotten—if indeed he had ever known—the number of her apartment, but located Willensky on the name board. Chieko buzzed him in.

"Look familiar?" Chieko stepped back from the doorway for him to pass. She had done her studio in Museum of Modern Art decor. More trendy than comfortable. Her sound system was well balanced and well hidden. The scent of sandlewood was muted.

"What…. what did you turn up?"

"A friend at the National Archives, who can move through the records like a ferret. Here's from microfiche of the Army newspaper,

Germany 1945." She dropped a sheaf of hard copy onto the Parsons couch. "You can skim these while you undress."

"Un—"

"You knew it was going to cost you, Mr. Downs."

"For a handful of Xerox pages?" He looked at the copies. News stories from *The New York Times* and *The Stars & Stripes*.

Chieko stopped, her blouse half off. She studied his face for a moment, then sighed.

"Look, Mr. Downs, you want information. World War II. In a hurry. Right?"

"I think we're agreed on that."

"The time lag at the Archives is four months. For a *rush* job. I've got contacts that deliver overnight."

"For a price."

"You've got the picture. You can hang your skivvies over my bedpost, or you can slip back into your unmentionables and go get in line at the Archives, Mr. Downs." She undid the last buttons of her blouse and stood holding her panty hose. "Take your pick."

"Why me?" Philip made a last grasp for some dignity before his surrender.

"Hoping for compliments, Mr. Downs?" Chieko was naked now. As she handed him a glass of Chablis, she chuckled. "No way. Because I've got you checked out and nailed down. That's why *you*."

She strode across the bedroom and dropped a pillow on the floor next to the bed. "Point A—you're in a jam with Morris Reid. You need information in a hurry."

As his sense of reality swept away, Philip watched her set her glass on the bedside table, open a drawer, and select a condom.

"Point B—you're married, forty-six, clean-living, and strait-laced. That means no talkies. No complaints. Right, Mr. Downs? Put this on, please." She handed him the condom.

"You know all this?" He fumbled, opening the plastic packet.

"Personnel records. Security checks."

"But...they're confidential."

"Right. On your knees, please, Mr. Downs."

"Wha—" Her voice had been so matter-of-fact that he was sure he'd misunderstood her words. The condom had misled him. Was this her revenge for last summer? A power trip? A joke?

"You heard, Mr. Downs." She pointed to the pillow by the bedside. "Pay up—or push off."

As he sank to the pillow Chieko straddled him and with a firm, gentle grip guided his head. Philip's mind stopped working. When she was finally satisfied, her thighs released him. Chieko sighed. Handed him his glass of wine.

"Like to brush your teeth, Mr. Downs? There's a guest brush in the bathroom."

"You...Checked me out." Philip came back from the bath and picked up the Xeroxes.

"And I can nail your butt to the wall, with one call to Mrs. Downs." There was no serious threat in Chieko's voice. Just the satisfaction of being in control.

"And the rest of the information I need?" Philip knotted his tie and checked his wristwatch.

"All yours. Whenever you need it, Mr. Downs." Chieko snapped the waistband of her pantyhose into place. "But you'll have to give me actual names or more details." She took the wine glasses into her Pullman kitchen. Chieko turned back towards Philip and smiled. "And naturally, Mr. Downs, you'll have to pay."

When Philip got back to his desk there was a phone note from Morris Reid's secretary. Reid wanted to see him at 3:00. He had just enough time to digest the Xeroxed news items, then he stopped in the men's room, checked his appearance, and went up to Reid's office.

"I've made this...tentative plan." Philip had learned it was well to be authoritative with Reid, but still leave Reid room to contribute.

Reid nodded. Agreement. Permission to continue. A paucity of ideas on his own part.

"We've got to accept the Hungarians' premise. There isn't time to do otherwise. Or resources."

Reid gave a diagonal nod. It was enough for Reid that the White House had asked for this. That validated any effort.

"First, we try to locate these men. Whoever they are. Wherever they are. *If* they are. Still alive, that is." Philip studied his notes.

"Second, we'll need to check with Web David, in Legal. What's the status of this thing, this icon? If they do have it. Is it theirs? Booty from the war? Or is it…well, you see the problem." Reid had put on his interested face, but his eyes were barely present. Boredom had set in. Philip speeded up his delivery. "What's the legal status of this picture? If we do locate the thing?"

Reid's face tightened at the "if". Phillip saw his mistake and quickly ended his report. "Finally, we need some art expertise. Who could validate this icon? We could find ourselves negotiating for a fake."

"Good." Reid woke up and shuffled through his folders. "I'm glad you've thought this through. I've got you some help on part A. One of the FBI's better people. Something of an expert on 'skip tracing'."

Reid passed a business card across his desk. "You'll want to meet with him as soon as you can. The White House called again this morning…"

"Right." Philip accepted the card. The White House called again. Asking for the near impossible. Now you're going to put the pressure on me.

"When do you think we can tell them something?"

"Ah." Philip smiled. Reid returned a grimace that recognized the futility of his own question.

"Well, it's their job to ask for the impossible, Phil. That's how these people get to the White House," Reid said. "Our job is to use imagination."

"Well, I can't imagine when we'll be able to tell them something—maybe after I've talked with this FBI man." Make no judgement until you have all the facts. He had learned that from his father.

"Get to him a soon as you can." Reid gave Philip a nod. He began to shuffle through his folders for the next problem. Philip studied the note on his way out of the office. A name. A phone number. Another chance to use imagination. Another chance for success.

^ ^ ^ ^ ^ ^ ^ ^

BAVARIA, Autumn, 1945

The girl could have been 15, 16, 17. She had breasts but no makeup. High cheekbones. Dark brown eyes that cautiously measured his uniform, inspected his jeep, took in the press camera he was holding.

"You wish me to get you a horse?" Husky voice, taut eyes.

"For an hour or so. I haven't been on a horse for quite awhile."

She slid from the Pinzgauer's back. The horse followed her as she strode to the fence.

"If I get you a horse, what do you give me?" She was all business. Her manner suggested she was mistress of the land on which she stood.

"How about a photograph?" Lewis slid the film holder from his Speed Graphic. His shot of her on the small, Tiger-spotted horse would be spectacular: the two of them against the autumn sky, an ancient schloss in the background. In the stem of Lewis's brain, complex chemicals had begun to form, seeping into his cortex to trigger commands to his glands, transform his view of her.

"*Cigaretten.* My mother is liking American cigarettes." She waited, her eyes level on his, to see if she had a deal.

"Yes. Fine. Cigarettes." He nodded. A tiny breeze lifted the leaves of the oak tree on the fence line. He watched her use the back of her hand to wipe the perspiration from her forehead. The smell of her sweat, mingling with the perfume of the newly mown hay field, hastened the chemical productions in Lewis's medulla.

"How *many* cigarettes, please?" The deal was not yet closed.

"One hour, one pack?" Lewis waited for an answer.

She slipped onto the horse's back. The curve of her thighs, swelling as she gripped the horse's sides, twitched Lewis's nervous system. He studied her as a possible lay. She evaluated him; a well scrubbed, neatly uniformed cigarette machine.

"As you wish." The deal was set. She was lady of the manor again. "Sunday. In the afternoon." The small horse swung around, answering the pressure of her calves. Lewis watched her turn the horse up the hill. She had hindquarters like a Shetland pony. When she squeezed the horse into a canter the two of them moved together, like a single animal. She would probably be good over timber.

∧ ∧ ∧ ∧ ∧ ∧ ∧ ∧

WASHINGTON, Spring 1990

The J. Edgar Hoover Building had always struck Philip as the ultimate monument to paranoia. It hung above Pennsylvania Avenue, the most expensive public building ever built, a looming concrete expression of J. Edgar's mind set. Philip was signed in and given a visitor's badge. Escorted to the proper area. Directed to the office of Alasdair Murphy. "Alasdair T. Murphy, III", as it said on his card.

"It's a matter of doing one's homework," Murphy's pudgy fingers tugged at his regimental striped tie. "We can find anybody. Dead or alive." Murphy's face, which appeared to be made of eraser material, moved as if fingers inside were shifting his features. He wore a shaving lotion that must have come from South America. "I take it this is a 'hush hush' matter?"

"We'd like to be discreet."

"I thought so. I can smell these things." His fingers worked at the knot of his tie. "Well, you've come to the right place. Who are we looking for?"

"Two American soldiers. From World War II."

"Military types, eh? I know the territory." Murphy's tie knot got another twist. "Done a few hitches, myself."

"I thought you might have." Philip nodded at Murphy's tie. "Your tie."

"Oh, that. Yes." Murphy looked down admiringly at the silk band with the wide blue and narrow green stripe. "A present from my opposite number—in British Intelligence."

"You were in Military Intelligence?" Philip almost let his surprise show.

"I came out as a Major." The fingers inside Murphy's face squeezed on a look of modesty. "So we're looking for Military. Duck soup. Names? Ranks? Serial numbers?"

"We're not certain." Try that flavor of duck soup. Philip watched as Murphy's face went shrewd, then cautious. "We know their unit. We know a date on which they were in that unit. We know a specific assignment they carried out."

"So. First we trace the unit." Murphy ticked off the steps finger by finger. "Then we get the morning reports. Serial numbers. Select our targets. Follow up with date of discharge. Track them through their GI insurance. Maybe they used the GI bill to go to college. It's labor intensive," Murphy put both hands to smooth his tie and smoothed the striped silk. "But we can do it."

"When might we expect some results?" Philip hated himself for using the Reid technique.

"You'll know as soon as we know." Murphy smiled, the good doctor reassuring the troubled patient. He rose, to let Philip know that the interview was over. "Just leave the details with us. I'll call you."

As they shook hands, the South American shaving lotion asserted itself with new rhythms. Murphy suddenly noticed Philip's tie.

"Navy?"
"Yale."

∧ ∧ ∧ ∧ ∧ ∧ ∧ ∧

GEORGETOWN, Spring, 1990

Clyde's Omelette Room was filled for Brunch. Not the best place to talk. But Leecie—*neé* Alice Newbold Wentworth—loved to get away from the children on Sunday mornings. They had given the Baxters a lift to Georgetown after attending Bethesda Friends Meeting, so it hadn't been possible to talk in the car.

"Of course he's given me some help. Reid isn't a complete ass. His idea of help, though, turned out to be some clod from the FBI."

"Well, then." Leecie returned the menu to their waitress and ordered her usual mushroom omelette.

"Well, then," he imitated her Bryn Mawr vowels, "I've only got to find these people, assuming any of them are still alive. Then shake this looted art treasure out of them. With threats, promises, sweet reason—God knows what. And then get it back to the Hunkies before their next election. Their *first* election, probably. Maybe their last."

"I'm sure you can do it." Leecie looked around the room for acquaintances. "Morris Reid wouldn't have given you the job, would he? If he didn't believe you could do it."

Philip looked at her face to be certain she wasn't teasing. No, Leecie was just oblivious to the trap Reid had dumped him in. He sighed. She was such a good lay. She knew everyone worth knowing. More important, she knew how to *get along* with everyone worth knowing. That patrician profile. The Bryn Mawr accent. Phil could thank God for giving him such a wife. But why had an otherwise generous God dumped all Leecie's brains between her legs?

"There's Tessie Winslow!" Leecie's hand wig-wagged a greeting across the room. A plumpish woman with auburn hair sent a return semaphore, then nudged the man beside her. The man looked up. Smiled. Nodded. He appeared to be considerably Tessie's senior. The tribal gestures between the women arranged for their parties to merge.

Phil stood up to make room for Tessie and her husband at the table. The waitress, informed of the change of *venue*, looked sullen but manageable. Phil was introduced to Tessie's husband, clearly a man Tessie had selected as a father substitute. At least she had picked a clean old man, Phil thought. Mr. Tessie had the tight cheeks and well-brushed hair that said retired military. A few oblique references brought a wry admission from Walter.

"Right. I'm a double-dipper. Did my thirty years in the Army. Now I'm counting beans at the Postal Service. The PMG's office. It keeps me off the streets. You're with—"

"State. Counting passport applications."

Walter Winslow gave a courtesy chuckle. He had the older man's eagerness to be accepted among the young. Phil was amused to find himself, Leecie, Tessie, considered "young". He felt older than God.

"Phil's been given one of those awful jobs that no one else could do, so he's being a bear these days," Leecie apologized to Tessie. Phil looked left and right without moving his head. Was there anyone who could hear? Washington was the worst place on earth to shoot your mouth off, even if your grandfather was a Senator. *Especially* if your grandfather was a senator.

"Why didn't he just refuse?" Tessie looked at Phil, but spoke to Leecie. She spoke with the wisdom of those who enjoyed generations of influence and a substantial private income.

"Well, you know. If you refuse, they shove you off into some little office somewhere, and you just sort of wither away until you retire." An unexpected breath of reality from Leecie. Maybe God hadn't planted *everything* below the Plimsol line.

"Well, I'm sure they wouldn't have given the job to Phil, if they didn't know he could do it." Tessie's comment sounded like a recording of Leecie's earlier comment, played back in a slightly higher register. Did they do a brain implant at boarding school, to give all these women the same set of clichés? "Walter's done all *sorts* of impossible jobs. Haven't you, Walter? He was even in World War II." The fact seemed to astonish Tessie.

Winslow flinched. Grimaced. Sighed. "Not all of it. Just the last part. And the occupation."

Phil's mind jumped to attention. He kept his voice as casual as he could. "Japan?"

"Germany."

"That must have been interesting." Philip wondered how far he could take the subject, before the women complained.

"It was a long time ago." Winslow had definitely learned not to bore his wife's friends with war stories.

Philip's caution stopped him from asking more. It wouldn't do to show too much interest, in this convivial situation. Phil also suspected that Winslow would resist discussing a topic that underlined his age difference with his wife.

Phil looked at Leecie again. The clear hazel eyes. The clean line of the jaw. For the hundredth time, Philip wondered. Was Leecie really smarter than he ever understood? Was there some visceral instinct at work, a genetic force locked in her DNA, that made Leecie's pronouncements wiser, more productive, than any intellectual reckoning of Philip's? He was still unable to decide.

∧ ∧ ∧ ∧ ∧ ∧ ∧ ∧

"Mr. Downs, there's a gentleman to see you." Kathie's voice on the phone was strained. Calling him "Mr. Downs" telegraphed wariness. "A Lieutenant Jenkins."

"All right, Kath. Show him in." Philip checked his desk for sensitive papers. Lieutenant Jenkins. He searched his memory. Someone from the Army? School? One of those parties at the Chevy Chase club? Possibly a relative of Leecie's.

Kathie ushered in a tall black man in a well-cut glen plaid. His tie was Liberty of London. The Lieutenant offered his hand as Philip rose from his chair.

"You seem surprised, Mr. Downs." Jenkins' voice and accent were Ivy League. Without being asked, he took a seat.

"I...was expecting Army." But they both knew what Lieutenant Jenkins meant. Philip had expected to see a white man. "How may I help you?" He reminded Lieutenant Jenkins that this was his office.

"Tell me about Tibor Szilágyi."

Tell me about Princeton, Philip was tempted to say. Or Harvard. Or wherever you picked up that cool accent, but failed to learn the manners that go with it.

"Shouldn't you be talking with the Hungarian Embassy?"

"I'm talking with you, Mr. Downs."

"I don't believe we've met, have we...Lieutenant?"

The Lieutenant slid a wallet from his inside coat pocket. The badge looked genuine. The photo ID card was District of Columbia Department of Police.

"What, precisely, did you wish to know about Mr. Szilágyi?"

Jenkins stretched out his legs until his feet touched Philips desk. "Precisely what I wish to know about Mr. Szilágyi is why he might have been run down by a hit-run driver. In Georgetown last night. With your card in his jacket pocket."

"Tibor is dead?" Philip felt the shock freeze his face. He saw the satisfaction in Jenkins' eyes, as his words hit home.

"Not quite." Jenkins crossed his legs. "But near enough."

"But a hit and run…In *Georgetown*?" Philip tried to picture a car racing through the narrow, crowded streets of the old town. It couldn't be done. Not unless someone purposely tried to—

"Oh yes. It happened." Jenkins reached into the side pocket of his coat. He drew out a card. Slid the card onto Philip's desk. It was Philip's official calling card.

"Yes. I see. And he's…" Philip didn't want to use the words.

"He might live. There's no guarantee. He's certainly not talking at the moment." Jenkins took the card back. Returned it to his pocket. "So perhaps you can tell us something."

Philip looked around the room. Baffled. Tibor had doubtless survived brushes with destruction in his career. But why would anyone wish to destroy Tibor now? In Washington? When the worst appeared to be over? Unless….

"Tell me what you're thinking." Jenkins had seen the thought cross Philip's face. The man would be difficult to lie to.

"Szilágy did have some business with us. Nothing cloak and dagger. We don't go in for that."

"But you can't tell me what the business was. Right?"

Philip felt a sudden urge to say No. You're wrong. I *can* tell you. It was a harmless search for a missing piece of religious art. But of course Lieutenant Jenkins was right. Without clearance from Reid, Philip could not talk.

"I'd be glad to ask permission from my superiors, Lieutenant."

"I don't think I'll wait for that." Jenkins made the disobliging innuendo his art form. His sudden smile told Philip that worse was coming. "Chevy Chase, isn't it?" The Lieutenant consulted a small notebook. "Your safety really isn't my problem, once you cross the District line." Lieutenant Jenkins shook hands warmly. He walked from the office like a victorious tennis player leaving the court. Philip sat. Absorbing the shock.

Georgetown. That would mean one of two hospitals. George Washington, or Georgetown University. Philip picked up his phone.

"Kathie? Could you come in here for a minute?"

∧   ∧   ∧   ∧   ∧   ∧   ∧   ∧

A call to George Washington University Hospital located Tibor in room 653. The nursing station reported his condition as stable. A phone call was possible. Philip dialed Tibor's room directly.

"Yes?" The voice on the was weak, but recognizably the Hungarian's.

"Tibor, this is Phil Downs. I just heard. Are you…all right?"

"You have some information to share with me, yes?"

Tibor's voice, drained of energy, still held a whiff of Middle European charm, an echo of Franz Lehar, a bit of dialogue from Schnitzler.

"Yes. Yes, I do. When would you like to meet, Tibor?" Philip found himself oddly glad to hear the Hungarian.

"At your convenience, yes? But as soon as possible. Please." On the final word, Tibor's tone dropped from The Merry *Widow* to *The Third Man.*

"Suppose we meet this afternoon. You can have visitors?" Philip hoped a hospital room meeting would avoid an hour of secondary cigarette smoke.

"It would be quite safe. You will bring papers, yes?"

"I will bring papers. Is there anything else you need?"

"Do not send flowers." Tibor was once more back among the *gemütlich*. "However if you could find a packet of Gauloise?" Tibor coughed weakly. "Until this afternoon. Yes?"

"Yes."

Philip re-cradled the telephone. Lieutenant Jenkins may have exaggerated Tibor's injuries. Tibor may have minimized his condition. And now Philip recalled the broken window in his car. Another Georgetown accident. He turned to the stack of hard copies, newspaper articles printed from microfilm. Chieko's contact at the National Archives had written the date and publication on each article. The first item was from the New York Times, December 12, 1945:

"3 U.S. OFFICERS DIE
IN GERMAN LODGINGS

FRANKFORT ON THE MAIN, Germany, December 10th (U.P.)—The charred bodies of three Military Government officers have been found in the ruins of their lodging at Passau in eastern Bavaria and military intelligence officials disclosed tonight they were investigating the possibility that they were killed by German 'werewolves.'

The bodies of a major, a captain and a lieutenant, whose names were not revealed, were found after fire fed by gasoline swept their three-story stucco building at the outskirts of Passau Monday night.

Signs that the victims might have been beaten were found on the bodies. The Stars and Stripes quoted soldier witnesses who said there were indications that there had been a fight inside the house. One officer, a major, reportedly escaped and has been sworn to secrecy by intelligence agents who rushed to Passau from here."

So Tibor's story had been correct. At least, the time and place were correct. The Times had more details in a follow-up story on December 13th:

"SLAYER OF 3 OFFICERS
HUNTED IN GERMANY

PASSAU, Germany, Jan. 12 (U.P.)—A peg-legged German is being questioned by Third Army counter intelligence officers in the slaying of three American Military Government officers. He was the personal was the personal chauffeur of Maj. Edward Coughlin, AMG officer in charge of the Passau district, who was slain with two officers from the Regensburg Military Government detachment in their quarters at 4:30 A. M. Monday. Gasoline then was spread through the three-story stucco house in which they were quartered and ignited.

An autopsy indicated that Major Coughlin was killed by hatchet blows. The other victims, a captain and a lieutenant whose names have not been disclosed, appeared to have been beaten with a heavy club.

Another occupant of the house, Maj. Howard Henry, was sleeping in a downstairs room and fled when he heard noise in the upstairs rooms. He declined to discuss his escape. Investigating officers had sworn him to secrecy.

Major Coughlin had strictly administered the denazification order. Intelligence officers said one or more resentful Nazis might have murdered the major and the other officers."

Philip began to form a picture in his mind. There was more substance to the Hungarian's story than Philip had thought. But this information was 45 years old. It would be hard to imagine a colder trail. The third photocopy was from the Times of December 14, 1945 and carried two stories in the same column:

"GI'S AT MURDER SITE
TOLD TO CARRY ARMS

REGENSBURG, Germany, Dec. 13 (AP)—All United States troops in the Danube resort town of Passau were ordered today to carry guns at all times as new security precautions were enforced as the result of the death of three military government officers.

Army agents investigating the finding of the burned bodies of the three officers in a riverside cottage at Passau a week ago indicated they had uncovered a lead as to the origin of the fire.

Meanwhile, the Army doubled the guard around officers' billets. Officers who were living alone in requisitioned homes were moved into two hotels in the town.

Curfew regulations for German civilians were tightened and only those with special passes were permitted on the streets after 10:30 P.M.

PASSAU, Germany, Jan. 13 (U.P.)—Three Military Government officers found hacked to death in their fire-swept quarter here last Monday had been investigating a food black market ring, and intelligence agents are working on a theory that they were slain by German or American ring members, sources here reported today.

Maj. Edward Coughlin, Passau district military governor, one of the three victims had been attempting to break the ring, it was understood. His German chauffeur was held for questioning."

Philip laid the photocopy down and glanced at his watch. It was time to leave for his meeting with the Hungarian. He would scan the story from *The Stars & Stripes* later. Philip slipped the photocopies into a manila folder. He told Kathy he'd be gone for an hour or two. Then he went to meet Tibor Szilágyi.

∧ ∧ ∧ ∧ ∧ ∧ ∧ ∧

Spring was always the most pleasant season of the year in Washington. Early Spring. Before the high heat and the foot-weary tourists arrived. This was one of those afternoons Philip especially savored. Sunlight, still welcome after winter, was not yet the burning scourge it would soon become. The air carried a scent of new growth that lifted the spirit. Bird song sounded through lulls in the traffic.

Tibor's stubby figure looked even smaller in the hospital bed, with the cast and the traction. The Hungarian waved a greeting as Philip entered the room. There was an ash tray, nearly full and easy to smell. Tibor's suit coat hung from on a hanger in the open closet. Philip wondered; why did every Eastern block diplomat and businessman wear a double-breasted suit? Was this the only style manufactured behind the formerly iron curtain? Socialist economies must cut all men's garments in size 42, portly.

"Magnificent accommodations. Yes?" Tibor's free arm embraced the room. "So good of you to meet me." Something between a nod and a bow went with his handshake. Even in the hospital Tibor carried the smell of Gauloises. "You have brought papers. Yes?" He tapped the folder in Philip's hand. "And now we talk, yes?"

"How are you feeling?" Philip wondered if man were in serious pain.

"Much more cautious than before. Yes?" Tibor's hand outlined the sweep of the city as viewed from the hospital window. "In such a place as this, I had imagined..." he looked up to see if Philip were paying attention, "—but I was wrong. Yes?" He drew in a large breath before lighting another cigarette. "Here, in such freedom, it is hard to imagine the dark times you will have found in your papers. In 1945. Yes?" Tibor pointed his cigarette at the folder in Philip's hand. "And that they should find me still..." he looked up quizzically.

"So you accident wasn't an accident, then."

"You are quite safe, yes? They would not dare to touch an American. Yes?" Tibor drew on his cigarette. He looked to see if

Philip understood. Accepted. "Only that I became careless. I will not become careless again. Yes?"

"Do they allow you to smoke in here?" Philip laid the folder on the bedside table.

"Of course not." Tibor looked warily towards the doorway as a nurse passed on rubber soles. "But back to 1945. You remember, yes?"

"I was born the following year." Philip opened the envelope and took out the photocopies. "My father had just come home from the war."

"A good year to be born," Tibor settled himself in the bed. "A war ends. A new world begins." He chuckled as he lighted a fresh Gauloise from the stump of his last. "But it is always a good year, if you are born in America. Yes?"

"We've been a fortunate country."

"So *now*, let us look back. Into those dark times, yes? Into your papers."

"There isn't much." Philip handed photocopies to the Hungarian. "Newspaper stories. Forty-five years old."

"Yes, yes..." Tibor scanned the Times articles. "But here. This article. You see?" He held up a photocopy from *The Stars & Stripes* Southern Germany Edition. "The newspaper for your army. You have read this article. Yes?"

"No. Not yet."

"Please. If you would.... Take a minute."

Philip scanned the printout from the Library of Congress microfilm. *The Stars & Stripes* had front-paged the story. A three-column headline read:

> "Man Killed Three Military Government Officers
> At Passau in Cold Blood, CID Agents Conclude
> By Douglas Gordon
> Staff Writer
>
> PASSAU, Dec. 20—Criminal Investigation Division agents announced today, 13 days after the murder of three Military Government officers in a house on the

Danube River, that the killer was a man, his crime was premeditated and he had an intimate knowledge of the victims' quarters...."

Philip scanned the story, then studied the photograph above the headline, three columns wide. The photo showed a charred bed, an open jerrican tilted against it. Three charred beams slanted across a hole in the roof, which gave a glimpse of the Danube river, the rooftops and church spires of an ancient city.

"This story seems much like the ones in the Times." Philip wondered what the point was here. Why did Tibor ask him to read this version? "A few more details, perhaps. Is there something in the photograph, Mr. Szilágy?"

"Tibor." The Hungarian spoke flatly.

"Tibor?" Philip was confused. "You're in the photographs—"

"No no no! Only that you will *call* me Tibor. Not 'Mr. Szilágy'. Please?" The Hungarian offered his pack of Gauloise. "And I may call you Philip. Yes?"

"If you like, of course." Philip waited while the Hungarian lighted a fresh cigarette. "I don't really see anything terribly conclusive in this *Stars & Stripes* article. The writer was probably on the scene. He could give his story a bit more color. Except for that—"

"*Exactly.*" Tibor's hand went into an elaborate dance, shaping an invisible substance. "The writer, yes?" He smiled at Philip. As if they now shared a secret.

Philip looked at the photocopy again. The byline.

"Douglas Gordon?"

"*Now*, Philip—we have agreed I might call you Philip, yes?—*now*, Philip, you know *one* of the men we are seeking."

All right. There was a certain logic to it. Philip began to re-read the article. Gordon's story did suggest that he had examined the murder scene in person. But even given that Douglas Gordon had been there, in 1945, where was he now? Was he even alive?

"Why didn't you tell me Gordon's name, when you came to us?" Philip was puzzled, ready to be angry.

"Philip, you were born in 1946. Yes? In a free country. Yes? You have not lived your life where every single decision can have, at a minimum, six hundred consequences. Five hundred ninety-nine of them will be unpleasant. Yes?"

"When first we met…in the office of your Mr. Reid…what could you think of me? 'Here is another crazy foreigner.' Yes? 'Come to cause me problems.' Yes?" Tibor automatically extended his pack of Gauloise, accepted Philip's head shake. "A natural reaction, yes? So then I tell you a story that must seem to you…beyond belief. Ridiculous. A fairy tale, yes?"

"Not *ridiculous*, actually. Some of the links are a bit tenuous, perhaps." Philip pondered. His father would have had to deal with men such as Tibor. His father would not have become angry.

"Tenuous?"

"Unsubstantial."

"It would be so, yes. 'Unsubstantial'. How could one, in such a place as this…" Tibor's hand stroked the view in the hospital window. The vast stretch of immaculate buildings. The fluttering flags and bright shop fronts. "…how could one find substance in such a story? Therefore, I am careful. Yes? I learn to play tricks. Yes? I lead you to make your own discovery. Then, *only* then, do you understand that my story is…is 'substantial'. Yes?"

"But you said there were *two* men. Two men who would have your icon." Philip was now consciously imitating his father's interrogatory tone.

The nicotine stain on the Hungarian's forefinger showed a deep brown as he tapped the newspaper article in Philip's hand. "The photographer," he said. "There had to be also a *photographer*. Yes?"

For a minute Philip stared at the photograph. There was no credit line. But obviously it had been taken by someone. Probably not the writer, Gordon. So there indeed could be two men. But nothing at all to show the photographer's name.

"That is your second man, Philip. A man who also may possess the icon."

Chapter 2

❀

A carousel of doubts revolved in Philip's head as he drove the VW Rabbit along the East-West Highway on his morning run to the office. Was Tibor Szilágy's accident not an accident? Or was the Hungarian winding him up? Hoping, perhaps, to dramatize? To create urgency? As if there weren't already urgency enough, with Morris Reid, prodded by repeated calls from the White House, baying for results.

And Chieko Willensky. She had delivered, for a price. For further information, would her price go up? Now that Phillip had the name of one of the veterans, Chieko might be able to find out if the man were still alive. She might also, Philip considered, have an agenda that included a closet full of whips and chains. And what waited when the job was finally over? Did Chieko have dreams of domination that ran well into the future? To buy information, he had given her the power to ruin his marriage. He was also beginning to like her.

There was something else that disturbed. If Chieko knew that he was under pressure, other people in the Department must know. How far had this knowledge traveled? Were his competitors for the Austrian Desk even now planting landmines for Philip to step on?

The morning traffic was still light when Philip turned the VW onto Connecticut Avenue. The Rabbit breezed by the Chevy Chase Club. He remembered that he and Leecie still hadn't used their minimum for this month. Leecie might wish to invite her parents for dinner. They hadn't seen the Wentworths for several weeks.

Philip slowed for the light at Lenox street. Two men and a woman were waiting at the bus shelter. One of the men, standing at parade rest, looked.... yes, it was Tessie's husband. Wallace?...no, *Walter.* Walter Winslow. Philip braked and pulled the Rabbit over to the curb.

"'Morning, Walter." Philip reached across to open the passenger door.

"Philip! Thanks for stopping." Walter boarded, adjusted his seat, fastened his seatbelt, stowed his briefcase and Washington Post. He brought with him the scent of Old Spice, shoe polish and Harris tweed. "I take it your job includes a parking place?"

"It took some negotiation." Philip put the Rabbit in gear and moved back to the fast lane.

"I thought that was all you folks did, in the State Department."

"At my level, we just beg."

Walter gave a "one of the boys" chuckle. "Tessie tells me you and...'Licia', is it?"

"'Leecie.'"

"You and Leecie did some time overseas."

"Here and there. Nothing exciting. Not like occupying Germany." Philip pretended to concentrate on passing a bus. He waited to see if Walter would take the conversational bait.

"That was a long time ago." A note of yearning crept into Walter's voice. Philip had cast the right lure.

"It's always fascinated me. That period. My...brother was there." It was only a small lie. Philip had switched 'father' to 'brother'. No sense in twitching Walter's age sensitivity.

"Was he?" Eagerness. A voice come alive. Walter would soon be trapped in the topic. "What outfit?"

Philip hesitated. He recalled the trophies in his father's library. Framed service ribbons. Unit insignia and shoulder patches. An autographed photo from Lieutenant-General George S. Patton, Jr.

"Was there something called the 'Constabulary'?"

"The Constabulary! Yes," Walter's voice went twenty years younger, bright with recall. "The Constabulary were headquartered in Bamburg."

"A General…—Herman?"

"Harmon! Ernie Harmon! Son of a bitch! Your brother served with Ernie Harmon, did he?"

"That's the family legend." Philip rounded Chevy Chase Circle with the dash of a fighter pilot swooping in for the kill.

"What a time that was! You know, for awhile, we expected the Krauts to put up some resistance. There were supposed to be SS units holing up in the Bavarian Alps. We heard stories of resistance groups. The 'Werewolves'. The 'Edelweiss Pirates'. But in the end, the Krauts were as law abiding under the Occupation as they had been under Hitler."

"My brother said there were some murders and things, though."

"Not the Krauts. Dps, maybe. Black marketeers. Scum like that."

"DPs?"

"Displaced persons. Germany…*our* zone of Germany…was crawling with DPs. Polish. Hungarian. Dutch. Russian. You name it. The Russkies kept their own German PWs for forced labor. The Krauts lost millions of men in the war."

"That left…" Walter was now firmly back in Bavaria, 1945. Probably the year Tessie's parents married. "…thousands of women who hadn't seen men for years. Never *would* see men. Then, in marches the United States Army. Loaded with nylons. Chocolate bars. Cigarettes. K-rations…."

"Horny as a herd of caribou." Philip braked for a bus pulling out.

"Phil, it was the greatest fuck-fest since Adam first showed Eve his snake."

Philip chuckled. He paid Walter off with an "us boys" confidence. "My brother told me some stories."

"They're all *true*. You had to be there, Phil."

They were crossing Calvert street, passing the Shoreham Hotel. Philip remembered that Leecie had invited the Watanabes to join them on Friday, for Mark Russell's show. Should he invite Walter and Tessie? Better check Leecie first. Mixing couples was a tricky business. At least Walter hadn't served in the Pacific. There wouldn't be any problems about a Japanese couple.

"What was the most remarkable thing you experienced there, Walter?" It was a talk-show of question, asked to disguise Philip's interest in debriefing a World War II veteran. Walter was too deep in the ecstasy of remembrance to notice.

"I suppose…" Walter looked out the window at McClellan's statue as the VW took the curve that descended past the Washington Hilton, "if you put aside the hanky panky…the cigarettes selling for fifty dollars a carton on the black market…the real shocker was the Russians."

Walter turned towards Philip and brought his voice back to the present. "Your generation only knows the cold war. My generation saw the Russians as allies. Good guys. 'Uncle Joe', the friendly Russian bear."

"All that ended in '45." Walter spoke with sadness. Was it for the lost illusion of Russian comradeship? Or for his own lost youth. "You wouldn't remember, but when Churchill made his 'Iron curtain' speech in '46, there was a terrific reaction against him. People thought he was trying to start World War III."

"I've read about it." Philip turned the car onto 18th street. "And Kennan's 'X article' in' Foreign Affairs."

"Don't know that one."

"The beginning of American resistance to Russian expansion. George Kennan's article laid out our containment doctrine."

"That may be the way it works on the diplomatic level." Walter hunched down in his seat. His voice lost even the warmth of sadness. "Where I was," he said, in a dull chilled tone, "it meant blood in the streets."

∧   ∧   ∧   ∧   ∧   ∧   ∧   ∧

BAVARIA, Winter 1946

"Keep that camera out of sight. No pictures unless I give the word. Understand?" The Colonel, a Captain, and a First Lieutenant wore helmet liners and sidearms. The atmosphere in the office was drumhead tight. Two sergeants and a corporal stood rigid, hands along trouser seams, faces as blank and hard as concrete.

Gordon looked out the second story window, watching the line of box cars being backed along the loading platform. The barracks marched in orderly rows beside the barbed wire fence. Guard towers, solidly built for a lifetime of service, loomed at regular intervals. This was Dachau.

"How many men are you moving out, Colonel?" Gordon held a folded wad of copy paper, ready to make notes.

"Just under three hundred." The Colonel checked his watch, settled his pistol-belt, took a long, slow look at the rows of single-story barracks. He spoke to the Captain at his elbow. "Koslowski has the Poles in position?"

"Yes, sir. Behind the mess hall."

"Good." The Colonel looked at his watch again. The line of cattle cars had stopped. American MPs, carbines slung, began to slide the doors open. "Let's move."

The Colonel led them down the stairs at a brisk trot. The sunlight was clear but there was a bite in the air. The screech of metal riding on metal sang across the barracks yard. The locomotive at the head of the line of box cars hissed out a jet of steam. The crunch of gravel stopped as the Colonel took up a position before the first barracks. The Captain motioned to one of the sergeants. A sergeant stepped forward and twisted the door handle.

The handle turned but the door didn't give. The sergeant pushed. Pressed his shoulder to the door panel. Drew back and kicked at the door. A second non-com trotted forward. Both men threw their weight against the door. There was barely perceptible movement. No sound from inside the building.

"Bring a jeep." The Captain's voice whipped across the yard.

The jeep pulled up with a swirl of gravel. A 30 caliber machine gun swayed on a mount in the back. The Captain signaled the driver forward. Gingerly, the MP angled the jeep's bumper against the doorway. He shifted the jeep into four wheel drive. Eased forward. Wood groaned. The door burst from its frame. The driver quickly reversed, pulled back to let the sergeant level his carbine through the doorway.

Deep silence flowed out of the darkened barrack hall. The sergeant looked in. Froze. Slowly turned back and sought the Captain's eyes. He opened his mouth to speak, said nothing, turned again to look inside.

The Russians hung like sides of beef in a freezer. Not uniform in size. Each an individual. Yet all similar in the deadly stillness with which they hung from the rafters. The smell of urine and black bread filled the room.

"Adams! Johnson! Cut them down! Double time!" The Captain's voice shook the sergeants from their stupor. Their boots clattered across the floorboards as they ran to get their squads.

A clamor rose from beyond the barracks. Shouted commands. Screams of rage. Glass breaking in the next building. The sounds of a riot starting came from several barracks at once. The Colonel turned, strode past the suspended bodies, kicked aside the door that hung on one hinge, disappeared into the sunlight.

Gordon and Davis moved quickly to stay within the Colonel's aura of authority, where their status as correspondents was established. If they found themselves among the lower ranks in a situation like this one, any frightened, self-important non-com was likely to bar their movements. By the time they could locate and appeal to higher authority, the story would be lost.

The fresh January air outside did nothing to cut the queasy knot in Gordon's stomach. MPs were trotting across the compound. A squad of riflemen—Poles in G.I. khaki and helmet liners—moved into position around building two. There was another crash of glass and a loud "pop" as the MPs fired a tear gas shell through the barrack window.

The Colonel moved faster. Noise and confusion spread. A nearby shattering of glass caught Gordon's attention. A man's head thrust through the barracks window. The head whipped violently left and right as the man tried to slash his throat on the jagged fragments of glass in the window frame. A clutch of half-naked bodies erupted from the back of the barracks. The Russians looked heavy-set, well muscled. Their peasant bodies were making motions that Gordon couldn't interpret.

Suddenly, he understood. The Russians were trying to disembowel themselves. Using shards of broken window glass. Bright arterial blood sprang across white bellies. MPs ran among the kneeling, groveling men, clubbed at their heads, battered a few of the Russians unconscious.

Smoke erupted from the barracks building. More Russians staggered out, choking from the tear gas. Even at this distance, Gordon's eyes began to sting. Six or seven Russians, completely naked, locked arms as the MPs tried to herd them towards the open box cars.

An American Lieutenant led the squad of Poles into position between the barracks. The American barked an order in English. The Poles leveled their M-1s. A Russian ran towards them, dropped to his knees, threw his arms wide and screamed in Russian, Polish, some

Slavic-sounding tongue Gordon didn't understand, but the Russian was desperately begging the riflemen to shoot him.

The Poles moved forward quickly. Gordon heard the hollow *thuck* as butt stocks smacked heads. The Poles pounded with their rifles until the kneeling men were stunned enough to be dragged into the box cars.

The shouts and screaming turned sporadic. Metal screeched on metal again. There was yelling from inside the cattle cars. The "incident", as it would be called, was almost over. It was time to get a casualty count from the Colonel and start back to Altdorf to write his story.

Driving along the narrow road from Dachau towards the Autobahn, Gordon's thoughts kept him busy until the unusually long silence from Davis caught his attention. He glanced at the youngster. Lew's face, drained white, looked somewhere between shock and pain. Beads of sweat dotted his forehead.

"Want to pull over a minute?"

"Yes." The urgent, strangled, single word was like the stopper in a volcano of vomit. Gordon barely had the jeep on the verge when Lewis leaned out the side. Gripped the door edge. Spewed his breakfast onto the frozen turf. The sour smell of stomach acid bit through the cold air.

Some of Lewis's color came back, as Gordon swung their jeep
back onto the autobahn and headed them north towards Nürnberg. Gordon repeated in his head the lead sentence he'd been formulating for his story: *Ten Russians committed suicide at Dachau today rather than return to the Soviet Union to face charges of desertion and treason.*

"Why did they have to send them back?" Lewis was clearly recovering, if he was thinking of someone besides himself.

"The agreement at Yalta. Any Soviet citizens accused of war crimes are to be sent back. Regardless."

"What a rotten way to die." Lewis sounded ill again.

"Shall we pull over for a minute?"

"No. No. You just wonder. How could they..." Lewis looked at Gordon as if Gordon could explain the whole world to him.

"They know what's waiting for them, back in Russia."

"God." Lewis held his head..

"Not God. Stalin." Gordon accelerated the jeep to 50 mph again. There was no hurry to get back. The story wouldn't run until Monday. But the higher speed brought fresh air into the jeep. Gordon badly needed cold, clean air.

∧   ∧   ∧   ∧   ∧   ∧   ∧   ∧

WASHINGTON, Spring 1990

"I got your note." D. Webster David, Esquire stood in the doorway of Philip's office, holding a copy of The New York Times. "Would you like to talk now?"

"Please." Phil offered the lawyer a chair. "Did my note make sense?"

"Your problem is clear enough. So is the answer. But I'm not sure there's much joy in either one."

Lawyers did not often, in Philip's experience, dispense joy. Web's announcement was at least concrete and direct.

"The legal principle is, 'You can't get good title from a thief'. Which is to say, anyone who buys a stolen painting has to relinquish the object to the rightful owner."

"If and when the stolen object is ever discovered."

"That's the *bad* news." Webster had the lawyer's gift of being philosophical about other people's problems. "You'll find this story interesting." Web laid the Times on Philip's desk. "An almost parallel case. American officer brings home stolen art treasures from Germany. Forty years later his heirs in Texas try to sell the stuff—the Germans get word and move legally to block any sale and reclaim their artwork."

"And succeed?"

"Yes—and no. The heirs got some of the items to Switzerland. They were able to sell—although they called it a 'finder's fee'—some illuminated ninth-century manuscripts. Back to the Germans."

"How large a 'finder's fee'?"

"Three million dollars."

"And all perfectly legal?"

"In Switzerland."

"*Christ!*"

"They *were* biblical manuscripts, yes." Web would have his little witticism.

"So the men I'm looking for can ship their icon to Switzerland. And they're home free."

"In simple terms, yes. When you look into the technicalities, no."

"Tell me the technicalities."

"Well, this case..." Web tapped the Times page, "...was between a German Cultural Foundation and a lawyer for an American seller." Web picked up the Times and read aloud from the story. "'Part of the deal—which they made in Switzerland where these transaction are protected by law—was that the American's name would never be revealed.'"

"So why couldn't my men use the same trick?"

"They could try. I don't know that the Hungarian Government would pay—or could pay—as much as the Germans have."

"But these Vets could sell to a private collector, surely?"

"Not the same. A 'finder's fee' for returning a lost object to its rightful owner holds up in court. Conveyance to a private collector constitutes a sale. Your title problem again. What private collector is going to pay big money for a shaky title?"

"Some must do. Or stolen art would never get stolen."

"There's your rub. Your men always have that option, if they want it."

"Any more good news?"

Web chuckled. "*You* asked the questions. I'm simply the virtuous bearer of truth." He handed back the folder of photocpies of the Passau murder stories. "One thing intrigues me. A major survived these murders. Have you tried to find him?"

"No." Philip thought for a minute. "Why should we?"

"He can't be any more remote than your other two veterans. He had an even more direct link with the case."

"By God, you're right." Philip had been concentrating on the two men from *The Stars & Stripes*, following Szilágyi's suggestion. But Web had put his finger on another possibility. Why hadn't the Hungarian mentioned the survivor? Perhaps Szilágyi already knew....

Web gave a cheerful wave and departed, as Philip's telephone rang. It was Alasdair Murphy, suggesting that the two of them meet for lunch.

"It might be better if we met at some casual place," Murphy's voice was ripe with portent. "Do you know *Au Pied de Cochon*? Wisconsin Avenue? Two blocks above M street?"

"It's a bit public, isn't it?" Philip sometimes took Leecie to the small French restaurant, when they went to the movies

in Georgetown. He wondered again about Tibor's "accident".

"That's the beauty of it." Murphy spoke as expert to amateur. "The place is so public it's actually private."

"What time?"

"Twelveish."

"Fine."

Au Pied de Cochon had the look of a native French bar-café. The high-ceilinged, wedge-shaped room had a dark bar, ancient tiled floor, marble topped tables. The waiters had accents. The menu was short, simple. *Ratatouille* came with everything. Garlic complicated the air.

Murphy had a table at the thin end of the wedge. He flapped a hand to catch Philip's attention. "Over here!"

"Hello. Good to see you." Philip offered his hand. Murphy slide aside a glass of wine to shake.

"I can recommend almost anything on the menu." Murphy tickled the air to call a waiter. "Drink?" He pointed to his empty glass for the waiter's benefit.

"Thank you, no." Philip wondered if Murphy's host-like manner meant that the FBI would pick up the check. Probably not. "I'd like the *steak pommes frites*," he said to the waiter.

"You won't be disappointed," Murphy promised. He was wearing a different tie today. Paisley pattern. Conspicuously rayon. "I thought this was a comfortable place to fill you in on our progress."

"A happy thought." Philip sipped his ice water. A hint of the chef's fondness for shallots sashayed from the back of the restaurant. The lunch time crowd began to scrape the metal chairs around, finding their places along the walls.

"You're probably not too familiar with trade craft." Murphy sampled his second *vin rouge*. "To check out your first man, the writer, we did a systematic survey. It's labor intensive. Not like the movies. We did a run down on…" Murphy drew a folded sheet of typing paper from inside his jacket, "…the Newspaper Guild, the National Press Club, and the press clubs in New York, Chicago, San Francisco, and LA. Then the American Legion, and the VFW."

Murphy gave the wine his full attention for a few seconds. Closed his eyes. Smiled in satisfaction. Set the glass back. "A nice little wine." He looked again at his list. "We checked the New York Times index for bylines. And the Reader's Guide for ten years after the War."

"You said you'd found something."

"Not Gordon. We found someone else."

"The photographer."

"Not bloody likely. You couldn't even give us the photographer's name. I mean…we don't work miracles, after all."

"And it's labor intensive."

"Exactly—but we did find a former CO of the outfit. A Major Caldwell. The officer in charge at the time Gordon and the photographer were serving on the paper."

"He's still alive?" Philip wondered. The Commanding Officer should have been a man senior to most of the regular staff members. A man of his father's generation. Even if the CO were only in his early thirties in 1945, he'd be in his seventies now. As old as Philip's father would have been. Should have been.

"Still alive." Murphy's face moved into a mask of contentment. "Still with us. It took some doing," Murphy drained his glass. "But we found him for you."

"Where?"

"Ah…" Murphy paused over his *coq au vin rouge*. "There's a…small but crucial complication."

"He's *non compos*? In jail? What?"

Murphy managed to steeple his fingers without letting go of his glass. "The Bureau has its constraints. You understand that, of course?" A quick, sharp look at Phil.

"I think so."

"We can't just track down American citizens. Invade their privacy. Make the information public. Without substantial reasons." He paused, watching to see if Philip grasped the logic.

"You're not making it public."

"We're letting it outside the Bureau. For purposes unknown. Possibly not licit. My Masters would need some assurance about the use of this information…." Murphy smiled. The man of probity. The guardian of truth and the American way.

'My Masters…' Philip thought. Murphy must live in a John LeCarré novel. With his regimental tie. His 'tradecraft'. You little bastard, Philip thought. You smell a chance to make some brownie points somewhere, and you want in on the deal. Fuck you.

"Of course. I understand." Philip cut a small section of steak and chewed with elaborate precision. What was Murphy offering, after all? The name of the outfit's CO? Not much. The man probably remembered little or nothing about two subordinates, 45 years ago—even if he'd had that much contact with the two men in the first place.

"It's possible we could handle this matter informally," Murphy signaled the waiter for a refill. "If I were personally satisfied that the use of this information was…within the proper constraints under which the Bureau operates…it could stay on a purely personal level. Between you and me. After all, one has one's code."

Murphy had switched from LeCarré to P.G. Wodehouse.

"Alasdair, I'm pretty far down the tree, myself. You know that Xeroxed cartoon they have in all the mailrooms? 'I feel like a mushroom—kept in the dark and fed horseshit'?" Murphy, eager to enhance his superior status, he might accept Philip's pretense of being below the salt.

"Take it up with your chiefs," Murphy took a mouthful of wine. Swirled the wine with his tongue. Chewed. Swallowed. "I wonder if I shouldn't be plugged in at a higher level with your people."

"Very likely. Let me look into it."

The waiter slid their check onto the marble table top. Murphy studied the mural on the back wall. He gestured with his empty glass. "Reminds me of a place in Marseille. When I was doing some undercover work overseas."

A malicious twinge flared in Philip. He started to ask Murphy what the French was for 'separate checks'. Better not. Philip laid his credit card on top of their bill. It was amusing to picture Murphy thinking he was passing himself off as a Frenchman. In Marseille. Undercover. Probably in a beret.

The check paid, Murphy's attention returned to the table. He raised his glass, found it empty, clicked it back on the table.

"Naturally, any exchange of information would remain *entre nous*."

"One has one's code."

"Exactly."

"I appreciate that." Philip struggled with an uncomfortable mixture of amusement and rage. Murphy was indeed more Wodehouse than LeCarré. Yet the rotten little bastard had the only live clue to turn up so far. "I'll see what we can manage."

Philip decided to walk back to the office. It would give him thinking time. He strolled down Wisconsin Avenue and turned left on M street. It was time to ditch Murphy. Put him on the back burner, at least. Philip would have to use Chieko Willensky if he was to succeed. Success again. That distant mirage that faded, like the illusion of water in the desert, the closer one came.

Walking around Washington Circle, Philip realized that he was facing another of the…. disappointments? No…realities. One of the realities that periodically overtook him, always as a surprise.

There had been Phillips Exeter. The tension of getting admitted. The certainty that here would be found a special wisdom, a light of knowledge, even the secrets of the world he inhabited. But Exeter was only a school.

Then there was Yale. A very special place. Special for his father, at least. There were indeed outstanding people at Yale. But no one had the secrets of the universe. Was it Buckley who said that "For God, for country, and for Yale" was the greatest anti-climax in the English language?

OCS was another pathway to reality. Getting his commission, he expected to find—at least among the higher brass—some of the inspiration, the brilliance and ingenuity, that the history books and the movies promised. There were some good men in the U.S. Army. But only men, after all. The Robert E. Lees, the George Marshalls, had all gone.

And at State, there was the promise of a world-wide scope for imagination, subtle statesmanship, a hand on the tiller of
destiny. That particular sense of an opportunity for contact with greatness had glowed in Philip for considerable years. In the end, he

found that the Dean Achesons had gone. Only the Henry Kissingers and the Morris Reids were left.

George Washington's equestrian statue loomed against the skyline. Another reality. The fox-hunting General sat his horse with the natural grace of the born horseman; but this was an historical fact, not just an artist's flattery. A sudden truth

rose in Philip's mind. It was the rare great man, his legend and his accomplishments, that shaped the institutions in which the Murphys and the Reids prospered.

Because George Washington had had an extraordinary depth of character, Americans expected to find a President of like calibre every four years. The Abe Lincolns, the George Marshalls, the Dean Achesons, set a standard that was mistaken for a norm. Whole establishments were organized on the assumption that such men were available to staff them. But when the real norm was voted in or appointed, it was usually a Murphy, or at best a Reid.

Philip considered the downside of this great truth and what it meant to his personal dilemma. He would have to succeed on this assignment without the help of brilliant men. Murphy was no accident; just the mean average. The upside? If there were no giants left, at least Philip was not a pygmy. His chances were as good as the next man's. He had Yale. He had Leecie's social connections. He had private means. He had Chieko Willensky. Philip had no excuse for not achieving success. Or at least, no excuse that his father would accept.

Murphy had mentioned checking the Press clubs for Douglas Gordon. Maybe a newspaperman would be better at finding these two men. *If* the two men still existed. But Philip would have to find help from someone who would keep quiet. Philip picked up his pace as he turned down 23rd street.

∧ ∧ ∧ ∧ ∧ ∧ ∧ ∧

The National Press Club was on the 14th floor of the National Press Building. From the visitor's lounge Philip could look out over Pennsylvania Avenue, the Washington Monument, the District Building, a large section of the Federal Triangle. An elderly gentleman dozed in one of the leather chairs. The top of his suspender-held trousers was unbuttoned. He looked like a fixture. Down on 14th street the noon day traffic was heavy, movement slowed by the cars of tourists befuddled by the radiating streets Major Pierre L'Enfant had laid out in the Capital. Across 14th street the colonnaded grandeur of the Willard Hotel, now restored, drew Philip's eyes. Lincoln was said to have made speeches from the second story balcony.

"Nice view, isn't it?" Gary Dobson was Leecie's cousin. Perhaps second cousin. Leecie didn't discriminate. Gary was a feature editor on The Washington Post and had spent years with Time-Life.

"You don't usually get this height, in Washington," Philip said.

"No. Only the power of the press permitted us to build this many floors. How's Leecie?"

"Fine. She asked me to see if you and Laura could join us at the club Saturday evening."

"Sounds good. Laura will know our schedule." Gary led them down a hallway paneled in oak, the walls lined with varnished stereotype-mats from the front pages of newspapers around the country and the world. A teletype machine whispered somewhere down the hallway. The fumes of ambitious cooking escaped through a suddenly opened door.

The *maitré d'* found them a table by the window. Philip shook his head when Gary offered a drink. Over lunch Philip explained his problem. It was not necessary to tell Gary to keep it quiet.

"Forty-five years? That's quite a time."

"You notice that."

"They may not have stayed in the business." Gary smiled across the room at a passing party of people who looked like fellow journalists.

"May not even have *been* in the business. Just assigned by the Army. Square pegs. Round holes. You know the Army."

"I only saw the one story they did. It looked pretty professional."

"Oh, I agree. The chances are they *were* professional. After all, The Stars & Stripes had the whole army to select from. But if your friends at the FBI—"

"Not my friends. And possibly overrated."

"Most police are overrated. They get their real clues from informers."

"So where should I start?" Where should *you* start is what Philip really meant.

"We'll start with some of my Time-Life friends. There're still some people around who were in World War II. Time-Life Books is over in Alexandria, now. Jim McLean edits their World War II series. I think he was on Patton's staff in the war."

"I don't have a lot of time."

Gary smiled.

"Sorry." Philip was asking a lot. But blood was thicker—at least Leecie's blood was thicker—than water.

"I know." Gary nodded. "Let me make some calls. At least you know the former CO is still alive." Gary's face suddenly lighted. "And there's Ralphie—right here in the club."

Gary led Philip down the hallway back to the visitor's lounge. The dozing elderly man—now blinking awake—was evidently Ralphie. Gary sat on the couch next to Ralphie's chair.

"Gary." Ralphie smiled.

"Ralph—you were in Paris during the war, right?"

"Paree?" Ralphie went into a slow-motion version of the "retro-view" effect, eyes journeying into the past. "Oh *yes. Oui oui, M'Sieu!*" A roguish smile tip-toed onto Ralphie's sagged features.

"You must have known some of the Stars & Stripes crowd, then, Ralphie."

Ralph's smile turned beatific. "Terrific poker players. Alec Woollcot. Granty Rice. Hal Ross—Ross married that Red Cross girl…Janet…Jane…." Ralphie looked up at them, his eyes flickering with memory. "Terrific poker players."

Philip was amazed at his good luck. He had sat in this same room with the very source he needed. Might well have left the Club without ever realizing how close he was.

"Terrific poker players." Ralphie repeated. He was back at a café table somewhere in wartime Paris, sitting behind an inside straight.

"You keep in touch with any of them, Ralphie?" Gary spoke with measured softness, trying to reach Ralphie through the glaze of nostalgia. Ralphie appeared not to have heard. The old man's eyes stared straight ahead into the past.

For a second Philip felt a desperate need to shatter the old man's reverie. But than Ralphie suddenly spoke.

"They're all dead, you know." His face put on forty or fifty years in a few seconds. "All dead."

"Ah. Well, *tempus fugit*, Ralphie." Gary patted the old man's shoulder.

"All dead." Ralphie said again, speaking to no one, just before he slipped back into the doze in which Philip had first seen him.

In the elevator down from the 13th floor Philip let his bitterness show. "I guess that ends that." Then, remembering manners, "Thanks for your time and effort, Gary."

"Ends what?" Gary waited until Philip stepped out into the Press Building lobby. "…your search?" Gary chuckled. "My God, no."

"But if they're all *dead*?" Philip saw nothing amusing.

"They *are* all dead. Harold Ross, Alexander Woollcott, Grantland Rice." Gary smiled and patted Philip's shoulder. "Cheer up. Ralphie was talking about World War *One*."

∧   ∧   ∧   ∧   ∧   ∧   ∧   ∧

BAVARIA, 1945

Major Caldwell waited until it was completely dark. The paper went to bed at nine o'clock. Most of the men would be busy until then. The Major switched off his desk lamp and the office light, shrugged into his overcoat. Leaves crunched as he walked to his jeep. The night air, moist with the smell of dead leaves, rustled branches. The sound and smell stirred the Major's memories of childhood Halloweens.

Burning leaves. That was it. The Krauts didn't burn their leaves in the gutters, as the citizens of Pennington, New Jersey, did. Caldwell stopped at the jeep and looked around. No one in sight. He looked up at the sky. Through a tangle of bare branches he could see a sprinkle of stars. A glance at his watch. Betsy would have the girls in bed by now. It was time to go. He collected the packet of sandwiches Wacker had wrapped for him. The Major walked down the drive and along the road that curved towards town.

Thirty years of living plus three years of war had taught Caldwell prudence. He considered again the risks and propriety of his action. It was no longer forbidden to 'fraternize' with a German woman. Betsy lived in an apartment in the basement of the Pickle Haus. There was a private entrance. She was 30 something, a mature woman. Discreet. Forthright. Her husband long since *"gefallen im Russland"*.

Under the covers, Betsy was like…he pondered, listening to the sound of his footsteps in the darkness. She was like fresh home-baked bread. Warm, wholesome, satisfying. And satisfied. Well satisfied. What was it the British used to say? "You never miss a slice off a cut loaf." Caldwell smiled. Cutting off a slice with Betsy, he got it buttered on both sides. These German women. *Kinder, Kuche, Kirche.*

The headlights of a jeep slapped him across the eyes as the vehicle rounded a curve in the roadway ahead. The driver braked, turned aside, eased up beside the Major.

"Major Caldwell?" Young Davis's voice came out of the jeep. Probably back from some photo assignment. "May I give you a lift somewhere, Sir?"

In the darkness, the Major couldn't see whether or not Davis had saluted. Probably, he had. His voice was properly deferential. Grammar upper middle-class. Accent East-Coast Anglo.

"Thank you, Davis." The Major made a casual salute. "I'm just out for an evening constitutional."

"If there's anywhere you'd like to go, Sir…"

Was Davis going to be a nuisance? Had he seen the packet of sandwiches and guessed? No. Davis simply wanted to be obliging. Caldwell shifted from his Infantry manner to the usages of affluent suburbia. "Good of you to offer, Davis. But I need the exercise."

"Yes, sir." Davis got the picture, as presented. "Well, good luck, Sir."

"Thank you for stopping, Davis."

The jeep eased ahead, Davis careful not to scatter any dirt or blow exhaust as he drove off towards the newspaper plant. Once again, the proprieties impinged on the Major's thoughts. Well, every man in the outfit was shacked up, one way or another.

The final argument, "Everybody's doing it", gave Caldwell a feeling of assurance as he strode towards the Pickle Haus. Even young Davis was rumoured to be having it off with some horsey Fraulein he'd discovered, somewhere out in the woods. On the photo department wall Caldwell had noticed an 11 by 14 inch blowup; this pigtailed Hun on horseback.

Betsy had left a tiny light in the front window. The girls were asleep. The Major knocked softly.

"*Guten abend.*" She stood in the doorway, waiting for his arms to go around her.

"Good evening." The scent of her hair against his face replaced the cool night air in his nostrils. "How are you?"

She presented her face to be kissed. Her arms slid up his chest and over his shoulders. Passion, with dignity. Tonight, he thought, he hoped, there might be time for two slices.

∧ ∧ ∧ ∧ ∧ ∧ ∧ ∧

WASHINGTON, Spring 1990

"You're in luck." Gary Dobson's voice on the phone sounded envious. "There's a retired managing editor from Stars & Stripes. He's doing a book about the outfit. He may have even been there when your two men were. McLean knows him. You can use McLean's name."

Philip wrote the former managing editor's name on his yellow legal pad.

"San Diego? Did McLean have his street address?"

"Even a telephone number. You must worship the right Gods, Phil."

Philip thanked Gary, asked him to thank McLean. He looked at his watch. A bit early to call California. When he did call, it would be necessary to strike just the right note. How should he present himself to this editor? It was important to sound

casual, important to move quickly. The one need defeated the other. Candor? Not really. Use the "brother" story again? It had worked with Walter Winslow. Philip went back to filling out his expense return. Could he take the luncheon with Gary as an expense? Probably wiser to pay for the meal himself, rather than get in a wrangle with the accounting people.

He looked at his watch. Almost noon. Nearly nine o'clock in San Diego. The man should be up by now. He picked up his phone. Dialed. The number rang once, twice, three times—had he called too early?

On the fifth ring, a man's voice. "Hello..." Elderly. A trifle vague. But awake.

"Mr. Zimmerman? This is Philip Downs. You don't know me, but James McLean suggested you might be able to help me. Do you have a moment to talk?"

Zimmerman did.

"My…uncle was in World War II, and he's asked me to help him locate two friends who were on The Stars & Stripes. Jim McLean, over at Time-Life Books, said you're writing a book…"

The newspaperman was well into retirement. Willing to meet with Philip. Having got that much, Philip arranged a date with Zimmerman and rung off. Zimmerman hadn't asked why Philip would be in San Diego—perhaps hadn't even realized Philip was calling from Washington.

It was easy. So easy that Philip wondered later if the telephone conversation had really happened. He looked at the phone he had just cradled. Screw you, Murphy, he thought. You and your 'labor intensive". Zimmerman had been managing editor of the paper for ten years, from '46 into the fifties. He'd saved many of the records and documents, was now using them to write his book.

The *frisson* of success raced along Philip's nerves. The lucky stroke, the short cut to—but then, there was still Murphy to be dealt with. And Reid. Reid would be eager for progress reports. Reid would want assurances that results were coming soon.

∧ ∧ ∧ ∧ ∧ ∧ ∧ ∧

"I don't see why you have to pay for your own plane ticket." Leecie pointed the Audi towards the 14th Street bridge. She drove with a precocious élan that always unnerved Philip—the more so since she had never had an accident. "You say Gary found this man for you?"

"If I try to get travel money from the Department, Reid has to approve it. He'll want to know why I'm going to San Diego. It may be only a false start. Yes, Gary found this man."

"We're supposed to take the Watanabes Friday. Do you think Tessie and Walter Winslow would like Mark Russell?" Leecie was a peerless practitioner of the *non sequitur*.

"Would the Winslows like the Watanabes?"

"I don't see why not. Tessie's second husband was a Mexican."

"Then I think she'd enjoy Mark Russell." Philip waited for a chuckle he knew would not come.

Leecie turned towards the airport. Fast. Accurate. She had a boldness that came from generations of assured ancestors. She cut into National Airport, out-maneuvered a cab driver, dropped Philip at the main entrance to the terminal.

"You'll phone from San Diego?"

"This evening."

Leecie's kiss caught him unprepared. She could turn passionate without warning. "Hurry back," she said, knowing well enough that she had already given him ample reason. That was better than a chuckle.

∧ ∧ ∧ ∧ ∧ ∧ ∧ ∧

SAN DIEGO, Spring 1990

Zimmerman showed the same reflex all these old timers had. Philip had watched it in Walter Winslow, Tibor Szilágyi, even his father in the old days. With Zimmerman the action was exactly the same. First, their eyes shifted focus, as if turning from outside to inside. Then their faces changed, the muscles reshaping to a position they must have held decades earlier. Years of age appeared to drop away, as the Zimmerman's face regained the Reichian mask of his youth.

"I remember there *was* a Doug Gordon. But he shipped home before I got to Altdorf. I was running the Pfungstadt Edition, outside Frankfurt, until May, '46. Caldwell was still there. But when I got to Altdorf, Caldwell had shipped home too."

Zimmerman was looking straight ahead, into the past where Douglas Gordon and his photographer covered murders and Ralphie once played poker with Harold Ross. Philip had found it easy enough to get him started. Zimmerman was a classic friendly sort, eager to help an old soldier locate a wartime buddy. Philip's initial caution about approaching Zimmerman now changed to guilt; he was exploiting the decency of this man.

"The photographers on the Altdorf edition. I was wondering about them. There never seemed to be credit lines on their photos. Would you recall their names?"

"There were two or three, I think. One was a fresh-faced kid…It should show in the duty rosters…" Zimmerman eased up from his chair, struggling with a bad hip. He used his cane to cross the room to an orderly collection of cardboard cartons that lined the study wall. The dusty smell of yellowed paper and stale mimeograph ink rose as he opened a box.

Zimmerman sorted through the papers with care. The mimeographed sheets were disintegrating around the edges. Philip struggled with his impatience. Here, possibly, was the name of the second man. The cameraman who had been with Gordon in Passau.

"Here we are…" Zimmerman held some pages apart while he adjusted his glasses and read from the sheet. "…Earl H. Dent, Jr., PFC." He looked up and grinned at Philip. "How's that for 45 years after the fact, eh?"

"Extraordinary. That was D E N T?"

"Yes." Zimmerman glanced at the sheet again. "Earl H., Jr."

"You mentioned a second photographer."

"Oh. Right." Zimmerman worked through the sheets again.

"Yes. I thought so. Davis. Lewis L. Davis, PFC."

"Would you have serial numbers for these men?"

"Possibly. It would take me some digging, though." Zimmerman's voice suggested that he was reaching the end of his energy, and perhaps his patience.

"Let me give you a telephone number." Philip wrote the office number, the direct line, on the back of his personal card. "You've been extremely gracious about giving me your time, Mr. Zimmerman. My uncle will be delighted."

"Only too glad to help," Zimmerman accepted the card, studied the telephone number.

"Please call me collect, too."

"Thank you, Mr. Downs." He shook hands with Philip. A sudden smile. "You know, it's strange the way pictures pop up in your mind, up years later. I *do* remember Davis. One of those odd flashes of memory."

Philip watched Zimmerman's eyes refocus on 1945. "There was a large round table in the dining-room of the Balzer Haus—where the editorial people lived. Five or six of us sitting around this table at lunch one day. Talking, the way GIs did. Somebody brought up table manners. Jerry Callahan—one of our cartoonists—commented that Davis was the only one at the table who was using his soup spoon correctly."

Zimmerman smiled. Shook his head. Came back to 1990. "Strange, the things you remember."

At the airport Philip calculated the time difference before calling Leecie. It was mid-afternoon on the East Coast. She answered after the third ring and for several minutes Philip listened to the latest developments in Chevy Chase. Tessie and Walter Winslow *were* joining the dinner party on Saturday, with the Watanabes. Both couples were delighted at the prospect of seeing Mark Russell.

"Oh, and the phone company was here this morning," Leecie suddenly recalled. "He fixed the problem with the phone in your den."

"The...oh, yes, that. Well, see you this evening, Leece."

Philip blew a kiss into the phone. Leecie made a succulent noise, chuckled, hung up.

There was no use alarming her, Philip reflected, as he boarded the TWA flight. He knew there *was* no problem with the phone in the den. He'd look for the telephone bug when he got home.

∧   ∧   ∧   ∧   ∧   ∧   ∧   ∧

WASHINGTON, Spring 1990

"What would one sell for? Difficult to say. *Impossible* to say." Dr. Theodore McC. Burns, Ph.D. waved his hand across the books lying open on his mahogany conference table. "You're talking about objects unique. Price would depend on period. Condition. Provenance." He gave a twisted smile. "The state of the market. Which museums are bidding. Which collectors."

"Could you suggest a range, then? What's the least that one of these icons might bring."

But Dr. runs had not earned his Ph.D. and achieved his ascendency at the National Gallery by advancing rash judgements.

"Impossible to generalize. Give me specifics..." he brought his fingertips together and pursed his lips, an icon of rectitude.

"Well, something from the 14th or 15th century. The sort of icon you'd find in a church in, say, Hungary."

"Hungary. *Ah*. Well, *there's* your problem. Hungarian civilization straddled Eastern and Western Europe. Your icon might be from the Eastern Church, Byzantine, Russian—or equally, from Florence. And between the 14th and 15th centuries, there were—"

"I understand, Dr. Burns. My question was poorly put. What I need to know is...." Philip searched for words that would not trigger another lecture. "...well, would a painting like these have any value at all, really? Except in the religious sense?"

"Good Lord, yes!" Burns snorted. Philip's reversal of approach annoyed the Doctor. "Anything genuine would be worth...thousands."

"And if it had an interesting history…say a miracle attributed to it?"

"Add a zero to the price. Add two zeros." Safe in his sufficiently generalized pronouncement, Dr. Burns removed his rimless spectacles. He opened a desk drawer, drew out a tissue, began to polish the lenses.

"You mentioned 'state of the market'. Is there much 'up and down' with these things?"

"These 'things', as you put it, are graphic representations of the devotional core of Western civilization. A supreme example of man's effort to know God. You referred to a miracle. These *are* miracles. Look at this…" Dr. Burns opened a folio volume, releasing the pungency of printer's ink on coated paper. A full-color page illustrated a Madonna and Child, the Child's head circled by a silver halo enclosing a *crux quadrata*.

"Florentine. 13th century. Artist unknown."

Philip studied the picture, wary of another lecture. The eyes of the Virgin, heavily stylized, seized his mind with their look of sadness and wisdom. She seemed to know the fate of the child she held. The artist had sent his belief across seven centuries, with a power no electronic medium could touch.

"This was purchased for the Getty collection. In 1954. For $80,000. Today, it could bring…three times that." Dr. Burns glanced at his watch. Philip hoped he was running out of time. "Today, with the drug cartels investing in art…heaven only knows what the price would be."

"But this is a famous icon."

"Not *especially* famous. *Good*, yes. But not stylistically significant. Not a landmark in the development of composition, for example. Not the work of a painter who was later canonized—such as Rublev." The Dr. closed the book, a sign that Philip's time was up. He gave Philip a superior smile. "Just another miracle, Mr. Downs."

∧ ∧ ∧ ∧ ∧ ∧ ∧ ∧

Philip walked from the National Gallery along Constitution Avenue, back towards his office. He was walking a lot these days. Walking was a good way to think, undisturbed. The eyes of that icon stayed with him. Telling him something. Maybe he should have studied art. Maybe genuine success was to be had there, among the underpaid and the dedicated. The Florentine artist who painted that Madonna and Child had surely succeeded. What was Philip doing, that anyone would care about in seven hundred years? Or even seven?

Three telephone message slips waited on his desk. Murphy had phoned, suggesting lunch. Ms. Willensky from the library had called. Reid wanted to see him. Zimmerman had left a message: Earl H. Dent's Army serial number. Philip slid Zimmerman's message into a folder and went to Reid's office.

"The FBI has located one of them." Philip didn't say which one. Reid wasn't interested in details. He wanted to hear "progress". If Murphy sat on his information, Philip could use Dent as the one he'd meant. "I've talked with legal. The National Gallery people were very helpful." No names, no specifics. Give Reid the strokes he wanted without pinning anything down.

"Don't let this drag." Reid accepted Philip's report. He must have had another call from the White House. Or it could be that the White House had forgotten completely. Reid might be eager because he wished to make his brownie points before a situation change killed the project. Eastern Europe was shifting by the hour.

"No, I won't. The Hungarians?"

"Leave them out of it. When we find something, I'll handle it from there."

"*If* we find something." He wasn't going to let Reid slip in that assumption of certainty.

"Yes," Reid said, without agreement. "Don't let it drag." Morris gave a joyless smile. "By the way. Had lunch with Pete Anderson today. He's going in June. I thought you'd like to know."

"Thank you." For nothing, Philip thought. IF Anderson went in June, they'd be picking his successor in a very few weeks. So Anderson could give his replacement a fill-in before taking off. Which meant that Philip had to produce quickly, to stay in the running for the Austrian Desk. "That's good to know."

∧   ∧   ∧   ∧   ∧   ∧   ∧   ∧

Philip sat at his desk staring at the lined yellow legal pad. What were his assets, at this point? Four names. Major Caldwell. Sergeant Douglas J. Gordon. Pfc. Earl H. Dent, Jr. Pfc. Llewellyn L. Davis. Plus one Army serial number. And the name of from Major Howard Henry.

Gordon was the only certain connection with the murders, with the icon which had disappeared, as Tibor Szilágy insisted, at that time and place. Gordon must have taken one of the photographers with him on the story. Which one? Caldwell was the CO of *Stars & Stripes*. Not likely to go out on a story himself. But Caldwell might be a man whose memory could be searched. Assuming Philip could reach Caldwell through some channel other than that treacherous little bastard Murphy. Maybe that was why Chieko had called. He picked up the phone and dialed the library.

∧   ∧   ∧   ∧   ∧   ∧   ∧   ∧

Philip finished shaving Chieko's legs and rinsed off the razor. He started to put his clothes on again.

"You do nice work." Chieko ran fingertips down the inside of her thigh, over her calf.

"For a price."

"Right." She slid off the bed and opened a dresser drawer.

"There's a Retired Officers' list. I found Major Caldwell there."

"That's it?" Philip buckled his belt and looked at her. She was still slim in her mid-thirties. Only her legs a bit heavy in the calf. Otherwise,

Chieko had the anatomy to drive a man to distraction. "Hardly top secret stuff."

"There's more." She squirmed into her black panties. "Your Major Caldwell had a considerable career in business. I've made you copies of his entry in Who's Who in Business." Chieko turned her back to Philip so that he could fasten her bra. "And I'm working on your writer. Are there any other publications he might have written for? Besides Stars & Stripes?"

"Damned if I know."

"I can't find the photographers listed anywhere. Even Army photographers. But I'll keep trying." She closed the jar of honey and took it back to the Pullman kitchen. "And I found that Major who survived the murders. He's listed in the Alexandria white pages."

"Look, this is pretty obvious information…. considering the price I'm paying."

Chieko walked from the kitchen and buttoned her blouse.

Then she took her time straightening the knot of his tie. "But you're having fun, aren't you, Mr. Downs." She was telling, not asking. And now, Philip realized, he had Caldwell taped. Plus the survivor's location. He could go to lunch with Murphy and enjoy himself. He'd be able to stall the treacherous little son of a bitch forever.

∧   ∧   ∧   ∧   ∧   ∧   ∧   ∧

Lunch with Murphy was easy. Philip had invited the FBI man to the Sulgrave Club. In the sedateness of the dining-room Murphy was so busy identifying Senators and a Cabinet Secretary at surrounding tables, he half forgot why he and Philip were meeting. Philip kept him amused with gossip and trivia until the meal was suddenly over. Murphy and Philip left, having got nowhere, each assuring the other that the pleasure would be repeated soon.

Back at his desk Philip found the morning's mail. He put the mail aside to concentrate on the directory entries Chieko had found for Major Arthur W. Caldwell. There was a page from *WHO'S WHO IN AMERICA*. "CALDERON...CALDERONE...CALDERWOOD...then, finally CALDWELL, ARTHUR WYKEHAM, investment banker, former manufacturer: b. Poughkipsie, N.Y., Nov. 16, 1903: s. Roger James and Amanda Frances (Wykeham) C.; m. Margaret Jane Wendt, June 6, 1928; children: Arthur Wykeham II, Margaret Wendt, Amanda Wykeham. BA Dartmouth College, 1926. With Greybar Electric Co. 1927; operating mgr. Newark plant, 1930-32. General Electric, 1933; product development mgr., Small Appliances Division, 1935-39; Newark Electrics, 1940-41, Ex. V.P. & gen. mgr. Served U.S. Army 1942-46, discharged as Major, 1946, with Bronze Star, Purple Heart. Caldwell Mfg.. Co., 1947: Pres. & CEO, 1947-63. Eastman, Dillon, New York office, 1965; Sr. Part., co-chairman capital committee, 1966-79. Trustee Dartmouth College 1977—; bd. dirs., Caldwell Mfg.. Co. 1963—; Union League 1970 - 74. Republican. Episcopalian. Clubs: N.Y. Racquet and Tennis, Union League, Metropolitan Club (New York), Short Hills Club (Short Hills, N.J.). Home: 37 Lake Shore Drive, Short Hills, N.J. 07078."

Caldwell had known real success. Home from the war and straight into starting his own business. Where had he found his capital? It would not have been possible to start a manufacturing company with only a Major's mustering out pay. The bare facts of Caldwell's biographical entries neither suggested nor denied the possibility of inherited wealth. His wife might have had money. Or equally, Caldwell might have found his grubstake by selling an art treasure. At least, the man was alive. Philip knew where Caldwell was. Caldwell might lead him to Gordon and whichever *Stars & Stripes* cameraman had covered the Passau murders with Gordon.

Philip turned to his mail. The usual detritus. Then, without warning, an official letterhead:

> Department of Veterans Affairs
> Veterans Benefits Administration
> Washington DC 20420
>
> Ms. Chikako Willensky
> Room 34508
> Department of State
> Washington DC 20260-0439
>
> Dear Ms. Willensky:
> This is in reply to your letter dated June 21, 1990, requesting information from the Department of Veterans Affairs (VA) about Earl H. Dent, Jr. I regret to advise you that Mr. Dent died on October 5, 1977, at the VA Medical Center, 5901 E. 7th Street, Long Beach, California 90822. His cremated remains were interred at the Bethesda Memorial Park in La Marada, California.
> I am sorry to convey such unfortunate news.
> Sincerely yours,
> Marvin B. Sakers
> Director, Administrative Service

Across the bottom of the letter Chieko had scrawled, "Sorry."

Philip folded the letter inside out, slipped it in the envelope, laid the envelop aside, with Caldwell's directory listings. Was he feeling sadness for the man deceased, or just his own disappointment? Dent was unknown to him. A "fresh-faced kid" that Zimmerman had half-remembered. Dent had been dead over a decade now, while men who were his seniors by many years were still enjoying life. Had Dent even been part of this? Or was Dent simply a blind lead, who never had a connection with the Passau story or the missing icon? Well, at least Philip knew where Dent was. It would be worthwhile to find out more about him. A cold trail. However a factual trail. He picked up the phone.

"Chieko? Your letter on Dent was just what I needed. Can you follow up for me? I want his obituary. Died? Long Beach, California. That's right." Philip opened the envelope to check the date. "October 5, 1977. In the VA Medical Center. Thanks, Chieko."

Philip turned back to the WHO'S WHO entry. Caldwell was a hot trail. Alive. Pinpointed. Defined and biographied. Would Caldwell know where Gordon was? The cameraman Davis? If there were a connection among the three, Caldwell undoubtedly knew their whereabouts. Though he'd also be unlikely to tell. And if Caldwell were hiding something, he'd be suspicious of Philip's "brother" story.

Success with Caldwell. Failure with Dent. And the survivor's envelope still to check out. He slipped the directory listings and the envelope into a folder, carefully locked them in his lower right drawer. Philip needed to move quickly now, before Reid got another call from the White House. The fear of a possible misstep filled Philip. He was at the danger point, where the temptation to act—the need to end weeks of uncertainty—could overcome prudence. Success—that bitch Goddess who teased you until you did something desperately stupid. Act in haste, repent in leisure. He who hesitates is lost. There is a tide in the affairs of men…etc., etc., etc. What would his father have done?

It was time to talk again with D. Webster David in Legal. That was an action Philip could take right now, without risking disaster.

^ ^ ^ ^ ^ ^ ^ ^

"You're going to leave the bug in place, then." Web David put on a non-committal look.

"If I yank it, they'll know I know."

"They?"

"It must be that clod from the FBI. They were ham-handed about it. Showing up as a Bell System repairman."

"Why? Why bug you, that is?"

"Murphy is slobbering to get in on the act. Reid probably dropped hints about the White House."

"And if it's not Murphy?" Web had an annoying habit of considering all angles.

"Won't matter. I don't do any crucial phoning from home." Then Philip caught the significance of Web's remark. "Besides—who else could it be?"

"No knowing. Art thieves? Your own people? Even the Commies—they didn't just dry up and blow away after the collapse."

"No matter *who*, it's safer if they don't know *I* know."

"The bug isn't just your phone line. Some of those devices pick up the whole room. House. Conversations with Leecie."

"Well, Leecie's forgotten the project. I think. My problem now is how to approach Caldwell." Philip waited in silence for Web's opinion.

"Well, I wouldn't just phone this Caldwell and ask him where he got his money." Web had the lawyer's habit of hearing out a question, however peculiar, with a straight face. He paused, not yet through speaking. Web angled his head over his left shoulder. His eyes screwed into a squint. He looked out his window at the Kennedy Center. "Why don't you call your broker?"

"Stockbroker?"

"Yes." Web unclenched his hands. He swung his chair towards Philip. "Financial gossip is their stock in trade."

"But Caldwell's been retired for years. The man's 77."

"If your Major Caldwell made any sort of financial splash, someone will remember him. One of the senior partners. Someone."

The practicality of Web's suggestion slowly sank in. The more Philip considered, the more obvious it became.

"But security?"

"All you're asking is where the man's money came from. That's not confidential. Especially not on Wall Street."

"You don't think word might get back to him?"

"If it does, he'll be flattered. He's sitting in Far Hills, wondering what to do with himself. His wife probably has him trimming the shrubs."

"But what about asking Caldwell for information on Gordon? Davis?"

"Your own assumption is probably valid. If there's anything funny, you'd tip your hand. If there isn't, Caldwell probably doesn't know any more about them than this…Zimmerman? ..knew." Web David turned his chair again, leaned forward, picked up a miniature saber letter-opener and began to turn the tiny weapon with his fingers. "Your methods of finding these men are probably as effective as the FBI's, after all these years. Why don't you look in the Social Register?"

"The Social Register?" Philip heard himself repeat Web's words and almost smiled. He was turning into a second banana. They would soon be doing the "Who's on First?" routine.

"Why not? Zimmerman told you that Davis used his soup spoon correctly. He might have come from money."

"Old money." How did Web do it? His mind picked up each detail of a situation. He turned any piece of information into a lead. Oh, God, Philip thought. We're back to Sherlock Holmes.

"Old money." Web conceded. "You could check it in five minutes."

"Without Murphy."

"That's another bonus." Web stuck the saber among the pencils standing in the polished brass casing of a 70mm cartridge. "And while you're at it, don't be seen with that Willensky woman too often. Word is spreading."

∧ ∧ ∧ ∧ ∧ ∧ ∧ ∧

Philip picked up his phone, read the slip Chieko had given him: "Henry, Howard P. 4297 Braddock Road, Fairfax, VA 22032 (703) 323-6014". He dialed the number and waited.

"Hello?" A woman's voice. Hesitant. Middle-aged.

"Mrs. Henry?"

"Yes." Her tone was cautious. "Who's calling, please?"

"This is Philip Downs, Mrs. Henry." He felt it safer to identify himself immediately. "I'm with the State Department. I was hoping to reach Major.. *Mister* Howard Henry."

There was a strained pause. Her accent was upper middle class. Her manner formal. She had not sounded like the class of woman who would be unnerved by a call from an official.

"You're with.. the government, Mr. Downs?"

"The State Department, ma'am."

"I see." She sounded resigned. Relieved. He heard her take a deep breath. "Then I believe you should come here in person, Mr. Downs. You have our address?"

"I do, Mrs. Henry." What was her problem? Was her husband an invalid? Unable to come to the phone? Rather than press his luck Philip accepted her suggestion. "When would it be convenient, ma'am?"

"Tomorrow afternoon? About three?" Her voice sounded as if she were already thinking of other things.

"Thank you, Mrs. Henry. I'll be there at three, then."

"Goodbye, Mr. Downs."

After she hung up Philip still held his phone. There was an echo of something in her voice. As if she had been expecting his call. But this simply couldn't be the case. Yet his call had meant something to her. He hung up, still wondering.

)

The housewife who answered the door at 4297 Braddock Road matched the voice Philip had heard on the telephone. She suited this townhouse, a residence designed for middle-income public servants or double-income couples with one child or less. Her barely tinted hair and pleasantly patterned blouse with Bermuda collar were the uniform of a placid personality, a self-contained life-style.

"Mr. Downs?" She offered him a courtesy smile. Accepted his official calling card. "Do come in."

Mrs. Henry led him through the front living room into a pine-paneled dining room. He took the chair she indicated.

"I have everything ready." She spoke over her shoulder as she opened the china cabinet. He wondered if she were going to offer him tea. Instead, she took a seat across the table from Philip and handed him a legal-sized manila envelope, sealed with brown paper tape.

"I intended to destroy it. But it must have meant something very important to Howard...." Her voice was far away again.

"I understand." Philip gripped the envelope, feeling the thickness of the contents. There was nothing on the outside to suggest what the envelope might hold. Philip was in a situation he still did not understand. She was mistaking him for someone, something—and he took care to leave the impression undisturbed. "I'm sorry."

"It's been nearly five years now." She looked at Philip for understanding. "It was cancer, in the end. Despite his other fears. So I never needed to do anything with it." "It" clearly meant the envelope Philip was holding. "And then your call...."

"Thank you, Mrs. Henry. I'm sorry about your loss." Once again, he was violating a social trust. She seemed to know nothing about the envelope, except that she was prepared to hand it over to "the government". Philip was trading on a false impression. It was time for him to withdraw and investigate later. "You've been most helpful."

As she showed him to the door Mrs. Henry stopped, as if struck by a thought. "I don't believe he was ever in any *real* danger. Afterwards, that is. But he had me keep the envelope ready." She looked at Philip again for understanding.

"A war always leaves its mark, Mrs. Henry. My father—" but he saw that she was no longer listening. He offered his hand, returned her formal smile, and carried the envelope to his car.

∧ ∧ ∧ ∧ ∧ ∧ ∧ ∧

Chapter 3

❦

BAVARIA, Spring 1946

"You have the manners from a gentleman. My mother likes it."

She stood by the window of his room. Afternoon sunlight struck the fine gold hairs on her skin, made a shimmering shell on her naked body. He could still smell the wet warmth from her armpits, the horsiness of her discarded clothes. She turned to look out at the budding trees.

"Your mother is very nice." Lewis rolled over on the bed. He studied her body, like a man buying a horse. The hefty buttocks curved into well-shaped thighs. Her rounded calves swept down to graceful ankles. When she turned and walked towards him an adolescent firmness jutted her breasts.

"Erda…."

She planted herself on his bed. Her eyes locked with his. She ran her right hand up his thigh and gripped him. "You wish to tell me something?"

"Oh, God!" He started to come alive again. It hadn't been ten minutes since they finished.

"That is what you wish to tell me? 'Oh, *Gott!*'?" She teased him with her hand.

"I...not so *hard!*...I'd.. like to...marry you. As soon as it's legal."

"*Aber* you cannot marry to a German girl." She pronounced it '*Tcher*man'. "You are an American soldier. To marry to a German girl is not permitted."

"But it will be. It's just a temporary...*ouu*, easy!"

She smiled, contented. Now she began to use both hands. "Poor Lew. Cannot to marry his darling *fraulein*. *Verboten. Strengsten verboten.* So sad." Her hands were soothing him now. She knew just how to make him helpless, while she drove him wild.

"Erda..." he words came as gasps. His hands shaped her breasts. "...will...you...marry me? When we *can*?"

She withdrew her hands. She let him hold her breasts, but her face went dull. "I can do nothing, until my father returns."

The subject dropped between them like a portcullis. SS *Oberführer* Wilhelm von Reichenberg was still being held by the Russians. Lewis hadn't said so to Erda, but he believed there was a very good chance her father never would come back.

Erda's father had been *Waffen SS,* the military force. Not one of the *Einsatzgruppen*, which carried out the exterminations in occupied countries. The Americans might consider this difference. It wasn't likely that the Russians would bother with such distinctions.

"When your father does come back..." he moved his hands until her breasts opened their eyes.

"*Vielliecht*...." "her voice was distant. Was her "perhaps" for his proposal? For her father's return?

Suddenly Erda's face was pressing into his neck. Her shoulders shook. Her tears came hot against his bare skin. She would be 17 years old in June.

∧ ∧ ∧ ∧ ∧ ∧ ∧ ∧

CHEVY CHASE, 1990

That evening at home Philip slid a CD-ROM into the D drive on his computer, punched up Windows, and waited until the row of icons appeared. He moved the mouse and double-clicked the PhoneCheck icon. The CD set was advertised as containing all the Bell System white pages listings for the U.S., in two CD's, East and West. In the name box he typed: Gordon, D., left the address, state, and zip code boxes blank. He pressed the Enter key again and sat back, while the green light on the D drive blinked and the machine ran through the entire directory.

After what seemed nearly half an hour the screen flashed a list of name, all Gordons, all with first initial D. Philip paged down through four, five screens. Then he clicked the button to get a count of items found. 189 listings of "Gordon, D."

Start again. This time with "Gordon, Douglas". Another lengthy pause while the machine churned. Another list. Count: 87. He had 87 Douglas Gordons, in the East alone. God knows how many would turn up in the West. Start phoning each Gordon? There wasn't time. Murphy had been right. It *was* labor intensive. Unless Chieko Willensky could use her contacts to find short cuts through military records at the national archives.

Just as an exercise in optimism, Philip started the program again, typed Davis, L. in the name box. 9,732 in the East. "Davis, Lewis" got a count of 243. No, he'd have to deal with Chieko. Whatever the cost.

Then he remembered Web David's suggestion, The Social Register. He turned off the computer and turned to the bookshelves. Leecie had been Secretary for her Bryn Mawr class in the early 80's. She kept a Social Register Locator somewhere in the den. Philip found the black book with the orange title, wedged between her 1971 Bryn Mawr College yearbook and a photo album. Davie…Davies…Davis. God, there were pages of them. Laurence L…Lavinia M…Leonard H…Lewis L. Phila, Pa. Success! Web David had hit it lucky. But. The twinge again.

Doubt soured his elation. Was this the Lewis Davis that Philip needed? Not an unique name, after all. Three and a half pages of Davises, in the Social Register alone. And Davis was a Welsh name; half the Welshmen in the world were named Lewis. Philip's feeling of success began the familiar fade.

Did Leecie have the Philadelphia Register somewhere? Philip scanned the bookshelves. *Jonathan Livingstone Seagull.* Dr. Spock, in hard cover and paperback. A sprinkling of parent directories from Sidwell Friends. The entire *Time-Life Encyclopedia of Gardening. Social Register Philadelphia 1984.*

Philip pulled down the book and quickly paged through. At the bottom of page 104 he read: "Davis Mr & Mrs, Lewis L. (Anne C Roberts) Me.Ul.Rd.Pa'50 Phone No 525-7719.. 309 Conestoga Road, Rosemont Pa."

He turned to the front of the Register, where the abbreviations were spelled out. Me—Merion Cricket Club. Ul—Union League. Rd—Radnor Hunt. Pa'—University of Penn Graduate.

"Pa' 50." The year was about right, if Davis had come home from the war and gone directly to college. Philip felt success returning—or was he reading too much into what might be simple coincidence? Web David's suggestion, though logical, was also the longest of long shots.

Still, the man named Lewis L. Davis was there. Documented. Nearby. Easy to locate. A cross-check should be simple enough. Someone from Philip's class at Yale would doubtless live around Philadelphia, belong to at least one of those clubs, quite possibly know Davis personally. Leecie had always insisted that a well brought up person was no more than one introduction away from practically anyone in the whole world. Philip had tried to refute her argument by asking her whom she knew who could introduce her to Mao Tse Tung. Leecie countered that one of the Soong nieces had been in the class below her at Bryn Mawr.

Philip found his 1989 Alumni Directory and began to scan the entries.

∧ ∧ ∧ ∧ ∧ ∧ ∧ ∧

There were phone slips waiting on the desk when Philip got to his office. Ms. Willensky from the library. His broker, Stan Kahn, from New York. A call from Tibor Szilágyi. Philip dialed Stan's 800 number.

"Gruntal & Company."

"Mr. Kahn, please."

"One moment."

Philip was not one of Stan's major clients. He had fed Stan small amounts of business from some of his and Leecie's friends. Stan, however, always treated Philip as if he owned a million dollar portfolio. Over the years a trusting relationship had grown, built on brief phone conversations, on the prudent buy or sell recommendations Stan made.

"Stan Kahn."

"Stan, this is Phil Downs, in Washington."

"Oh, yes, Phil. I was calling you because I've asked around about this…Arthur Caldwell. He retired a few years back, Phil. But one of our senior partners here knows him. *Knew* him. Caldwell actually worked in Wall Street for some years. He sold out his electrical manufacturing company somewhere back in the 60's. Then came to Eastman, Dillon as a partner. Basically, raising capital for various enterprises. He retired with a second fortune in '81 or thereabouts."

"So he had the knack of raising money, then."

"Quite a knack, evidently. *Where* his original stake came

from our partner didn't know. Could have been family money. Caldwell may have taken over the manufacturing company from his father. The business was in operation back in the 30's."

"Stan, you've been most helpful. Thank you very much." It was 9:30. The market was open. Stan would be anxious to get on to calls that would produce commissions.

"Glad to pass on what I could find out, Phil. Let me know when you need some investment suggestions."

Philip put down the phone. Another fading success. Caldwell's ability to find capital was probably all he needed for his successful career. It was not likely that Caldwell had sold an art treasure to finance his manufacturing company. Yet he still had some value to Philip. Caldwell was a direct link with Gordon and with Davis. A definite factor in the equation. Importance unknown.

Philip dialed Tibor's number at the hospital.

"Ah, Mr. Downs. *Philip.*" Sizilágyi's voice quivered with welcome. Philip got that absurd vision of gypsy violins. Paprika. "I am—how does one say?—'ambulatory' once again. I believe it is important that we should lunch together, Philip. Yes? *Soon*, if possible. What do you think?"

"Alright, Tibor. Today?"

"Today! Yes. Delightful." Tibor made the words a blessing.

"Can you manage the Old Ebbit Grille? At 12:30?"

"A trifle public, yes? Especially as I am now on crutches. Would you permit me to persuade you to...."

"Of course. Would you prefer the Sulgrave Club?"

"But how pleasant! And so discreet, yes? You are most thoughtful, Philip." Tibor sounded like a B-movie vampire. Philip could almost smell the Gauloise over the phone.

"12:30, then? At the Sulgrave."

"So kind of you. 12:30, yes? Until then...."

Before Philip could telephone the library, Chieko called him.

"It may be *him*." Chieko's voice was tight with restrained excitement. "I was just browsing through the New York Review of Books when this name leaped out at me. An article on 'Medieval Symbolism in Modern Painting'. And then the name 'Douglas Gordon.'"

"He's mentioned?"

"He *wrote* it. There's a section in the front where they give backgrounds of the contributors. Here, let me read it to you, Mr. Downs...'Douglas Gordon is engaged in a series on the influence of Medieval symbolism in Western European painting during the last half of the 19th century and the first half of the 20th. He is Emeritus Professor of the History of Art at Princeton University.'"

"Chieko, you're a wonder."

"That's why you couldn't find him in Journalism, Mr. Downs. He's an academic."

"Then there must be more information about him. Somewhere."

"Oh, yes. Publications. Directories. Everything. I'll start digging right after lunch. Oh, by the way—they've got the entire Stars & Stripes on microfilm at the Library of Congress. I could see what else Professor Gordon might have written, when he *was* in journalism."

"Chieko, you're a wonder." Philip caught himself too late. He'd have to find another cliché.

"Pay up time tomorrow, noon?"

"How about after dinner, tonight?" Leecie would be going to a DAR meeting at eight, probably not get through until after eleven.

"If you find that more convenient, Mr. Downs, by all means." Chieko's voice told him that someone had come within earshot of her desk. "Bring a jock strap," she whispered.

"Right." Philip hung up the phone and unlocked the drawer in which he kept the Icon file. It would pay to review the papers before meeting Szilágy at lunch. One by one, Philip went through his notes, memos, even the letter from the VA announcing Dent's death. Then a memory nagged. After receiving the VA letter from Chieko, he had folded it inside out, before re-inserting the sheet in the envelope. It was a habit designed to speed location of specific correspondence. Now, the letter was folded inside *in,* exactly as it had arrived from the VA.

Kathie? But she had no key to the drawer. No reason to go into the papers.

No one else had a key to his—but that was a frivolous sense of security, he realized. The desk drawer lock could probably be jimmied with a nail file. Morris Reid would hardly need to pick the lock, if he wished to check Philip's files. No. Someone else had a reason for checking Philip's correspondence. The next time, Philip decided, they would find a few red herrings.

∧ ∧ ∧ ∧ ∧ ∧ ∧ ∧

"An excellent club. Exclusive, yes?" Tibor's tone hovered between confidential and conspiratorial. His left arm was still in plaster. His speech was a tad slow, probably from taking pain-killers. "To belong to such a club, one must have…connections? Yes?"

"My wife's father," Philip admitted.

"Just so. You have had the intelligence to marry well. Yes?" An agreeable smile, half-joke, half-compliment.

"The good luck. Not the good sense."

"It is often better to have good luck than good sense. Yes?" Tibor could turn anything into a compliment. He had not survived to his age, and reached his position in the slippery world of Middle European politics, without knowing which buttons to push.

"It's sometimes hard to tell the difference, Tibor." Philip waited to see what the Hungarian wanted. A progress report, no doubt. Philip had already decided how much—or rather, how little—he could safely tell the man.

"It could be said that there is no difference. Yes?" Szilágyi played with the words, but there was a sadness beneath his levity. "It is lucky to be smart. It is smart to be lucky."

Tibor leaned back in his chair, carefully adjusting the cast on his left arm. The aroma of brandy and a good cigar floated from an adjacent table. He looked around the dining-room, seeing much more than the handful of legislators and the odd cabinet member that Murphy had noticed. Tibor appeared to see an entire world, in which he was both a stranger and a beggar. His eyes returned to Philip.

"And with your search, Philip. You have had…'good luck'?"

The temptation to be honest tugged at Philip. Especially seeing the man in such banged up condition. Tibor had the gift of knowing exactly which tone to take, so that his listener would feel sympathy, confidence, trust. Philip had already cautioned himself against such temptations. But Tibor was getting a fix on him. Philip paused. Moved his knife and spoon casually. Covered his moment of recovery with the appearance of a man choosing words with care.

"The hardest thing in the world to recognize is good luck when it first arrives." Philip heard his own words and smiled at their portentousness. He was aping his father. "That sounds like postcard philosophy. What I mean, Tibor, is that…well, we've probably located the two men. More than probably. But there are three 'candidates', as it were. One of them has been dead for years. Of the two others—the probables—one may not be the man involved. The other may be a mistaken identity. I'm not making this very clear, am I?"

Tibor had gradually leaned forward in his chair. The cast grated on the chair arm. The casual pose was gone. His voice remained steady, but his eyes were quick and probing.

"You think you have found the writer. You are uncertain about the photographer. Yes?"

The surprise must have shown on Philip's face. The Hungarian lowered his soup spoon and made a pacifying gesture with his left hand. "Forgive me. I did not mean to plunge to conclusions Yes?"

Philip realized that the Hungarian had no inside information. Using only what Philip had just told him, Tibor could figure it out quickly enough. They had known Gordon's name from the beginning. Gordon would be the possible mistaken identity. The other two had to be the cameramen. One dead. The other might or might not have been on the Passau murder story.

"But you're right. That's about where we are." Philip gave himself credit for having decided, well before lunch, just how little to reveal to the Hungarian. Philip knew now that he was playing with a mind swifter than his own.

"And you cannot tell me where or who these men are. Correct?" Tibor was taking care not to frighten Philip again.

"Correct."

"But I congratulate you. Yes?" Tibor was again assuming a casual posture, somewhat hampered by the cast on his arm, draped back in his chair. Smiling warmly. "That you have done even so much is remarkable, yes? You are lucky *and* smart, I think."

"One wonders." Philip braced himself for another wave of flattery.

"Oh, yes. You have encouraged me very much, Philip. And now. I hope to encourage you, yes?" He reached down and unzipped his leather briefcase. "You have worked very hard. You will be wondering, 'Is this a wild duck chase'? Yes?"

"Wild *goose* chase."

"Thank you. 'Wild *goose* chase'. Of course. And so I show you that this is not a 'wild goose chase'." He extracted a glossy 8 x 10 inch color photograph from his case and slid it across the table to Philip.

Philip studied the picture. Against a black background, the top of an elaborate gold candlestick appeared to burst like an explosion of light—something between a huge gilded snowflake and a dazzlement of fireworks. In the center of the golden starburst was a small round window or mirror. The baroque design, ornate stem, and rococo base suggested a goldsmith of supreme skill; a Benvenuto Cellini.

Philip looked up from the photograph. Waited for an explanation.

"You are not a Catholic. Yes?"

"Yes. That is, yes, I'm not."

"You will not be familiar with a monstrance, I think. Yes?"

"True."

"This is the Monstrance of St. Emeric. Such a device is used to…show? *display*…the consecrated host. To the worshipers. Yes? The tiny circle of bread…" Tibor searched his English vocabulary,"…the wafer that has become the body of Christ, during the ceremony of the mass."

"Much like our communion."

"Quite the same, I think. Yes." Tibor leaned across the lunch table. Philip noticed again the nicotine stain on the forefinger, as Tibor tapped the photograph. "This monstrance is the work of Johann

Khunischbauer and Matthias Stenger. 17th Century. Vienna. Taken from the Church of St. Emeric in October, 1944. When the Nazis departed from Hungary."

Tibor waited while Philip studied the photograph once more and absorbed these facts. The golden rays of the monstrance had a breathtaking quality, an exquisite physical expression of the magnificence of Christ's presence, contained in a pale wafer of consecrated bread.

"This appeared in Zurich. In 1957. A private collection." Tibor reached into his briefcase and drew out a second photograph. Smaller than the first photo. Black and white. He laid the picture on top of the color photograph of the monstrance.

It was an ornate cup elaborately decorated with precious or semi-precious stones. The picture reminded Philip of King Arthur's knights, of the way the Holy Grail might have looked.

"A chalice."

"Precisely. You have a good eye. Yes?"

"From St. Emeric's."

Tibor smiled his compliment. He nodded. "Appearing in São Paulo. An auction. In 1962." Tibor took back the photos and slid them into his case.

"The vestments—the highly decorated garments worn by the priests at mass, yes?—these were found in Amsterdam. Offered to the *Rijksmuseum*. By a dealer sadly unable to remember the address of the client who had left them with him. That was in 1959. His memory has never improved."

"What do you conclude from all this, then?" Philip could see no way that these church treasures, appearing at intervals throughout the world, made the search for the icon less chancy.

"We know that all those items in the possession of people willing to sell, *have* been sold. Yes? The last sale was nearly thirty years ago. Therefore, the persons holding the icon clearly do not wish, probably do not need, to sell. Yes?"

"Or have already sold it." Philip resisted the Hungarian's conclusion. It was like Reid, drawing him into an agreement from which there would be no escape. "It could be hanging in some millionaire's private gallery."

"A possibility. Yes. However, Philip, I promise you. Had the icon been sold…as you suggest…we would know of the sale. Not to *whom*. Not even the price. But we would know that such a sale *had* taken place."

"But a private sale…"

Tibor raised both hands, pushed the air, spoke with the experience of years of dealing and double-dealing.

"In such a world, nothing is truly private. Yes?" He smiled suddenly. "Because we, also, have information to trade. Imagine." The Hungarian pushed aside his coffee cup and spread his hands flat on the tablecloth. "The millionaire buying for his hidden collection. He wonders. 'Is my purchase genuine?' 'Have I been cheated?' And so he seeks to be certain. Yes? Through dealers who have bad memories, but many contacts. So *we* trade *our* information for *their* information. We do not learn *where*. Not *who*. Not *how*. But we learn *if*. Yes?"

"I see. So you're convinced there hasn't been a private sale of the icon." Philip wondered if there was even more that the Hungarian hadn't revealed. Was this conversation constructed to tempt Philip into sharing information? No matter. There were legal constraints. Practical cautions. "There are no 'if's, then."

"No 'if's, Philip." The Hungarian stamped his Gauloise into the porcelain ashtray. Folded and laid aside his napkin. "For nearly 45 years. Yes? No 'if's at all. I promise you."

∧ ∧ ∧ ∧ ∧ ∧ ∧ ∧

"Shouldn't we be using first names?" Philip looked up from drying Chieko's leg.

"Don't be forward, Mr. Downs." She used the big toe of her right foot to jiggle his privates. Her thighs widened. "A little further up in the crotch, please. Yes.... there. That's it."

She had the taut, smooth musculature of a teenager. Japanese women must age more slowly than Western females. Did they suddenly turn into the wizened creatures Philip had seen in Tokyo? When did the process start? Chieko was 35, without a wrinkle. She pointed to the shelf above the sink.

"I think the sandlewood scent this evening, Mr. Downs. With the jasmine oil." She leaned back so that he could apply the lotion effectively. "Are you enjoying this?"

"Are *you*?"

Chieko giggled. "I've always wanted a slave."

"A white slave."

"Right."

"Does the reality match the fantasy?" His hand slipped on the oiled surface of her thigh and poked her into a twist.

"We haven't gone the whole route yet, Mr. Downs." She ruffled his hair. Pushed her forefinger between his lips. "You'll get you a report at the end of the trip."

"I've got to pick up…Mrs. Downs at eleven." He picked his wristwatch from the bedside table and checked the hour.

"Don't worry." Chieko looped her brassiere around his head and tugged. "I'm already starting to come."

Her prediction was accurate, her climax quick and noisy. She released him and sighed. "Let me get you the papers, Mr. Downs."

As he re-dressed she walked naked to the dresser, opened the top drawer, fished among the lingerie. The insides of her thighs glistened as she flopped back on the bed and held out a manila envelope.

Philip took the envelope, buckled his belt, opened the envelope flap. A sheaf of Xeroxed directory entries. Clipped to them was an item photocopied from the obituary column of a newspaper, and a microfilm printout from *The Stars & Stripes*. Handwritten across the top of the obituary was "Buena Park News, Thurs., October 8, 1977."

> "DENT, Jr., Earl H, age 51 of Montana Street, Buena Park, passed away at VA Hospital, October 5. Survived by his wife, Mary. Daughters, Marilyn and Linda Dent. Two Brothers and Three Sisters. Mr. Dent has been a resident of Buena Park 7 years. At the time of his death, he was employed at Omega Data in Hawthorne, prior to that, he was employed at Porter Cable in Anaheim for 20 years. Services will be held at 2pm Thursday, October 8, 1977 at Richardson Mortuary in Buena Park."

Zimmerman's "fresh faced youngster" had only made it to 51. The spare details in the obituary were almost the clichés of a middle class American life. A life cut off short. But with nothing to suggest exceptional circumstances. Dent had probably been exactly what Zimmerman remembered. A fresh faced kid. Dent's life had been played out in wholesome, regular fashion. Wife, two daughters. Regular job. Then some debilitating illness, a long session at the VA medical center. Cremation and burial.

The dry factual account of Dent's death, burial, survivors, left Philip with a sadness for which he could find no reason. Had Dent known success? Philip had never known Dent. Never would. But, death at 51? 51 was only six years ahead for Philip. Elizabeth would be out of Wellesley. John would still be in Sidwell. Philip shook off the oppressive thought.

"You're getting nowhere," he said aloud.

"I'd say you were home free." Chkieo's voice interrupted his reverie. She was standing, still naked, admiring herself in the mirror on the back of the bathroom door.

"Time to take off, Mr. Downs." Chieko handed Philip his necktie. "I won't see you to the door."

"You better hadn't, with that showing," he made her a Bikini with the palm of his hand.

"A perfect fit, Mr. Downs." She nuzzled his palm with her pudenda. "I'll take a two."

Parked in front of Constitution Hall on 17th street, Philip used the car's ceiling light to go through the papers Chieko had dredged up. He turned to the directory entries on Professor Douglas Gordon.

CONTEMPORARY AUTHORS, New Revision Series, gave Gordon half a page:

> GORDON, Douglas M(McKirdy) 1917-
> PERSONAL: Born, December 12, 1916, in Chardon, Ohio; son of Arthur Kenneth and Flora Elizabeth (McKirdy) Gordon; married Janis Sarah Stoughton, June 25, 1942. Education: Amherst College, B.A. 1939., L.H.D., 1968; attended Princeton University, 1939-41; Harvard University, Ph.D., 1947.
> ADDRESSES: Home—95 Crestview Drive, Princeton, N.J. 08540. Office - Art & Architecture Department, Princeton University, Princeton, N.J. 08540.
> CAREER: Brown University, Providence, R.I., began as instructor, became assistant professor, 1948-55; Princeton University, Princeton, N.J., assistant professor, 1955-56, associate professor 1956-60, professor of fine arts, 1960—, chairman of department, 1963-66, 1976-77. Military Service: U.S. Army, Artillery, three years.
> MEMBER: College Art Association, Society of Medieval Historians (director, 1960-63, 1965-68, 1978-80). Medieval Society of American, Medieval Society of Great Britain.
> AWARDS, HONORS: Guggenheim fellowship, 1955-56; National Endowment for the Humanities fellowship, 1978-79.
> WRITINGS:
> Ligier Richier, Lorraine Sculptor of the 16th Century, Yale University Press, 1952, reprinted, Shoe String, 1970.
> (Contributor) Artisans of the Middle Ages, McGraw, 1960.

(Editor with Arthur Noyes) William of Wykeham, 14th Century Genius, two volumes, Harvard University Press, 1961.
Medieval Buildings and Their Architects, Doubleday, Volume III: Academic Architecture at the Turn of the 15th Century, 1970 and Volume IV: The Impact of New College on the Architectural Development of Oxford Colleges in the 15th & 16th Centuries.
The Medieval Town: 1066-1966, An Architectural Tour in Bayeux, Normandy (pamphlet), Princeton Preservation Society, 1971.
(Compiler with Morley P. Christopher) Medieval Buildings on Paper: Surviving Architectural Drawings, 1225-1945, Stockton Gallery, Mercer Art Center, Princeton University, 1982.
Contributor to art and architectural publications in the U.S. and England.
WORK IN PROGRESS: A study of medieval symbolism in abstract art in Western Europe during the 1920's and 30's.

The newspaper article that Chieko had provided was dated October 5, 1945. Gordon had written a feature story, boxed on an inside page of *The Stars & Stripes*. Above the headline - "Army Sleuths Trace Stolen Masterpieces"—was a black rule,

with the words "Hitler Loved Art". Gordon's piece was illustrated by a photograph of GIs displaying Titian's "Danae" and Bruegel's "Parable of the Blind Men".

> *Munich. Oct. 5 - More than 18,000 priceless works of art looted by the Nazis from collections throughout Europe have passed through two marble buildings, which once housed top-ranking leaders of the Nazi Party, on Munich's Koenigsplatz, but now serve as headquarters for the Army's fine arts detectives.*

Coming from American museums and art history classrooms, knowing nothing about fingerprints and little about pistols, the detectives for the 3rd Army Arts and Monuments Section vary greatly from the Pinkerton variety.

The stolen goods they recover, however, are usually worth many times the value of a missing string of pearls or a filched mink coat.

Hitler, Art Thief

Nazi records, detailing Hitler's art thefts as carefully as other files have listed concentration camp atrocities, are the principal clues for these detectives, who are charged with undoing the work of the Einsatzstab Rosenberg (Cultural Task Force Rosenberg), which carried on the most wide-scale plundering the world has ever known.

Following orders from Alfred Rosenberg, former Reich minister for culture and one of the 21 top Nazis now in the jail at Nürnberg, this task force looted Europe to fill the Adolf Hitler Museum, which the Fuhrer projected for his birthplace town of Linz, Austria.

Wholesale Looting

Rosenberg's experts followed the Wehrmacht. They took every art object they could get in Poland and Russia. They cleared out all Jewish collection in western Europe. But they were afraid to steal big national collections, like that in the Louvre, however, for fear their own people might object to such outright burglary.

When the Hermann Goring division finally retreated from Monte Cassino, the SS troops took a huge part of the art collection of the Naples Museum, which had been hidden in the monastery by the Italian Government. The division magnanimously offered 150 world-famous paintings to the Luftwaffe chief for his private collection. They were so well-publicized, however, that even Goring turned down the gift, preferring that the "hot" loot should be stored in Germany.

Cash Purchases

Some of the better-known works of art, which could not be seized as Jewish property, were bought by Rosenberg's agents under what the Arts and Monuments Section terms "forced purchases". Several items left the Louvre in this manner.

Contrary to popular belief, says Capt. Edwin Rae, who taught art history at Illinois State College, the Nazis frequently paid extremely high prices for these works. The attempts of Hitler's various agents to curry favor with their boss accounted for this generosity. Nazi art dealers outbid one another for the privilege of being the one to hand the Fuhrer a sought-after Rubens, Titian or Rembrandt.

Cultural Rivalry

Another boon to art auctions under the Nazis was the rivalry between Hitler and Goring to enlarge their collections with the same picture. Rosenberg's task force was divided into two camps.

The first, headed by Rosenberg himself, favored Hitler. The second consisted of agents Goring had managed to slip into Rosenberg's organization. The two factions bid against each other, while Rosenberg, who was outranked by both of Nazidom's greatest art patrons, maintained a timorous middle position.

The collecting point possesses a file of letters between Rosenberg and Hitler, however, which settled which of the two would have first choice of all works of art.

There was still another art agency which worked against the entire Rosenberg task force. It was a section on fine arts and monuments attached to the Wehrmacht, and was composed of soldiers who had been art historians and museum *directors in civilian life, very much as is the fine arts section of the U.S. Army, and has an excellent record for preserving art objects.*

While this Wehrmacht agency was, of course, less powerful than Rosenberg's task force, it managed by obstructionist tactics to prevent the Nazi chiefs from obtaining some objects they desired. For example, Goring was particularly eager to get the famed Bayeux tapestries from the Louvre, but was blocked by elaborate administrative red tape devised by the Wehrmacht art section.

Well Preserved

On the whole, says Lt. Craig Smythe, a naval officer who uses experience with the National Gallery in Washington, to head the Munich collecting point, the art works now being unearthed from cellars and mines are in an excellent state of preservation.

The Nazis moved their art, as they moved all other resources, into the redoubt area in front of the advancing Allied armies. Since the 3rd Army collecting point also serves USFA, most of the unearthed masterpieces are now being returned.

Very little has been lost. The biggest difficulties in this respect stem from soldiers' looting, carried out both by GIs and Germans. Particularly large concentrations of art objects were lost in Munich, where 500 paintings, which could not be removed before the city surrendered, have disappeared into the same hands that picked up watches, lugers and cameras. An unnamed castle repository, which served as an American billet, was looted of 116 paintings.

The art works, some of them worth several hundred thousand dollars to their uninitiated owners, will be confiscated whenever they are brought to light. It is virtually impossible to sell a masterpiece which has been obtained illegally, since experts are well versed on the original ownership and legitimate sales of all first-rate and most second-rate and third-rate arts objects.

The GI who wanted to keep his masterpiece would have to hang it in how own home. But he probably would not be able to keep it long.

The innocent looter will not be punished , but the crook who knowingly tries to profit through a stolen work of art has little chance of success.

Philip laid aside the Xerox copies. Gordon's success in the groves of academe was solidly built on superior intellectual power, an uncommon ability to write well. Doubtless Gordon had work habits and political skill that added to his success. Above all, knowledge. The *Stars & Stripes* article proved that even in 1945, before his impressive academic career, Gordon would have known the Hungarians' icon for what it was. Maybe even known where it came from. Gordon would have had a clear idea of the price such an artwork would bring. He would have appreciated, might have valued even more highly, the cultural significance of the Mother of God of St. Emeric's.

Philip then began to play his own Devil's Advocate. Only the most circumstantial evidence connected Gordon with the icon. The man had knowledge. Sophistication. And also—if Szilágyi were to be believed—Gordon had had opportunity. That was all Philip had been able to verify. And no evidence, so far, connected Lewis Davis with Gordon, the murders in Passau, the icon. Dent could easily have been the cameraman covering the murder story with Gordon. Possibly Dent and Gordon shared possession of the icon between them. It was even possible that—but Philip stopped himself. Enough desperation for one evening.

What would his father have done, with a problem such as this? The old man's words, in the old man's judicial voice, came back to Philip. 'When in doubt, collect information.'

Grand. Just what one needed. A rousing cliché. As if Philip had not been collecting information for weeks. 'Collect more.' All right, you old bastard. I'll go after some more information, Philip agreed; resentful, reluctant, grimly aware that the old boy's maxim was right. Dead these fifteen years, was Father Downs. But still right, beyond the grave. That was success.

Philip heard women's voices. The DAR meeting was over. He watched Leecie's form break from the gaggle of chattering pre-dowagers and move towards the car.

∧   ∧   ∧   ∧   ∧   ∧   ∧   ∧

"I don't doubt she's a great fuck," the slap of running shoes against the concrete set the rhythm of Web's words," but I don't think you want to scuttle your marriage to Leecie—or do you?"

"Certainly not. I've *got* to do it. Willensky has the only pipeline into the archives that works." He tried to keep up the pace and control his voice. "How would you like to be turned into a sexual trinket…for a Sensei divorcée?"

"Sensei? Sounds kinky." Web gave a merciless chuckle. "I sense a fortuitous concatenation of duty and desire at work here."

"You wouldn't believe what's in her head. Willensky must have run for his life. But she's turned up the information. She's found the writer." Philip halted and squatted by the curb. "Could we take a break? I'm pooped."

Web turned and continued to jog in place. Web David liked to jog early on Sundays. The stretch along Reservoir Road was usually quiet until late in the morning, when the yuppies started flocking towards Georgetown for brunch. By jogging with Web, Philip could pick the lawyer's brain without feeling guilty about using Web's working day. Web had a framed print in his office that showed an old-time lawyer, conversing on the courthouse steps, over the scrolled motto, "A lawyer's time is his capital and his livelihood".

"Am I in danger of 'invasion of privacy'? Tracking down these people?" They started up again and hit the forward slope of the hill. MacArthur Boulevard branched off to their right. They could still see across the Potomac, where Sunday morning traffic droned along the George Washington Parkway.

"Invasion of privacy? Not likely. You're not publishing anything. You're not tapping telephones or breaking into houses. At least, I *hope* you're not, Phil. If you *are*, don't tell me about it. Invasion of privacy covers people who've become…infamous in some way. Established new identities. Or at least gone to ground somewhere. Then you come along and expose their whereabouts in some way."

The hill became steeper, slowed their pace. Philip kept doggedly on as they neared the German embassy. He began to suck up lungs full of air, fresh with the odor of newly green growth. Was this helping his health? Or simply hastening middle age?

"You're also covered by the 'immunity of a public officer carrying out his duties'."

"But I don't know that these people really have this icon. This might all be somebody's paranoia."

"True."

"If I start poking into their lives, they may find out. And take offense." Philip pulled off to the side of the walk. He was not in as good shape as Web. His breath was coming harder and harder as the grade steepened. Web stopped with him, jogging in place. The lawyer looked back at the water shimmering in the reservoir. He studied the trees along the roadway.

"Phil, you've got two advantages. One, they don't know you have any reason to be after them."

"But the guilty fleeth where no man pursueth."

"I doubt if they feel guilty. Not after half a century." Web stopped jogging, stretched leisurely. "Had enough rest?"

Philip nodded. He was still panting when Web started along the road again.

"And that's your second advantage. Assume they *do* have this icon. Assume they *are* paranoid. They still won't be expecting someone like you to come after the icon. They'd be worrying about the FBI. Or Interpol. Or the IRS. Not the State Department."

"I *could* be FBI, for all they'd know."

Web looked back at Phil and smiled. "You look like just what you are. You couldn't fool a tourist."

"Thanks."

"It's a compliment, Phil." Web stopped at the corner of Foxhall Road and studied the terrain. Left meant a steep upward climb, right a sharp descent. Or they could continue toward Georgetown University. Web indicated the University direction with his chin. Philip nodded. They resumed their jog. "You don't want to look like Sam Spade."

"I don't want to look like an absolute ass, either."

"Then do the social bit. Catch one of them at a party. If they're like most old soldiers, you won't be able to stop them from telling you their war stories."

"Most old soldiers aren't hiding stolen art treasure."

"Think of Raskalnikov, then. Guilty secrets are even more likely to be revealed."

The stark grey buildings of Georgetown University began to loom ahead. They would soon be able to see the Gothic revival lines of Healy Hall.

"So I find these people at a party?"

"Why not. Gordon's *emeritus* at Princeton? Try going up there for Alumni Day." Web kept up the pace. Philip knew they were going for the full five miles. "You'll probably find your other man—that Philadelphian—at a Hunt breakfast."

That, Philip decided, was the principal advantage of legal training. Lawyers were schooled to reduce all matters to the elementary, then to the obvious. Perhaps that was why his father had always proved to be right.

"I wouldn't get too paranoid about people breaking into your files. Or that Hungarian's accident, either. There must be five or six thousand reckless drivers in DC." Web grinned and jutted his chin at 35th street, where it ran up the hill towards Wisconsin Avenue. "There's one now."

"But hit and run?"

Web had already jogged on ahead and didn't hear Philip's question. Or didn't choose to answer.

∧   ∧   ∧   ∧   ∧   ∧   ∧   ∧

"And then when Trish was presented at Court, Queen Elizabeth asked her where she was from. 'The Main Line, Mum,' Trish said. And then Her Majesty answered, 'Ah, of course.'"

The young cousin of Leecie's Bryn Mawr roommate, with whom they were staying in Haverford, Pennsylvania, was driving them down Conestoga Road. The cousin's name was Amanda or Amantha Ashbridge. Philip could never quite catch which. She was variously addressed as "Manthy", "Manna", "Mans". Blonde. Clean jaw-line. The adenoidal vowel sounds that echoed coming-out parties and summers at Bar Harbor. She wore a perfume that reminded him of prep school proms.

"I remember reading in a McReady Huston novel once, 'All Main Liners are created equal—to any occasion.'" Leecie returned Amanda/Amantha's conversational serve with the practiced backhand of an old pro. The cousin gave a throaty chuckle. Philip tried to recall the house number. If the Social Register address had been correct, they should eventually pass Lewis Davis's house.

Philip tuned out the women's conversation so he could concentrate on the driveways and mailboxes they were passing. Conestoga Road wound uphill and down through a series of colonial curves and Native American short cuts. The road never went straight up a hill or directly down a slope. They passed a restored 18th Century farmhouse—or a good counterfeit of one. Walls of fieldstone mortared in spiderweb pattern. A cedar-shingled roof and pent roof with classic lines. Dormers with six-over-nine windows. A split-rail zig-zag fence in front.

The road dropped into a sharp curve. Amantha/Amanda steered the Volvo gracefully down the slope. Her forbears had probably driven oxen along this road. Some genetic imprint remained. Was this where the Conestoga wagons had come from? Philip studied a low, square, single-story stone building that looked as if it had grown out of the hill they were now climbing. Inside a lichened stone wall massive oak trees were posted around the edge of a graveyard. Three or four rows of uniformly low marble headstones marched up the slope of the hillside. A signboard lettered in subdued colors announced the Radnor Friends Meeting.

The numbers on mailboxes were getting close. 417. A vast example of stockbroker Tudor. 390. Small, 1930's Colonial. 340. A late Victorian Gothick frame farmhouse, tarted up with contemporary pastel colors. 309. Philip turned his head to catch as much detail as possible. A quick flash of house, down a circular drive. Spiderweb stonework. Ancient poplars. A property on which money had been spent, to make wealth look ancient and unobtrusive. The Davises lived well.

"I was out with the Howard County last season." Amantha/Amanda's voice slipped back into Philip's consciousness. "The Master's daughter was in my class at Wellesley." She turned the Volvo down a rustic road, past a clutch of Colonial houses. Philip read the road sign. Sugartown Road. At the top of the next hill, Philip could see ahead to what must be the Radnor Hunt. Cars were parked along the grassy slope that lined the roadway. Horse vans and trailers were parked in ragged rows behind a long, low, stone stable. Horses of various types and colors were being led or ridden, to and from the paddock and the race course.

The Volvo parked, Amanda/Amantha distributed two-inch yellow buttons that read "Radnor Hunt Races Patron 1990". She led them into the clubhouse, a squarish brick three-storey farm mansion from the middle of the last century. While Leecie went upstairs to the ladies' room, Philip drifted to the bar.

Wearing his Patron's button and the protective coloration of a cord jacket and tattersall vest, Philip felt confident enough to take a risk. "Have you seen Mr. Davis this afternoon?"

The barman squeezed the wedge of lime before he dropped it into the glass of tonic.

"Mr. Lewis Davis?"

"Yes."

"He's right over there, Sir." The barman slid a paper napkin under the glass and handed Philip the drink.

"Which...?" Philip passed the barman a five and waved away the change.

"In the grey jacket, Sir. With the yellow tie. Oh, thank you, Sir." The barman sounded genuinely grateful. Probably a mistake to over-tip. Philip didn't want to be remembered later by one of the Hunt servants.

"Thank you." Philip cradled the drink and started to move through the crowd, as if going to meet Davis. The barman turned to his next customer. Philip edged through the press of people and found a corner from which he could study Lewis Davis.

Grey herringbone tweed jacket. Bright yellow tie. Holding a highball glass in his left hand. Engraved gold signet ring on the fourth finger. Davis was tall. Six feet at least. Slightly stooped. Well, the man must be well over sixty by now. Didn't look it. Davis was in deep conversation with a woman obviously not his wife. The man's face was lined. He still had most of his hair. When the crowd shifted Philip saw that Davis was slim beneath the grey tweed jacket. When the woman talked, his face came alive. Davis looked like a good listener. The woman was pouring out her feelings about something. Probably the servant problem, by the look of her. Or some difficulty with one of her horses. The crowd gave off a faint aroma of saddle-soaped leather, single-malt whiskey, Chanel, Irish tweed.

Davis glanced towards Philip, one of those quick looks that seem to be triggered by a crude telepathy. Philip looked away and studied the room. A series of paintings in gilt frames. Portraits of former Masters of Hounds, resplendent in scarlet. Some hunt scenes. One or two horse portraits, painted in the manner of Stubbs or Herring. A certain shabby elegance made the place comfortable. Like the members themselves, wearing tweeds especially woven to look old.

Philip's eyes were drawn back to Davis. It was important not to read too much into appearances. This search and stalking easily could make Philip see clues that weren't there. Too many assumptions, built on too few facts. The 'availability fallacy'. Davis had an unmistakable aura of the secure, mannered, aging gentleman. The way he stood, head attentively tilted, carefully taking in the woman's monologue. A thoughtful nod. A sympathetic chuckle. This might well be the man who had used his soup spoon correctly, in 1945.

The woman talking with Davis was distracted by a youngish man in breeches and boots; one of the gentlemen jockeys. Davis was looking around, the body language of a person open to engagement. Without hesitation, Philip approached him.

"Good afternoon." Philip smiled his formal reception smile.

"More or less." Davis half returned the smile. Uncertain whether or not he knew Philip.

"The paintings here—they look like a series by the same man."

"Charles Morris Young. Done in the 1920's. When the Radnor country was still open." Davis talked easily. He seemed content to accept that Philip and he might be acquainted.

"How many are there?"

"Never counted them. Half-a-dozen, I suppose."

"And they're all of the Radnor country?"

"These are. You can see what a magnificent place it must have been, back before the war." Davis turned to a large canvas on the South wall. In the painting a huntsman on a well-muscled grey led his pack of hounds down a stony road. Behind the huntsman's scarlet figure the road wound up a low hill, over a narrow stone bridge, past a rolling meadow fenced with post and rail. The scene was late Autumn. Bare trees threw lengthening shadows over the brownish-green of the adjacent field. Clouds of pale ivory sloped across a chill blue sky. A gaggle of riders, some in scarlet, some in black, followed the hounds at a distance. At the top of the hill a square brick building—Philip recognized it as the Radnor clubhouse—divided two lines of chestnut trees. Charles Morris Young brought Autumn to the eye as successfully as Verlaine brought it to the ear.

"Richard Mellon wanted to buy the set for his collection. The Hunt very nearly decided to sell." Davis sounded, within the limits of what he was prepared to reveal to any outsider, dismayed.

"You have a feeling for art."

Davis hesitated. He switched to the diffident tone of a man who has said too much. "For this art, yes. I suppose it reminds me of the past. What was. Before the developments and the subdivisions. As art, I don't know good from bad."

"The composition is awfully good. The way he's grouped the hounds. The road running back into the picture. That's this clubhouse, there on the hill, isn't it?"

"Hmmn." Davis had relaxed again. "You're right. It is well composed. I hadn't analyzed it." Up close, his expression lacked the full quotient of self-satisfaction so apparent in the faces surrounding them. These were the people Morris Reid was trying ape, in his Potomac subdivision.

"Like a good photograph."

"I doubt the artist would have been flattered by the comparison." Davis smiled. "Well, it's been nice talking with you." He smiled again. Turned towards the archway into the hall. Philip started to protest. Ask another question. Spill his drink on the man. Pretend interest in…what? But Davis continued to move away. Philip had learned nothing.

"Mr. Davis!" Amanda/Amantha paused at the bottom of the stairs, left hand on bannister rail, right hand waggling towards them. She jinked through the crowd, towing Leecie. "Mr. Davis, this is Alicia Downs and her husband, Philip. From Washington. Leecie and Phil, this is Lewis Davis. Mr. Davis is my Trust Officer." She gave Davis a conspirator's smile, linked her arm in his. "May we sit with you at lunch?"

Tribal. That was the word Philip settled on. Everyone in this crowd looked in some way alike. Not like one family. There was too much variety for that. Like a single tribe. The men with almost juvenile faces, until at a later age they turned into Toby jugs. As if their flesh had been boiled by too much alcohol and fresh air. The women looked fresh, clean, strong. Until age desiccated their features and rasped their voices. Both sexes spoke with the hearty volume of people used to conversing on horseback. These people and their forbears doubtless had been riding to the hounds since the days when Pennsylvania had been a British colony.

Leecie's "one introduction" theory had proved out again. The four of them sat at one of the round tables in the dining room, finishing steak-and-kidney pie. Davis brought the ladies and himself glasses of a yellow port, which he explained was bottled especially for the Hunt. Philip preserved his sobriety with lime and tonic. Through the chatter and laughter, Philip recalled a writer who had observed of this class of people that, 'Gaiety was their art and risk sports were their discipline'.

"You mentioned the war. Was that Korea? Viet Nam?"

"The big one. WW Two." Davis was mellow now, softened by the port, secure among his ilk.

"My...father was in that war."

"He wasn't alone." Davis's voice went into the time-resonant timbre that Philip had heard from Walter Winslow and Zimmerman. The old boy was mentally shifting back to his Army days. It was time to move in for the...the clue.

"Yes, my father still had copies of The Stars & Stripes he saved, from Paris."

Davis hesitated. Cautious? Philip panicked for an instant. He had gotten too cocky. Played it too close. Davis was suspicious. Philip felt panic sweep away his sense of good luck and near-success. What if Davis realized? What if Davis went directly home. Made a phone call. Started the icon on a quick trip to Switzerland? The whole game would be ruined because Philip had made one clumsy move.

"I was *on* The Stars and Stripes." The old man's voice was low with suppressed pride. He was making a boastful admission. His hesitation had been modesty, not suspicion. Philip fought against a feeling of guilt. This was too easy. Once Philip said the right words, Davis was practically defenseless. Philip felt a twinge of anger, such as con men are said to feel towards their victims, because the victim makes the scam so easy that the con man cannot resist. Davis's vulnerability was leading Philip to break the tribal trust of social acquaintance, of class, of gentlemen's behavior. Philip knew now how Kim Philby must have felt. Or Burgess and MacLean.

Philip thought of Morris Reid. Pete Anderson. The competition for the Austrian desk. He thought of success. He thought of his father. Reluctantly, Philip cast his conversational bait.

"You must have covered some exciting stories."

"Not really. I was just there at the tail end. A tourist in khaki."

"But during the occupation of Germany...."

"The Germans were amazingly passive, at the end. No resistance movement. No Bavarian redoubts. I got caught behind the Russian lines, once. Back before we realized there was going to be an iron curtain. That, and a series of murders down along the Austrian border, were about it."

Davis was staring across the table, past the crowd of diners, the fox masks and hunting horns on the wall, straight back into the American occupation of Germany.

Philip struggled with himself. Had Davis just told him that he was indeed the photographer with Gordon on the Passau murder story? Or were there other murders? Separated from certainty by the merest breath, Philip hesitated. He had to sound natural. Casual. Carefully, he delivered each word.

"The Austrian border?"

It sounded fake. A line from the straight man to a burlesque comic. Too suggestive by half.

"Yes." Davis accepted the cue. Phil thanked God for that special Port the Radnor Hunt Steward had had bottled. "A place called 'Passau'. One of those dark, medieval towns along the Danube. The murders were never solved." Davis mused awhile. Then he brought himself back to the present.

"Then I came home. Finished school. Never picked up a camera again. Except for family snapshots."

"But you've made a successful career in finance."

"Successful? Well, yes. I suppose." Davis drained his third glass of port. "A very narrow success."

Philip tried to appear casual, to suggest no more than polite interest, as he concentrated on the man's words and manner. The tone as Davis spoke suggested some great opportunity missed. Perhaps some possibility that still tempted him. A priceless icon, hidden away? Waiting to be cashed in? Or was Philip taking the reveries of an old man for more than they really meant?

Bankers, for all the money they handled, were not always well paid. Philip knew trust officers who managed millions but worked for thirty or forty thousand a year. Not a salary that would provide the home Davis lived in on Conestoga Road. But a sizeable sum of money—the price of a rare icon—in the hands of a skilled financial man, might have been the foundation for Davis's lifestyle. If he and Gordon had already disposed of the icon in the 1940s or 50s…Yet if the two men *had* sold the icon, then Philip's chances of finding the Madonna of St. Emeric's were nil.

The party was breaking up. Good-byes exchanged. Promises to call, write, lunch, floated through the flurry of collected gloves and hats. Davis shook hands and disappeared towards the bar.

Amanda/Amantha zoomed her Volvo back up Conestoga Road towards Haverford and the comforts of a family dinner at the Merion Cricket Club. She poured out a stream of comment and local gossip as she drove. The afternoon had been a great success. She knew two of the winners, had once been engaged to the boy whose father's horse had gone so brilliantly over timber.

Philip left Leecie to swim upstream through the social babble. A twinkle of hope had set him to fantasizing. Davis had in some way used the value of the icon to start his fortunes rolling. Through the fifties, sixties, seventies, shrewd investment purchases had built wealth. Otherwise, how could a modestly paid Trust officer sustain Davis's lifestyle?

"Isn't that your Mr. Davis, from lunch?" Philip pretended to notice the mailbox decorated with foxhounds, "L. L. Davis" painted in clear black letters across the bottom.

"There? Yes. That's the Davis's." Amanda/Amantha's mind switched to a different track. "He married a Roberts. Anne Roberts."

It was meant to convey something. What?

"Which Roberts are they?" Leecie backhanded her cue.

"The Pencoyd Ironworks Roberts. They came over with William Penn. At least, Anne and her daughter are in the Welcome Society. I think Anne's great-grandfather started the Ironworks."

Which explained the money. Which then shattered Philip's fantasy. A/A continued her genealogy, but Philip had already let his thoughts drift. He watched the rustic country houses give way to manicured suburban lawns, punctuated by occasional massive gate piers marking the entrance to someone's former estate.

Slowly, a second fantasy began to build in Philip's mind. Davis didn't need money. He and Gordon had kept the icon. Somewhere. Possibly the icon was hanging in the Davis living room right now. Philip might already have driven past the icon twice this very day. It was just a matter of…but Philip stopped himself.

Both fantasies were equally unlikely. And yet, and yet…the icon had to be *somewhere*. Tibor's people had had nearly half a century to narrow down the possibilities. Davis was definitely a man who could be one of them. At least *that* far, Philip had succeeded.

∧ ∧ ∧ ∧ ∧ ∧ ∧ ∧

Chapter 4

❀

WASHINGTON, Spring 1990

"It's all turning to shit."

D. Webster David's office had a leather couch. The lawyers were able to negotiate better digs for themselves. Philip dropped onto the couch, bent forward, rested his hands on his knees.

"I talked with one of them. Got nowhere. I even began to wonder if I was sane. My secretary's beginning to wonder why I'm out of the office so much. My marriage is in danger. If I could just find *one* damned fact that would tell me they have the damned thing...."

Web steepled his fingers, went into a preparatory silence. "Could be, you should reverse your field."

"What?" Philip was not in a mood to entertain gnomic advice.

"Try to prove that someone else has the painting."

"No, no. The Hunky's already been checking that out. For fifty years. Nobody else *can* have the icon. He claims they've checked out every other possibility."

"I'm sure he does believe it. That doesn't make it true." Web unsteepled his fingers. Cleared his throat. Rubbed the back of his head. "If you could establish that someone else has that painting, you'd be off the hook with Reid."

"How do I do that? Run an ad in the personals column? 'Wanted, Mother of God of St. Emeric. Cash paid. No questions asked.'"

Web David continued as if Philip had not spoken. "There *are* dealers for this type of art. If the right sort of person made a serious offer, I think you'd find them responsive. It's their business to be."

"The 'right sort of person'?"

"Someone who's demonstrably able to afford art of this kind. Who might have a legitimate interest. Someone on the board of the Corcoran, for example. Or the National Gallery."

Philip had learned to respect Web's judgement. He nodded slowly. At least it was a chance to get out of Reid's trap.

"What if a dealer does come up with the icon? How would I get out of the deal? They might even go straight to the collector. Or sue me."

"You wouldn't necessarily reveal the name of the person you were inquiring for. *You*'ve got sufficient credentials to pass as someone fronting for a rich collector. Any deal can be aborted later. Over price. Over terms. Happens every day."

"And where do I find this dealer?"

Web David thought for another long moment. "Well…your man at the National Gallery—Burns?—might know." Web's phone rang. He turned to answer. Listened for a few seconds. Then he looked at Philip. Held out the phone for him. "It's Reid's secretary. For you."

∧   ∧   ∧   ∧   ∧   ∧   ∧   ∧

"It doesn't seem to be moving very fast. Would it be better if I got you some more help?" Reid laid his cigarette in the malachite ashtray. He knew Philip would be perfectly aware of the threat. "More help" meant somebody else in the Department. Someone who would share—probably monopolize—the credit.

Philip felt his lips tighten and go numb. He recognized this as a dangerous moment. The threat came from his own temper, more than Reid's veiled coercion. What the hell did Reid expect? 'Not moving very fast'. How the hell fast was Philip supposed to track down survivors from World War II? Find their identities? Establish that they had this "Mother of God"? Get them to part with it?

"I've located the two men." Philip heard the unmistakable rancor in his own voice. "That took some doing, as you can imagine."

"The FBI man?"

Philip hesitated. Better to leave Reid in the dark about Murphy and his treacheries. "A combination. Good luck. Some spadework in the library. Chieko Willensky was a great help."

Reid looked satisfied with that. All Reid cared about was the bottom line. Reid had built his career by being responsive to the corner offices. It was important now that Philip not let his temper push him into another of Reid's traps. A time commitment. A promise to deliver.

"I've got to find out whether or not these men actually have this 'Mother of God of St. Emeric's.'"

"But didn't the Hungarian—"

"That's all hearsay. Process of elimination. Not fact." Philip felt himself coming under control again. "We're also in a questionable legal position. Even if these men do have the icon. I've been consulting with Web David."

"How soon can we tell the White House something?" Reid stubbed out his cigarette.

You can tell them right now that this is a piece of shit, Philip thought. "I'll know better once I've seen the men in person." Philip tiptoed around the open trap. "That's scheduled for the next several weeks." Reid wouldn't know about the Radnor Race Meet; Philip had gone to

Philadelphia on a weekend, paid his own expenses. Alumni Weekend at Princeton was coming week after next.

"Don't sit on it." Reid was prepared to be satisfied for the moment.

Philip tried to re-establish an air of cordiality with his voice. "Of course. As soon as I get to a definite conclusion, I'll let you know."

He left Reid's office wondering, again, if he might not have been happier in the brokerage business

∧ ∧ ∧ ∧ ∧ ∧ ∧ ∧

NEW YORK, Spring 1990

"So Dr. Burns thinks highly of me, does he?" Nicholas Menelakos was all ego and a yard wide. Silk suit. Thick neck. Panama hat. Menelakos gave off a faint odor of lavender, talcum powder, and bay rum. "He *should*. I have provided some of the most important items in your National Gallery."

"I told him I wanted to start at the top. He said you were the best." Philip had met the Menelakos type before. Around the Mediterranean. In Europe. Their suits could be less expensive than this man's. Their diamond rings fewer. Or more. Some had gold teeth. Others had facial scars that did not come from student days at Heidelberg. But with their quick eyes, their arrogant, accented English, they were always the same man. Always selling. A house. A contact. Information. A woman. Menelakos was familiar enough. But it was a novelty for Philip to be sitting in a New York restaurant with such a man.

What Burns had *actually* said was that Menelakos was a sly, slippery devil who would know, assuming anyone did know, if and where one might purchase the St. Emeric's Mother of God. Philip had chosen *La Côte Basque* as protective coloration: people who could afford to purchase from Mr. Menelakos would inhabit such restaurants. The lunch tab would exceed $100. No chance Menelakos would pick it up. Philip would have to pay, and make up from his own pocket the difference between the check and the government meal maximum of $25.00.

"So, now you are at the top. And what do you seek from the top, Mr. Dance?" Menelakos flipped the massive menu to the waiter. "As you can see, I prefer to be direct."

Direct. Oh, yes. Menelakos was as direct as a spider's web. The dealer was also saying "Don't waste my time."

"I appreciate your directness, Mr. Menelakos." Philip played to the man's pretense of being straight forward. It had worked before with these types. Men of this background often saw the Anglo-Saxon mind as child-like and simple, easily gulled. "I'll come right to the point. I've been asked to locate, for possible purchase, a 14th Century piece of art. An icon from Eastern Europe."

Menelakos watched the waiter pour half an inch of a *Gris d'Alsace* into a glass. He picked up the glass, swirled the wine, sniffed it. Then took a sip. Chewed the wine briefly. Nodded. The waiter filled both glasses.

"Then you should approach the owner. Make him an offer." Menelakos looked up from his glass. His left eyebrow rose. "You do not expect that I have this painting stolen for you?" He laughed deep in his chest. "I do not do such things."

No. Of course not. A man of your character and charm, a thief? Perish the thought. "We don't *know* the owner. That's why we came to the top."

"A wise move, Mr. Dunns. You saved yourself much time. Not money..." Menelakos took a quick sip, set his glass aside. "...but time." He studied the plate of vichyssoise the waiter placed before him. "This painting of which you do not know the owner. Where does it come from? What does it show? Who painted it, in what century?" He laughed again, the chest-deep laugh of a man satisfied with his own expertise. "They painted 14th century icons in many different centuries, Mr. Duns. Some of them even in the 14th century."

It was time to show Menelakos that Philip had a serious commission. "It's known as 'the Mother of God of St. Emeric's.' Attributed to a 14th century Greek artist named Theophanes, or one of his pupils. Possibly Rublev."

Menelakos suddenly seemed to put on mental sun glasses. He gave the soup full attention. When he spoke, he sounded like a man ripe with power. "Who wishes to have this 'Mother of God', Mr. Dance?"

You're not conferring the thing, Menelakos, he thought. You're selling it. But Wed David had prepared Philip for the question. "You'll appreciate, Mr. Menelakos, that the buyer prefers to remain anonymous. I believe that's not unusual in purchases of rare art."

"Someone of Hungarian parentage, possibly. An American millionaire. Eager to possess a memorabilium from his ancestral homeland."

Burns had been right. Menelakos was the top drawer. Philip began to feel the same unease that Tibor Szilágyi stirred in him. These Eastern Europeans had quick minds, ancient knowledge, no matter how tacky their clothes or manners. There was one major difference between Tibor and Menelakos. Philip felt in no danger of liking Menelakos.

"There would be sufficient funds to make a substantial offer." Money was the *lingua franca* of these people.

"But if you do not know the owner...." Menelakos started on his *quenelles*. Philip realized another common trait of these men. They were all voracious eaters.

"But if *you* do know."

"My knowledge would double the price, Mr. Dunns."

Or triple it, Philip thought. Do you have the knowledge, though? Menelakos was now at his smoothest. Impenetrable.

"As it indeed should., Mr. Menelakos" Philip gave a smile he didn't feel. "That's why I was sent to you. The top."

"You do not know how fortunate you are, Mr. Dunns." Menelakos settled himself for an extensive ego trip. Philip knew all the signs. The shift of shoulders back against the banquette. The cocking of the elbow.

The self-satisfied tilt of the head. It didn't matter, as long as Menelakos came up with positive knowledge that the icon was available somewhere else, not hidden with the two Americans veterans.

"You are fortunate. First, because I am talking with you. Usually such a discussion would not be available for you. But Dr. Burns is an important customer. Also he knows other important customers.

"You are even *more* fortunate that I am an honest man, Mr. Dunns. I have honesty like a disease. Otherwise, I would quickly promise you this 'Mother of God'. We would haggle over price for a few months. First, the owner would agree to sell. Then the owner would decide not to sell. Finally, the price would reach the highest figure I could squeeze from your client. Then I would produce this 'Mother of God' for you. A convincing fake. A *very* convincing fake, painted while we haggled. One that would fool even your Dr. Burns."

The dealer wiped his mouth with special care and put the napkin aside. He shifted his body on the banquette. He pushed away his empty plate and leaned forward. Philip waited in silence. The ego trip was nearing its end.

"You wish to have the 'St. Emeric Mother of God', Mr. Dunns? Then I will tell you where it is." Menelakos laughed his deep Middle-Eastern laugh. Smiled his charmless smile. Then his face went serious. "The icon you seek is in some…what do you say? loft? Garret?"

"Attic?"

"Of course. Attic. Your icon is in an attic. Somewhere in America. Brought here by an American soldier. Who does not know what he has. Or had. It could be that he sells it. For a few dollars. To someone who *also* does not know what he has."

Menelakos watched Philip to see the effect of his words. His barbershop odor had increased. Without speaking, Philip looked around the room. The expensive people. Finishing expensive lunches. None of them had to work for Morris Reid. None of them had to chase a painting that had disappeared half a century ago. Philip searched his mind anxiously. Were there reasons that Menelakos could be wrong? Was it possible that the dealer couldn't really know *that* much about what was and was not available? He turned back to Menelakos.

"You're certain." Philip let his voice sound discouraged. Ordinarily, he would not have revealed so much emotion to a stranger. He laid his credit card on the luncheon check and handed them to the waiter.

"Mr. Dunns, only one person in the world would know for certain if your 'Mother of God' could be purchased—at any price whatsoever." Menelakos was now lecturing a not too bright student. "You have just dined with that person."

Philip listened to Menelakos repeat his self-satisfied chuckle. It was an ugly moment. Because he knew the sly, slippery, tacky-looking old devil was right

∧ ∧ ∧ ∧ ∧ ∧ ∧ ∧

PRINCETON, Spring 1990

Philip had discovered, over the years, a selection of minor pleasures he could enjoy without guilt, shame, or putting on weight. One of the most lasting was the pleasure of removing the pins from a new shirt. After getting off the two-car Dinky from Princeton Junction, Philip had walked up to Nassau Street. Stopped at Langrock's. Purchased a shirt before he checked into the Nassau Inn. Now, with an almost sensuous satisfaction, he drew the pins, one by one, from the blue button-down Oxford cloth shirt. The fresh scent of virgin Oxford cloth stirred memories of presents opened, boxes of laundry delivered.

The shirt unfolded like a body coming to life. Philip undid the buttons and slipped his arms into the sleeves. It was like putting on a uniform again. He would shortly join battalions of Ivy league graduates, swarming across the Princeton Campus for Alumni Weekend.

A late breakfast at the Inn. A brief look at the Times. Then Philip walked up Palmer Square, crossed Nassau Street. He entered the Princeton campus through the massive, ornate gates on the flagstone walk that led to Nassau Hall. Somewhere on the face of the building was the scar from a cannonball. A round

fired by Alexander Hamilton's five-pounder, when British Grenadiers holed up in the Hall during the Battle of Princeton. The invaders today wore many different uniforms. Each returning class had its own costume: the class of '84 were dressed as kilted Scotsmen; '67 wore white tie and tails, like a hundred ill-matched Fred Astaires turned loose in the crowd. There was a sprinkle of clowns, too far off for Philip to make out the year on their class badges. What looked like Colonial infantry had clustered at the North end of Nassau Hall. Probably another class, but looking like a re-enactment of the Battle of Princeton.

A carnival mood animated the crowd. Old grads met each other with exaggerated greetings. Presented spouses. Watched offspring scamper around the grounds in tee shirts reading "Princeton '97", "Princeton '98" or later years. The old grads were busy appraising each other's women, deterioration, status.

Was it any different, really, from Yale? Philip thought back to when he was at Branford, Web David at the Law School. It was the younger people here who had changed most. It would be no different at Yale. Years of being away, years of living aboard, had altered Philip's vision. A progression of time was visible here, as the Alumni formed up for their parade. The class years would shortly pass in battalion review; a living chronology of the social change that ran through the middle decades of this century.

The march-past began. The most recent class led the parade, a mixture of fresh, exuberant faces, energetic strides, pride and self-consciousness in equal measures as they paraded to the lively music. Philip studied each passing class with the interest of a man facing middle age. The further back the classes went, the more uniform they looked; the Twenties and Thirties were pure Anglo-Saxon. The Forties began to show more mixed types. Jews. Italians. Some Slavic faces. The people who would have had a hard time making it into the eating clubs.

The Fifties and Sixties had broken the Wasp ascendency. The Wasps were still there. Still in the majority. But no longer a solid phalanx as they marched past behind the banners of their class years. And with the Seventies came blacks, women. The end of civilization, as Old Princetonians knew it. *Sic transit gloria ethnic.* There was indeed room at the top.

Philip turned his thoughts to Gordon. There were to be open houses at the various departments. Art & Architecture...he unfolded a map of the campus. Art & Architecture was in a late Victorian building, on the North edge of the Campus. Philip strolled through several quads of Gothic pastiche. He passed a stone market-cross replicated from Medieval Suffolk and erected near the University Chapel. Gargoyles scowled down at him. Flagstone walks led him beneath arches patterned from the 14th century.

The witch-burning stench of hamburgers being charbroiled turned his head as he went down a series of steps towards Art & Architecture. Laughter rang around stone corners. The shouts of children rattled leaded panes in windows of Gothic perpendicular.

Inside the brick Victorian building there was a welcome coolness, a smell of floor polish and old books. Grads of various ages and their camp followers were scattered through the halls. A cased exhibit in the main lobby displayed Louis Kahn's 1930's plans for a model town. A varnished directory board gave Prof. Douglas W. Gordon's room number: 134. It was down the hall to the left. Door open. Burble of conversations leaking out into the paneled hallway.

The thin-faced man with the quick smile must be Gordon. He was the only one in the room who had the age to be Emeritus. When he spoke, there was polite attention from the gaggle of grads, less from the sprinkling of their wives, girlfriends, children. The man's voice carried the skill and authority of the practiced lecturer. His delivery made the most of each operative word. Philip listened as the man artfully delivered what must have been a favorite classroom joke.

"Never forget that Adolf Hitler was really a failed architect." The assembled grads chuckled, though most of them were far too young to remember Hitler at first hand. "It gives you an idea of the sort of ego the profession attracts." The chuckles grew into rueful and recognizant laughter.

The man who was probably Gordon looked up. Caught Philip's eye. Smiled. His deeply lined face was very much alive.

"Welcome!" He extended his hand.

"Thank you, Professor." Philip moved through the group to shake his hand. He could feel a look of curiosity from several of the grads. Philip didn't give his name. That might cause the Professor to search his memory for a connection that wouldn't be there. It would soon be necessary for Philip to account for his presence, unless… "Did you know Hitler personally?" he smiled at Professor Gordon.

Philip heard the laughter around him. The joke had worked.

"We were not close friends." Professor Gordon's eyes turned mischievous. "He was just closing up shop when I got to Germany. I looked upon his mighty works, and despaired."

The Professor was paraphrasing some quotation. But what? Philip wished he had paid more attention in Lit. I.

"Your quotation is from…" Philip let his silence spur the Professor.

"You have a good ear. Shelly. 'My name is Ozymandias, king of kings: Look on my works, ye Mighty, and despair! Nothing beside remains of that colossal wreck, boundless and bare. The lone and level sands stretch far away....'"

Gordon's voice made Shelly's words live. A somewhat awed, appreciative silence followed. Philip felt, rather than saw, why Gordon held his prominence. The man could touch your mind, expand your perception.

"Thank you, Sir. Very apt." Philip let the conversation shift back to the grads competing for their former teacher's attention. Once Gordon was sufficiently engaged, Philip casually turned to the pictures and book shelves that covered the office walls. He half-hoped to find the Mother of God hanging among these pictures on the wall. A Piranesi etching of the Nymphaeum of the Gardens of Licinius. Two framed pages from the Nürnberg Chronicles. A small oil painting of a Roman aqueduct. Portrait photographs of men Philip took to be art experts. He recognized Bernard Berenson's picture, and a squarish face that was probably Lord Clark.

The books on the shelves were arranged by types of art. Medieval sculpture. Tomb art. Painting. Architecture. Then a section filled with Gordon's published works. *The Violence of Picasso; Echoes From the Middle Ages. Tilman Reimenschneider and the Tyrolean Ideal. The Architecture of War: Bernard de Rughe's Fortification of Rothenberg. Renaissance Remnants of Gothic Themes.* Nothing to suggest icons or the earlier centuries.

One very thin volume, bound in dark buckram, untitled, extended higher than the other books on the top shelf. Philip looked over his shoulder, saw that more old grads had joined the Professor's audience. Suddenly Gordon spoke to Philip, from across the room.

"We're off to the President's reception for half an hour, Mr.—"

"Downs, Sir. Philip Downs."

"Mr. Downs. You're welcome to join us, if you like."

"Thank you, Sir. But I'll have to be leaving shortly."

"As you wish." Gordon gave him a departing smile. The Professor led his group briskly out into the hallway and off. It didn't seem to occur to Gordon that he should lock up his office. But then this was Princeton. Gordon was of an age to remember when gentlemen trusted each other. Philip's father had often quoted an earlier Secretary of War—possibly it was Henry Stimson—who had refused to permit intelligence surveillance of foreign embassies, making the comment, "Gentlemen don't read each other's mail." It was never clear to Philip whether his father had admired or pitied the Secretary.

Philip took advantage of Gordon's departure to linger, reach up, and gingerly pull out the thin volume among Gordon's books. It was a bound copy of Gordon's Ph.D. thesis. From Harvard, 1950. As he read the title, adrenalin shot into Philip's bloodstream.

Miraculous Attributions of Middle European Icons and their Psychological Consequences

Philip thumbed quickly through the paper. He ran his eye rapidly over the pages. St. Adauctus…St. Basil…St. Nicholas…St. Emeric, Mother of God.

Philip stopped at page 48. Halfway down the page, it began: "Amongst the Hungarian shrines to which pilgrims journeyed in the Middle Ages the monastery Church of St. Emeric, at Nádudvar (Tolna County) was prominent, the attraction being the relic of Christ's blood preserved there[90], and the Mother of God icon[91] that was undoubtedly the work of Feofan Grek[92] (Theophanes the Greek), probably a Cretan[93] who reached the Russian Empire via Constantinople[94]. Although the shrine at Nádudvar was probably not confirmed as a place of pilgrimage by the ecclesiastical authorities until 1434[95], it had in fact…."

Philip glanced up from the page to see if his actions could have been noticed. Gordon and his gaggle of former students had still not returned from the President's reception. The building was silent. He turned back to Gordon's thesis.

"…emotional charging of the Holy Features is epitomized in the Mother of God of St. Emeric's. Compared with the spectral rigidity, the hard monotony of the conventional Byzantines, these more animated eyes, the little touch of sweetness in the still, mild face, must have been like a smile out of heaven."

Tense with excitement, Philip fought the urge to press his luck. He had read enough to know that Gordon was familiar with the icon. An illustration of the icon would confirm that Gordon had, or had once had, possession of the Mother of God of St. Emeric's. Philip flipped rapidly through the pages. There were no pictures at all in the paper. Probably back in '50, before Xerox machines, there would have been no economical way to include illustrations in a doctoral thesis. Philip had to be cautious about making judgements on the technology extant, at a time when he would have been only four years old.

But elation sang through his system. Even a man with Gordon's obvious eloquence could never have written such a detailed and moving description of the painting, unless he had seen it himself. If Gordon had seen the Mother of God, he must have seen the painting after it disappeared from the Church of St. Emeric. There was simply no way Gordon could have been in Hungary, in the church of St. Emeric, while the icon was still there. Once the icon had been looted, Gordon's only chance ever to see the picture was if he had had his hands on it.

A sudden sound of opening doors. The burble of gathered voices. Multiple footsteps down the hallway. Philip re-inserted the bound thesis between two of Gordon's more recent books. He slipped quickly out the door of the office. Turned left. Waited around a corner until the group had resettled themselves in Gordon's office again. Then Philip quietly walked towards the building entrance.

Passing Gordon's office, Philip's look was drawn irresistibly to the small group of grads inside, gathered around Gordon. There was glow on their faces. Their voices sounded rich with shared feelings, common memories. Sunlight streamed through the Victorian window frames. Fell on the Piranesi print. The sunlight stirred dust motes. Etched Gordon's features as he smiled, parried witticisms, appraised comments.

Philip hesitated, watching the man. Fascinated by his own discovery in the thesis. Held by the attraction of Gordon's wry wisdom, personal warmth. Entranced by the knowledge he now held, about Gordon's connection with the Mother of God, the power this knowledge might give him. The opportunity for success.

Philip slipped down the hallway and out onto the campus again.

∧ ∧ ∧ ∧ ∧ ∧ ∧ ∧

BAVARIA, Winter 1945

Southeast of Regensburg the road dropped to the river level, curving with the Donau's edge. Strips of mist snaked across the roadway at irregular intervals. Whenever the jeep shot through a patch of mist the whiteness blinded them for a few seconds. Gordon was tired of braking each time the headlights brightened a new swirl of haze. It was almost midnight. No other traffic on the road. Inside the jeep there was a dull glow from the speedometer light, the gas and temperature gages. Gasoline fumes cut through the smell of sweaty woolens. Lewis had been silent for the last ten or so kilometers. Gordon could think about how he was going to write his story.

"How soon do you think it might be legally possible to marry a German girl?" Lew's voice was at its most serious, most tentative, most adolescent.

"Are we talking about that young lady where you dropped off the cigarettes? With the horses?"

There was a silence. Gordon had tread on serious, sacred ground. Maybe these kids didn't know how obvious they were. Did Gordon really want to spend his life teaching youngsters like Lewis Davis about culture and art? All these kids really wanted to do was screw. Davis was an exact specimen of what would be waiting for Gordon, in the classrooms of the Ivy League. The thought took his mind away from mentally writing his murder story.

"We might be." Davis spoke at last. He was really hooked.

"Well…" Gordon hesitated. He was now acting *in loco parentis*. Gordon sensed that his audience would not react rationally to a direct negative. He sought an oblique line of attack. "At least by the time you finish college, the regulations will probably be changed."

Silence. That had been the wrong answer. Had Davis already got the girl pregnant? Gordon was hesitant to elaborate on his answer.

Too much responsibility was involved. The grind of the jeep motor filled the silence. When he swung the jeep into a sharp curve, the jerricans in the back bumped softly, sloshed their contents. Another patch of mist. Gordon braked, then picked up speed when they cleared out of the mist.

"Somebody else might get her. If I wait that long." Davis was in real pain. Gordon resigned himself to an in-depth discussion.

"They'd have to find her, first. That's not easy. Not in those Bavarian hills." A pale hope might distract the lad. There were still strict regulations against marriage with a Fraulein. This particular *Fraulein*, in the brief glimpse Gordon had of her, looked like a classic junior Junker. Probably had a swastika tattooed on her ass. A father in the SS.

"You think so?" Hope stirred in Lew's voice.

"Well, there aren't any German men of her age left. They're all dead. Or PW's in Russia. They won't be home for years. The GI's will be pulling out soon. No GI is likely to find her, out on that farm. How did *you* find her?" Distraction might work as well as obliqueness.

"On the way back from Hof. I got lost. She was exercising a horse along the roadway."

"So you stopped and took her picture."

"Something like that."

"Love's old, sweet song began."

Silence again. He had hit another nerve.

"She's not knocked up, is she?"

"No." The "no" was not tentative. Lewis was just young, not stupid. And in love. The youngster rode along in silence.

"I think she'll wait for you." Gordon hesitated. This was tricky ground. Back in the States, Davis would probably forget her quickly enough. Nothing lasts long, at nineteen. But Gordon did not intend to be the one to tell him that. "Feel like a piss call?"

"Yeah."

Gordon took his foot off the accelerator, slowly steered the jeep onto the verge of the roadway. Cut the lights. Switched off the ignition. The doors of the winterized jeep squeaked open. They stood outside the vehicle and stretched for a moment.

Where the mist was broken, moonlight fell like a thin frost on the darkened ground. A vast silence wrapped around them. Faint metallic belly rumbles sounded beneath the jeep's hood as the motor cooled. Somewhere far distant, a somber bell rang the half-hour. The sour iron sound came at them from ahead and behind in the darkness.

Each of the men moved in a different direction. Took a few strides, stopped. The hiss of urine sounded on the frozen ground. A tendril of steam rose, making the odor distinct in the chill midnight air.

"We got anything to eat?" Davis's voice carried clear in the frozen air. If adolescents weren't screwing, they were anxious to eat. Gordon made a mental note to delay parenthood as long as possible. Possibly forever. Except that Janis wouldn't stand for that.

"There're K-rations in my musette bag. Some Hershey bars."

"Thanks!" Davis scrambled back into the jeep. Gordon heard him begin to fumble through the baggage in the rear. Moonlight etched the large encircled star stenciled in white on the jeep's hood. Gordon smelled pine needles in the damp night air. It had been a mistake to mention the Hershey bars. With chocolate in his hand, Davis would probably want to drive straight to his *Fraulein*'s farm.

"What's this?" The photographer's voice came muffled from the jeep's interior.

"What's what?" Gordon buttoned his fly and walked back to the jeep.

Davis climbed out into the moonlight. He held a bundle, about the size of an attaché case, wrapped in blanket material. "It was on top of the jerricans. Next to your bag." He laid the bundle on the jeep's hood. In the moonlight, the rough blanket material looked like Wehrmacht grey. Davis climbed back into the jeep, eager for food.

Gordon touched the coarse grey cloth. He prodded the bundle carefully. Took it in his hands. Hefted it gingerly. Not metal. Light. Nothing likely to explode. Carefully, he turned the bundle until he found where the cloth folds met and were tucked together, like a paper-wrapped package. He untucked the folds, opened the material.

Her eyes caught him immediately. Gripped him. Looked into his own soul. The night, the frozen air, the mist that drifted up from the Danube, all faded. The monochrome moonlight had drained most of the color from Her face. But Gordon was seeing something that reached across centuries. Touched him with a sadness deeper than words.

"Mother of God..." Gordon heard his words whisper into the frigid night. He knew Her. As surely as if someone had wrapped an oil portrait of Janis in a blanket and left it in the jeep. Her curving nose was familiar. The small, sad mouth. The eternal eyes, that saw with unmeasurable grief what Her infant Son must become. It was a face that, despite every sorrow to be, accepted God's will.

Gordon knew Her of old. But from where? His mind searched back through the years. Past the murders, the war, his marriage. An image floated up from Amherst. The library, late afternoon sun sliding across the paneled room onto an open book. Wynkoop's *The Birth of Western*

Painting. A full-page color illustration of a mosaic in the Hagia Sophia. "Head of the Virgin from a Deesis of the 13th Century." This was the same woman. The mosaic in the book had been fragmentary, no trace of the Child remained. Yet the Mother and Child in front of him now were surely drawn from that Greek original. And the Greek original had been based on St. Luke's portrait of the Virgin Mary, painted from life.

"What is it?" Davis held out some crackers from the K-ration. There was cheese on his breath.

"Early 14th century. Based on a Byzantine original."

"Looks like something from a church." Davis continued to munch as he studied the painting in the moonlight. "How did it get in our jeep?"

"How, indeed."

"You didn't buy it or anything?" It was a time when a carton of American cigarettes could be exchanged on the black market for anything from a Luger to a 16-year old's virginity.

"Or nothing."

"How do you know it's 14th century?" Stirrings of curiosity. Possibly Davis and his ilk might be educable after all. Gordon searched in his head for facts that placed the icon in the 14th century.

"Can't be precisely certain. Style. Costume. See the cross in the halo behind the Infant's head? That's Greek. The Madonna's headdress is a clue. That small cross, with the flowers projecting from it."

"You know all that?" Davis sounded impressed. He had stopped eating.

"I'm guessing. This could be a copy." Gordon raised the icon and turned the back up. The moonlight was too soft to reveal details. He felt the texture of the back; hand-hewn wood, varnished or gessoed, an ancient dustiness. "But I don't think so."

"What do we do with it?"

"What indeed?" Adore it, Gordon wanted to say. Stand mute before one of the miracles of an artist's mind. Run for our lives, before whoever left this comes to kill us for it. Or shake our heads, and watch this marvel disappear, back into the mists of our imaginations that produced it.

Gordon thought again of the library at Amherst, the pale New England winter sun bringing up the colors of a 13th Century mosaic. He recalled himself, in 1939, sitting at the oaken table, book open, studying the face of God's Mother in a 13th century mosaic from the Hagia Sophia, Istanbul. He thought back further, to the 14th Century artist who had also once beheld the face in that mosaic, and then painted that face onto the icon now in front of Gordon. Gordon considered himself, standing now in the December midnight along the Danube, centuries later, looking at the painted face with wonder. His thoughts made a triangle in time, a pattern that placed him in some eternal equation. Perhaps with art. Perhaps with God.

"Do you wanna' keep it?" Davis was apparently ready to relinquish any claim of his own to the painting.

"I don't see that we have much choice." Gordon's mind was running back through the past two days. They had unpacked the jeep in Passau. The icon must have been put in the jeep before they reloaded. Because once loaded, they had never left the jeep unguarded. Where might that have happened? Only at the murder house. When they had been inside, making photographs.

"Let's get moving." Gordon listened for a moment. He half expected to hear the growl of a motor in pursuit. The night air was still. Only the voice of the Danube murmured as the river ran alongside the road, flowing towards Passau. He climbed into the jeep and pressed his foot on the starter. Davis latched his door. He had finished the canned bacon and cheese from the K-ration and was peeling a Hershey bar.

Their jeep swung back onto the roadway. Gordon switched on the lights and picked up speed. The bands of mist were thicker now, but he was determined to drive straight through to Altdorf. In those two or three hours, driving through the darkened Bavarian countryside,

Gordon would have time to decide what he was going to tell the Major. If anything.

∧ ∧ ∧ ∧ ∧ ∧ ∧ ∧

WASHINGTON, Spring 1990

Monday morning. Philip walked up from the garage eager to get to his office and call Chieko Willensky. The feeling of elation had lasted from Saturday afternoon in Gordon's office almost until Philip got off the elevator on the 5th floor. As he marched towards his office, a favorite maxim of his father's floated across the horizon, blurring the vista of success. "The hardest thing in the world to recognize is good luck, when it first arrives."

Jesus, how he wished the old man would shut up. Roger Cecil Downs, Esq., had had his own large share of good luck, right up to the time he spun his Cessna 170 into the ground, flying too low over the beach at Hatteras. Looking for the remains of wrecked sailing ships? Or had his father spotted a sunbather who deserved a closer look? The investigation never established a cause. Now, the old boy sent his maxims back from the sky, to take the bloom off Philip's success.

Surely Philip had now found his fox. Gordon's Ph.D. thesis was proof unmistakable that the St. Emeric's Mother of God had once been in his possession. And probably still was. This was not good luck in disguise. This was pay dirt. Manna. The real article. A bird almost in the hand. As real and live and touchable as Leecie's—"Hardest thing in the world…." came back again. Philip felt, with anger, his sense of success start to slide away.

Quickly, he dumped his case on the desk. Waved to his secretary. "I'll be in the library."

Chieko Willensky was prim, fresh, untouched by a weekend she had probably spent flogging a pickup from the Third Edition, or trying her ice cube technique on an aging Congressman.

"...well, a thesis is published. In the literal sense. But finding a copy isn't all that simple. Where did he take his Ph.D.?"

"Harvard."

"A copy should be on file at Harvard, then."

"Don't you have a friend there? Don't librarians help each other in a pinch?"

Chieko smiled. She used his eagerness. "I'm sure something can be arranged. It might be oblique, Mr. Downs. We don't wish to make waves, I gather?"

"Chieko, you're a...a marvel!"

She smiled contentment. Answered her ringing phone. Smiled again. "For you."

Kathie's voice was conspiratorial. "Reid's office called for you. You're to go straight there from the library."

"Right. Thanks, Kathie." He hung up. Patted Chieko on the ass. Walked to the elevator and heard once more his father's precept on the difficulty of recognizing good luck. Chieko took a quick glance around, then gave Philip the finger

∧ ∧ ∧ ∧ ∧ ∧ ∧

Philip knew, even from the back of the man's head, who was sitting in the leather chair in front of Reid's desk.

"You remember Alasdair Murphy..." Reid was smooth, offhand, cordial.

"Yes, indeed. A pleasure." Philip tacked a smile on his face. Shook hands with Murphy. Looked inquiry at Reid.

"Have a seat. Mr. Murphy—Alasdair—has just been filling me in. He has some developments for us."

Was this the arrival of good luck? Not bloody likely. Murphy would be bad news at any time, any place, on any matter. Philip watched as Murphy adjusted himself in the chair, an act of theatrical self-importance.

"You were going to get back to me with some information...." Murphy steepled his fingers. "Meanwhile, I did some investigation on my own. It doesn't pay to let a trail go cold."

You pompous, conniving ass. Cold indeed. The trail was already 45 years cold. You wanted in on whatever the deal was, you rubber-faced little prick. Philip felt his temper slide into the danger zone: that numbness around the lips, a rush of adrenalin to his viscera. He might soon be angry enough to say what he thought. Which would definitely not bring good luck. Carefully, he took a grip on his feelings. Another maxim was delivered from the sky: "Never act on emotion."

"Of course. We appreciate your efforts." The frigid politeness of Philip's words signaled his anger to Reid. Murphy missed the cue.

"So I had a word with this Major—well, now he's Mr.—Caldwell."

"You talked with Caldwell?" Philip lost all sense of reason. What could this ham-handed schmuck possibly have said to Caldwell, that wouldn't blow the whole situation apart. Philip's voice lost all reserve. "About what?"

Murphy expanded, bathed in the attention he was getting. "We're both old soldiers. We talked about this and that. Old wounds. Old outfits."

"And why did Caldwell imagine you were contacting him?"

"I handled it socially. Dropped in at the Short Hills Club. Found Caldwell having a drink before lunch." Murphy consulted his fingernails. Looked up at Reid, then Philip. "I've established a relationship, of sorts, with the man. Now it's a question of what you want out of him."

"Very well done." Reid sounded as if his pleasure were genuine. He shook his head. "You people certainly are remarkable, when it comes to running down someone."

"Part of the job. Always glad to help." Murphy was not wearing his tie from British Military Intelligence. He had on a Liberty of London flowered pattern that clashed nicely with his pinstripe suit. At that moment Philip would have given his trust fund for the opportunity to seize Murphy by his flowered tie and choke him to death.

"Now if you could fill me in on your mission, I'd be glad to…." Murphy over-acted a pregnant pause. Philip was too angry to speak. Reid took the question as his own.

"Yes. We're very near that point, I believe. One or two loose ends to tuck in, first. Then Phil will get back to you with the details. I must say," Reid rose to cue the end of the interview, "I'm most impressed by your performance, Mr. Murphy." He came around the desk. Shook hands with Murphy. Ushered the FBI man to the office door.

Murphy turned at the doorway to smile at Philip. "See you at the club?" He gave a farewell wave of elaborate pleasantry.

Reid, seated again, looked silently at Philip. Philip took a deep breath. Then another.

"Does he know we've had an inquiry from the White House?"

Reid smiled. "From a 'foreign source'. Through Diplomatic channels."

Relief. Reid was no fool. He would have read Murphy faster and more precisely Philip.

"He may have blown the whole show."

"It's up to you to see that he doesn't."

"If he runs around talking to these people on his own…." Philip hesitated. Reid liked action. Results. If Reid thought Murphy could make faster progress than Philip…"Of course, he doesn't know I've located the key people, already."

Reid looked at Philip in a new way. It would be necessary now to tell him more. "The reporter, the cameraman are both still alive. One's a retired professor. The other's a trust officer."

Would Reid ask where? Who? No. Reid wanted only results.

"Does either of them have the painting?"

Philip paused to select his words. Tell Reid enough. But not give away the store. "There are strong indications…." Philip created his own pregnant pause.

Reid looked out his window. He had focused on a point beyond infinity. When he swung back towards Philip his voice was soft, almost seductive. "When can we know for sure?" Reid looked at Philip with the eyes of an executioner.

"Before Murphy gets loose again." Philip put it all into his tone. Keep that bastard Murphy out if it, his tone said, if you want anything from me. Philip waited to see how Reid would take this.

"Don't let it drag." Reid nodded. The interview was over. Philip had a free hand until…until the next call from the White House.

∧   ∧   ∧   ∧   ∧   ∧   ∧   ∧

The wait had seemed forever to Philip, but it had taken Chieko less than a week to produce a Xeroxed copy of Professor Douglas W. Gordon's Ph.D. thesis, from the Widener Library at Harvard.

"Chieko, you're a wonder!"

"Ice cubes, Mr. Downs," she said, dismissively. She held out the copy. Neatly bound. Complete from the title page: *Miraculous Attributions of Eastern European Icons and Their Psychological Consequences.*

"There's something odd…." Chieko tapped the cover of the thesis. "Or at least, it appears odd to me."

"What's that, Chieko?" Philip looked up from the document. She was wearing a scent she must have found in some oriental bazaar, the olfactory equivalent of a G-string.

"Professor Gordon's speciality is Western European Medieval art. This thesis topic is…well, not something a specialist in Medieval Western art would write."

"Medievalists don't care about Russian icons?"

"They may or may not, Mr. Downs. The point is, one doesn't usually begin an academic career with a Ph.D. thesis on an Eastern European topic, and then wind up as a specialist in Western art."

"So what does that suggest?"

"Don't know. It just puzzles me."

"Maybe the mystery will clear up after I read this." Philip hefted the thesis. "Thanks again, Chieko. You're—"

"A wonder, Mr. Downs. With ice cubes."

"How did you guess!" He mimed a kiss as he left the library. She glanced quickly around, then gave him the finger.

Philip closed his office door. Asked Kathie to hold his calls. He laid the thesis on his desk. Turned to page one. Began to read:

> "Of the icons in our galleries, private collections, and used as architectural adornments of those majestic edifices which sprang up in the Middle Ages (where they have not been despoiled or desecrated by a zeal as fervent as that which reared them), the greatest and most expressive portion have reference to the Madonna; Her character, Her person, Her history.
>
> The ethics of Madonna worship, as evolved in icons, might be likened not unaptly to the ethics of human love; but only as long as the object of sense remained in subjection to the moral idea—as long as the appeal was to the best of our faculties and affections—as long as the image was grand or refined, and the influences to be ranked with those which have helped to humanize and civilize our race. As soon as the object became a mere idol, then worship and worshipers, icon and artist, were together degraded.
>
> Because of the need of a personal communication between the supplicant and the sanctified, the authenticity of the image was of great importance. Often, to establish the authenticity of the image, legends were created about icons "not made by human hands"—the *acheropoietoi*—most important of which was the Edessa image of Christ[1]. These legends were used in support of the holy images in the eighth and ninth centuries, when the iconoclastic movement shook the foundations of the Byzantine empire[2]. The iconophiles used these legends to

assert that the countenance of the Mother of God on an icon was an epiphany, because the first icon ever to come into existence was made miraculously[3]. This is why an icon can perform miracles, listen to prayers, and provide answers.

It is not my intention here to enter on that disputed point, the origin of the worship of the Madonna. Our present thesis lies within prescribed limits: the psychological effect of miracles attributed to icons of the Madonna, the "Mother of God". We should start, therefore, with the earliest representation of the Virgin in art; the fourth century[4]. St. Augustine says expressly that there existed in his time no authentic portrait of the Virgin[5]; but we can infer from his account that, authentic or not, such pictures did then exist.

The condemnation of Nestorius as a heretic by the Council of Ephesus, in the year 431, was based on his insistence that in Christ the two natures of God and man remained separate, and that Mary, His human mother, was parent of the man, but not of the God; consequently the title popularly applied to her, *Theotokos* (Mother of God) was improper and profane[6]. The Council of Ephesus decreed that Mary was indeed the Mother of God[7] and henceforth the representation of the "Madonna and Child" became the accepted expression of the orthodox faith.

It is just after the Council of Ephesus that history first records a supposed authentic portrait of the Virgin Mary[8]. The Empress Eudocia, when traveling in the Holy Land, sent home such a picture of the Virgin holding the Child to her sister-in-law, Pulcheria, who placed it in a church at Constantinople[9]. It was at that time regarded as of very high antiquity, and supposed to have been painted from the life[10]. It is certain that a picture traditionally said to be the same which Eudocia had sent to Pulcheria, did exist at Constantinople[11], and was so much venerated by the people as to be regarded as a sort of *Palladium* (i.e. a sacred object having the power to preserve a city or state possessing it), and borne in a superb litter or car in the midst of the imperial host, when the Emperor led the army in person[12].

The fate of this icon is not certainly known. It is said to have been taken by the Turks in 1453, and dragged through the mire; but others deny this as utterly derogatory to the majesty of the Queen of Heaven, who would never have suffered such an indignity to have been put on Her sacred image.

According to the Venetian legend, it was this identical icon which was taken by the blind old Dandolo, when he besieged and took Constantinople in 1204, and brought to Venice[15], where it has ever since been preserved in the church of St. Mark, and held *in somma venerazione.*

The history of the next three hundred years testifies to the triumph of orthodoxy, the extension and popularity of the worship of the Virgin, and the consequent multiplication of Her image, in every form and material (most especially iconographically), through the whole of Christendom.

Then followed the schism of the Iconoclasts. Such were the extravagances of superstition to which the image-worship had led the excitable Orientals (i.e. those of the Eastern Church), that, if Leo III, the Isaurian, had been a wise and temperate reformer, he might have done much good in checking its excesses[16]. But Leo himself was an ignorant, merciless barbarian[17]. The persecution by which he sought to exterminate the sacred pictures of the Madonna, and the cruelties exercised on Her unhappy worshipers, produced a general destruction of the most curious and precious remains of antique art[18]. In other respects, the immediate result of Leo III's persecutions was, naturally enough, a reaction which not only reinstated icons in the veneration of the people, but greatly increased their influence over the imagination[19], for it is at this time that we first hear of a miraculous picture[20].

St. John Damascene, who most strongly defended the use of sacred icons in the Oriental Church[21], was according to Greek legend condemned to lose his right hand, which was accordingly cut off; but he, full of faith, prostrating himself before an icon of the Virgin, stretched out the bleeding stump, and with it touched Her lips, and immediately a new hand sprung forth "like a branch from a tree[22]."

Hence, among the Greek effigies of the Virgin, there is one, uniquely commemorative of this miracle, styled "the Virgin with the three hands[23]".

The second Council of Nice, under the Empress Irene in 787, condemned the Iconoclasts, and restored the use of the sacred icons in the churches[24]. Nevertheless, the controversy still raged until after the death of Theophilus, the last and the most cruel of the Iconoclasts, in 842[25]. His widow Theodora achieved the final triumph of the orthodox party, and restored the Virgin to Her throne[26]. We must observe, however, that only pictures were allowed; all sculptured imagery was still prohibited[27], and has never since been allowed in the Greek Church, except in very low relief. The flatter the surface, the more orthodox the image[28]."

Philip yawned. Gordon had been writing for his academic peers. Presenting his thesis with lucid, measured sentences. Each statement of fact footnoted for source. Philip began to flip the pages. He didn't wish to know all this much about miraculous icons. He only wanted to know what Gordon had revealed about the Mother of God of St. Emeric's. He found it on page 27.

"In the late thirteenth and early fourteenth century it is curious to trace in the Madonnas of contemporary, but far distant schools of painting, the simultaneous dawning of a sympathetic sentiment—for the first time something in the faces of the divine beings appears responsive to the feeling of the worshipers. It was this, perhaps, which caused the enthusiasm excited by Cimabues's great Madonna, and made the people shout and dance for joy when it was uncovered before them[89].

This emotional charging of the Holy features is epitomized in the Mother of God of St. Emeric's. Compared with the spectral rigidity, the hard monotony, of the conventional Byzantines, the more animated eyes, the little touch of sweetness in the still, mild face, must have been like a smile out of heaven. As we trace the same softer influence in the earliest Sienna and Cologne pictures of about the same period, we may fairly regard it was an impress of the spirit of the time, rather than that of an individual mind.

Amongst the Hungarian shrines to which pilgrims journeyed in the Middle Ages the monastery Church of St. Emeric, at Nádudvar (Tolna County) was prominent, the attraction being the relic of Christ's blood preserved there[90], and the Mother of God icon which was undoubtedly the work of Feofan Grek[92] (Theophanes the Greek), probably a Cretan[93] who reached the Russian Empire at Constantinople[94].

Although the shrine at Nádudvar was probably not confirmed as a place of pilgrimage by the ecclesiastical authorities until 1434[95] it had in fact been fulfilling such a role on a considerable scale for some time before that date[96].

Nádudvar was not the only place in the Middle Ages where it was claimed that traces of the holy blood might be revealed or miraculous icons worshiped: the same claim was made at Kassa[97] (now Kosice in Czechoslovakia) and in Gyor.

The tomb of the royal saint, King Ladislas, at Nagyvárad (Oradea, Rumania) was also a famous shrine which attracted huge numbers of pilgrims[98], mainly people in search of a cure for their disease.

The first miracle to be credited to the Mother of God of St. Emeric's, Nádudvar, took place when Turkish invaders swept across Hungary in 1539[99]. As the vanguard of Turks approached, the women and children of Nádudvar took refuge in the Church of St. Emeric. Huddled in darkness, a single candle burning before the Mother of God, the townspeople listened, terror-struck, in the night as the marauding Turks swept through their village on the way West, touching nothing, harming no one. In the morning light the villagers, suspecting a trap, sent a small boy as lookout up into the church tower. The child saw hundreds of hoofmarks and footprints in the freshly fallen snow, where the Turks had passed. But not one door or window was broken open, not one horse or pig taken. The Mother of God had blinded the Turks so that they marched through Nádudvar without ever seeing the village[100].

The first cure to be recorded in Nádudvar dates from the 17th century[101], when conscious efforts were made to reestablish those old places of pilgrimage[102]. According to legend[103] a woodcutter from Mihályhalma was passing near the village accompanied by his mute child. The child went off to look for water, when the Mother of God appeared before him from between the branches of a tree and pointed out the sparkling waters of a spring, lying in a depression in the earth in the shape of a horse's hoof. The boy drank from the water and then for the first time was able to speak. When his father took the boy to the Church of St. Emeric, to give thanks for this miracle, the child instantly identified the icon as the Lady who had directed him to the miraculous spring.

The psychological impact of the Mother of God of St. Emeric, even before the miraculous attributions made to the icon, came in major part because the artist—almost certainly Theophanes the Greek[104] who also painted the icon of the Virgin of the Don for the Cathedral of the Dormition at Kolomna[105], and who influenced the work of Andrei Rublev[106] (an artist later canonized[107]) when they collaborated on the icons in the Cathedral of the Annunciation in Moscow[108]—had the genius to convey a sense of the spiritual vision of his century. The icon transmits a sensation of benevolence, elevates the spirit to the world of the Divine Prototypes, opens the way to participation in eternal life. A spirit of sacred quietude dominates the icon—at once at odds with the time of disintegration and conflict in which the St. Emeric Mother of God was painted."

Philip laid down the manuscript. Could Gordon have written that description, without ever having seen the icon? Possibly he was quoting from sources. But if so, there were no attributions. Nothing in the footnotes. A man of Gordon's academic achievement would not, smack in the middle of his Ph.D. thesis, suddenly stop documenting his sources. No. Gordon must have seen the St. Emeric Mother of God with his own eyes. When Philip picked up the manuscript and turned to the next page, he had final proof.

It was not terribly clear in the Xerox copy. But the photograph was large enough to show the features of the Virgin, exactly as Gordon had described them. Why hadn't Philip seen this picture when he flipped through Gordon's bound thesis, back in the office at Princeton? Had Gordon been covering his tracks? No. That was absurd. More likely Gordon had—in the days before inexpensive Xerox copies—only put illustrations in the copy of the manuscript he submitted to the academic committee for his degree. Economy. Not subterfuge.

∧ ∧ ∧ ∧ ∧ ∧ ∧ ∧

CAMBRIDGE, MASSACHUSETTS Fall 1947

Douglas Gordon studied the folders, notes and books that crowded his desk. Late afternoon sun washed out the flowered design on the aging wall paper. In the sun's warmth a potted geranium sitting on the windowsill gave off an earthy scent. A wall clock ticked steadily towards 4 PM. Janis would soon be home from the Bursar's office. In a month or six weeks she'd be too far along to continue working. The baby was due early in December.

Gordon's look moved from one stack of papers to the next. So much lost time to make up for. Three years claimed by the war. A career delayed in that critical period of life when most academics did their seminal work. And most of his chosen subject was now locked behind the iron curtain. He might never be able to get into Russia, Eastern Europe. The sources and scenes needed to pursue his field of knowledge were frozen in the grip of Communism. On top of everything else, a baby coming.

Gordon's eyes stopped at a folder thick with notes and reference publications. Several inches of a glossy photographic enlargement stuck out from among the pages, revealing the black and white image of a child's foot, a woman's hand. Gordon reached across the desk and slid the photo from the file. He turned the picture so the sunlight fell full upon the image. Even in black and white, the picture stirred him. The Mother and Child appeared almost as he had first seen Them, that moonlit midnight on the Regensburg road.

Davis had done a careful job making the photograph. The picture was dead sharp. The surface of the icon evenly lighted. The texture of the wood showed through where the paint was chipped. The artist's brushwork was clearly defined. And the eyes. The Mother's eyes still caught Gordon in their infinite sadness.

Did he dare include the Mother of God of St. Emeric's in his thesis? This icon would add an important dimension to his work. Obscure, yet significant. Now almost unobtainable. Exactly the type of rarefied detail for which academic committees had a weakness. And God knows, Gordon thought, no one else would be using this example.

But did he dare? Those murders in Passau had never been solved. Could some arcane bit of bad luck lead the unknown killer or killers back to Gordon? Or Davis? Gordon shook his head. Ph.D. theses were published in obscurity, relegated to archives. The worst that might happen was some academic, years from now, would recall a reference in Gordon's thesis and pass the word to…to whom? Someone from the Hungarian Church, seeking their icon? Hungary was now firmly in the grip of Godless communists. Churchill's "Iron Curtain" had become impenetrable.

And yet…suppose someone on the academic committee questioned the sources Gordon had used? No. The general information on the icon was neither confidential nor inaccessible. Only this particular photograph could connect Gordon directly with the icon. And this photo could have come from anywhere. At any time. Only he and Lew Davis knew that the picture had been made of the icon in December, 1945.

Gordon smiled. Davis was now at the Wharton School burrowing into Finance. Lew had written Gordon several times over the past year. Letters mostly about going back for that Bavarian girl, who made her living breaking horses.

Gordon chuckled. She must have had something between her legs more powerful than a horse.

Gordon opened the file folder from which the photo had come. He had a career to make. "Publish or perish." The war had done him out of precious years. Put Eastern Europe in Communist control. But the war had also dropped this gift into his hands. The Mother of God would permit him to complete his Ph.D. thesis

successfully. Once he had his Ph.D., he could move into another time period. Make a new start with a new academic subject. Western European Medieval art. A subject well outside the Iron Curtain, with no language barriers, and far less chance of a Communist takeover. Gordon turned up a fresh page on the lined yellow pad and began to write: "Amongst the Hungarian shrines to which pilgrims journeyed in the Middle Ages, the monastery Church of St. Emeric, at Nádudvar…."

∧ ∧ ∧ ∧ ∧ ∧ ∧ ∧

Washington, 1990

"Mr. Downs, we have a problem." Chieko must be calling from outside her office. Her agitated tone would not pass unnoticed in the library. "I've been broken into. *Very* professionally."

"God damn! What did they take?"

"Sweet fuck all. They were looking for information." Chieko sounded angry more than frightened. "It had to be something to do with you. Your search. They didn't touch another thing."

"So what *did* they get?" Was it Murphy's people, he wondered? Or the people who may—or may not—have tried to run down Szilágyi?

"Nothing. It was all at the office. But somebody means business."

"You're certain it *was* a break-in…."

"Had to be. I only noticed because there was purple water in the toilet—I just put one of those blue tablets in the tank this morning. And didn't flush before I left home."

"Your cleaning lady—"

"Not until Wednesday. And there's a Japanese way of folding blouses. They couldn't match it exactly, after they went through the drawers. Plus a Venetian glass paperweight. I always keep it with the clown facing North. For luck. They missed that when the put it back. Plus there were no finger prints on it."

"So they didn't get any information."

"No. But what if they come back?"

"I don't know."

"You better know, Mr. Downs. This is getting to me."

"Certainly, Chieko." What would he do, if she lost her nerve and refused to help him further? "I understand."

"And the price is going up, Mr. Downs. It's payola time. Tomorrow. Lunch. My place. Right, Mr. Downs?"

"You don't mean…"

"I *do* mean, Mr. Downs." Her voice was businesslike, but he was relieved to know she would still play. Philip groped for a response that made sense.

"What if…if they walk in on us?"

"They can join the party, Mr. Downs."

"Yes, but—" and before he could think of a reply Chieko hung up. His mind was soon scuttling after any connection that would explain exactly who had been after information in her apartment.

∧ ∧ ∧ ∧ ∧ ∧ ∧ ∧

CHEVY CHASE, 1990

"What I can't figure out is, why did they keep it? Selling the icon would be understandable. Even showing the thing off at home or something. Why bury an art treasure somewhere and forget it?"

The veranda at the Chevy Chase Club was almost deserted at this hour. The distant sound of a mowing machine explained the smell of freshly cut grass that drifted in the air. Web David set their drinks on a small round table from which they could look out over the 18th hole. He sat. Picked up his drink. Swirled the gin and tonic as he stared into his glass. He looked up with a shrug.

"There must have been two of them involved, at the very least. It's possible the two could never come to agreement."

"If it was just Gordon and Davis, I can't see them disagreeing very much. They don't look like that sort of people."

"Most disagreeing people don't look like that sort of people." The ice cubes jingled in Web's glass, reminding Philip of a promise to spend tomorrow's lunch hour Chez Willensky. Web snorted. "Spend a morning in divorce court sometime."

"They must have known what they had. Gordon's thesis proves that."

"Perhaps that's just it. They *did* know."

"And therefore?"

"They couldn't sell it. Too obvious. They couldn't display the icon. Too risky. So they waited."

"For what? Perpetual care? They're old men. It makes no sense."

"Could it be they forgot it?"

"Very funny."

"All right. Look at what you've found out. They're too well off to need the money. Too old to for a thing like that to make any difference in their lives. And your Professor Gordon was—*is*—thoroughly conversant with the significance of the painting. What does that suggest?"

"Nothing." Web's Socratic pedantry irritated Philip.

"Politics."

"Politics? How."

"Intelligent, sophisticated men. They've just come through a major war. They've watched the 'iron curtain descend across Eastern Europe'. They couldn't very well return a sacred painting to a country ruled by Godless communists. Any more than they could sell the painting."

Philip watched a distant golfer poise for a putt on the 18th hole. The caddie lifted the flag from the cup. The man's body moved. After a pause the man broke his stance, walked to the cup, bent to retrieve his ball.

"That's an interesting thought. Politics."

"Remember, these men come from a time before we were born. Their values might be the same as ours. Their experience has been quite different. Old timers have strange loyalties. Strange to us."

"Do they still have the icon? That's the question. If I don't find out soon, Reid will have that ham-handed FBI man chasing them."

"Reid has nothing to gain by that." Web David had dealt with Reid himself. "If he didn't have confidence in you, you wouldn't be on the assignment. I can assure you."

"Thanks a lot." Philip drained his drink. Another gin and tonic would be imprudent. Leesie would be along shortly. She liked to share a glass of wine with dinner. There was still a dent in the Audi from his last experience with an extra drink before dinner. He turned to Web and admitted his real fear. "Web, I don't even know that they do have it. Let alone how to get them to part with it."

"True. You do have some imponderables. But you're certain they had the icon, once. Your professor is definitely acquainted with the painting. With its history. So you've made some progress. If they don't have the painting now, they're certainly a good lead to where it went. You've got that much joy."

"How do I approach them, though? What leverage do I have? What can I possibly say?"

Web set his glass on the table. He shook his head. Chuckled. "That's a question for a diplomat. I'm just an ambulance chaser.

∧ ∧ ∧ ∧ ∧ ∧ ∧ ∧

BAVARIA, 1945

Major Caldwell's office was in the corner of the printing plant. The morning sunlight came through the east window. It fell on his desk, a battered piece of furniture that must have been brought out to Altdorf when Julius Streicher moved the printing plant for *Der Stürmer* here, to escape the American bombings of Nürnberg. Caldwell had come to the office in a mood of contentment. He didn't even mind the smell of printer's ink that filled the room. Betsy had been in especially good form the night before. He would shortly be shipping home. Christmas was nearly here. He was wearing class A uniform: Betsy had sewn on the Stars & Stripes shoulder patch embroidered in gold thread—the special one he'd bought in Paris—and the two rows of ribbons, ETO, Bronze Star, Purple Heart running across the top.

Now the two of them stood waiting to see what he would say.

The painting lay on his desk. He looked at Gordon, then at Davis. There was a strong urge to ask them, "Why are you telling me all this?"

But he knew why. Sergeant Gordon was a mature, intelligent man. Educated. Literate. Davis was young but instinctively honest. Davis took his lead from Gordon. Neither one of them was a thief.

"You think this was looted, then?"

"Well, Sir, it *had* to be." Gordon was studying the painting as he spoke. "These artworks properly belong in a church. They're devotional objects, Sir. If they're not in a church, then they're in a museum."

"Or a private collection." Caldwell looked at the Mother and Child. He didn't know art, but he knew what was impressive.

"Of course, Sir. But in any case, not floating around the back streets of Passau."

"Unless it's connected with those murders." Caldwell watched Gordon look up from the painting and meet his eyes. The sergeant's expression endorsed Caldwell's train of thought. The Major looked at Davis. The youngster waited to see what his seniors would decide.

"It must be. In some way. But how? Should we turn it over to the CID?" Gordon waited for the Major to speak.

Caldwell hesitated. This was no time for complications. It was definitely not a time to present implausible stories to the Criminal Investigation Division. If Gordon and Davis became involved, Caldwell would have to back them up. An investigation could take months.

"Whoever dumped this on you…they wanted to get rid of it. Why?" Caldwell spoke to focus his own thoughts. It was not likely that murderers would plant crucial clues in the jeep of two newspapermen. It was more likely that some Kraut, frightened of being caught with the goods, had off-loaded his loot on the nearest GIs, hoping never to see it again.

"Yes, Sir. That is the question." Gordon was still entranced by the painting. He was more absorbed by art than murder. Davis simply waited to see which way the discussion would go. Probably anxious to get back to that nubile Kraut.

"I don't want you two mixed up in a murder case." Caldwell had reached a decision. If the painting was a clue, it would be impossible to connect it with anyone. Anyone except Gordon and Davis. Who were clearly not murderers. Unfortunately, if the painting were turned over to the CID, the story that Gordon and

Davis would have to tell would be implausible. Almost absurd.

"So what *do* we do, Sir?"

Major Caldwell re-folded the Wehrmacht blanket material over the front of the painting. He handed the bundle back to Gordon.

"The first thing we do, gentlemen, is keep our mouths shut. Get that thing completely out of sight. And then keep our mouths shut."

Caldwell looked at Davis to be sure his words were clearly understood. Davis and Gordon exchanged looks. Gordon placed the blanket-wrapped bundle under his left arm. They both saluted. Caldwell returned their salute and sat down at his

desk. Three years of war and killing were enough. It was time to complete his redeployment papers.

∧ ∧ ∧ ∧ ∧ ∧ ∧ ∧

Chapter 5

❖

"It was probably his life insurance." Web David bent over the photocopies and carbons spread across Philip's desk. "What's a '*Froggerbogen*'?"

"A questionnaire. Used right after the war. In the Military Government de-Nazification process." Philip pointed out the sequence in which he had arranged the documents from Major Howard Henry's envelope. "Our man was cleared, then given permission to immigrate to the U.S."

"Like thousands of others." Web wrinkled his nose at the fumes that wafted from the ancient photocopy paper.

"But he wasn't *like* thousands of others." Philip handed Web the photo copy of a Nazi *soldbuch*. "He was in the Medical detachment at Bergen-Belsen."

Web read inspected the *soldbuch* carefully. "The concentration camp? This *was* your Major Henry's life insurance."

"Evidently. But he never needed to use it."

"How about this Huberman?" Web flourished the *soldbuch* copy. "Could Henry have been blackmailing Huberman?"

"Perhaps. There's no apparent link. Except that Henry survived the murders. But look at this…" Philip handed Web David a carbon copy on legal sized paper. "…Huberman's clearance papers were signed by two of the three American officers killed in the murders. Major Henry was the only survivor. That says something."

Web nodded. Philip waited for him to comment. When Web finally did speak, it was with his usual lawyer's caution.

"It *might* have worked like this…your icon was a payoff for getting this Huberman cleared. Somebody then tried to murder everyone who knew this. Major Henry survives—and keeps these papers as his life insurance."

"Which doesn't get me any nearer the icon." Given Web David's confirmation of his own surmise, Philip swallowed another taste of defeat. Wasted effort. Another blank trail.

"It gets you nearer Huberman."

"Huberman?" Philip wondered if he had mis-heard. "*This* Huberman?"

"This Huberman." Web nodded. "There's a mid-sized, highly profitable drug firm, HB Pharmaceuticals. It's controlled by Uwe Huberman. I have their annual report somewhere. It's one of the growth stocks in my portfolio."

"So what should I do now? Invest?"

Web ignored the sarcasm. "Talk with him."

"And get myself killed? *Please*."

"You've got the same insurance that Henry had. You might get information that would help you. His company's just down the road from Princeton."

"You're serious." Philip wondered if Web was testing his credulity.

"I'll go with you, if you like." Web was serious.

"Yes. All right. What have I got to lose?"

∧ ∧ ∧ ∧ ∧ ∧ ∧ ∧

"Mr. Huberman, Senior, is no longer active in the Company." The woman's voice was professionally polite. An executive secretary handling a nuisance call. "I'm afraid we do not give out Mr. Huberman's home number."

"Let me give you *my* number. 202-678-3459" He gave her his direct line. "If Mr. Huberman, *Senior,* could call me at his convenience, I'd appreciate it."

"May I tell Mr. Huberman the purpose of your call?"

"You may tell Mr. Huberman that I'm calling about a regimental reunion. An SS unit. From Bergen-Belsen."

"Will Mr. Huberman know—"

"I'm certain he will. He can feel free to call me collect."

"Thank you." She chose to ignore his irony. "I'll see that Mr. Huberman gets your message, Mr. Browns."

∧ ∧ ∧ ∧ ∧ ∧ ∧ ∧

Philip had driven to New Jersey in the Audi. More comfortable for long distances. The drive gave him time to think. Thoughts muddled by hope, by ignorance, and by fear. On the telephone Uwe Huberman had been short and direct. He would discuss nothing with Philip except in person. Understandable, of course. But off-putting.

It was a nasty situation for both sides. Chieko's apartment broken into. Major Henry's collection of papers, a deadly threat to Huberman's position, now in Philip's possession.

The Gruntal & Co. investment report on HB Pharmaceuticals spelled out how valuable that position was. HB Pharmaceuticals made drugs that patients needed long-term. No quick headache remedies or heartburn cures. Expensive prescription items. A highly efficient form of adrenalin that gave diabetics longer relief between shots. A blood pressure reducer that didn't have impotence as a side effect.

At number 3062 Rosedale Road there was an electronically controlled gate. Philip identified himself through the intercom and the gate swung open. The mock-Tudor mansion stood around a curve of a driveway lined with professionally arranged rhododendrons. He parked the Audi beside a balustraded veranda and walked to the massive front door.

Philip was relieved to see a uniformed maid answer the door. No burly, possibly armed, butler. She took his hat—he had learned to wear a hat when dealing with the older generation—and showed him across a tiled hall to the library.

"Good afternoon, Mr. Downz." Uwe Huberman, white haired, wearing rimless glasses, sat in an elaborate wheelchair behind an 18th century walnut desk designed to accommodate two people. In the sunlight slanting through the study windows Huberman was a chiaroscuro portrait of age, dignity, perhaps even wisdom. "Forgive me that I do not rise to greet you." Huberman's gesture indicated the wheelchair or his body. "Time and nature take their revenge. Sit down, please."

"It's good of you to receive me, Mr. Huberman." Philip dropped into the chair placed before the desk. The room was shadowed. Polished walnut paneling gave a strong smell of lemon oil.

"My pleasure, Mr. Downz." Huberman's eyebrows shot up. "I hope you do not smoke? My oxygen supply...." Philip noticed the green valved cylinder behind the wheelchair. Huberman wore a clear plastic tube to feed oxygen into his nostrils.

"Thank you, sir. I don't." Philip paused. Where to start on his subject? He was instinctively reluctant to break the cordial tone Huberman had established.

"I know nothing of your icon, Mr. Downz." Huberman's voice dropped a register. He spoke the words crisply, to close the subject. The old man took a breath before speaking again. "Nothing whatever." His eyes looked directly at Philip. The old man's face formed a European expression of impassivity....

Philip nodded, to be agreeable. He had not been brought up to cross-examine his seniors. "However, sir, there has been a recent burglary—"

"Just so." Huberman cut him off. Took another breath. "That will be my son. Eric is an American," the old man stopped, breathed—or perhaps sighed—and shook his head. "He uses American ways." Another breath. "Also he is an art collector."

"So he got word from Mr. Menelakos…"

"It must be so, yes." The old man shifted in his chair. Leaned forward with an effort. Looked directly at Philip's eyes. "Eric knows something of my former…experience. Not so much as you will know, Mr. Downz." Huberman felt for the valve on the oxygen tank to adjust the flow. "Only of Alois Gruber—my late uncle—his bargain with the American officers." He slumped back in his chair. His left hand flicked the air. "Eric shall not interfere with you again."

Philip looked at the old man collapsed in his wheelchair. A medicinal smell surrounded the desk. Or was Philip smelling his own fear? The Hubermans could be capable of anything, to protect their name. Better to have it out now, than wonder what they might do.

"And the rest?"

Huberman knew what Philip meant. "Such things hardly matter for me, Mr. Downz." He leaned forward, tugged open a drawer, slid a paper across the desk to Philip. "Long before any consequences can befall, I shall be gone."

Philip picked up the paper. A lung specialist's letter to a consulting doctor, confirming diagnosis, prognosis, termination. Philip scanned the medical phrases that meant "no hope".

"I see." Philip laid the letter back on the desk. He looked at Huberman, seeking the old man's reaction to the interview. Huberman was not what he had imagined. The doctor's letter defused any threat of exposure. The icon was no closer. "I had expected…"

"You had expected to find an icon." Huberman twisted in the wheelchair to look out the window. "There is no icon." He turned to Philip and an unamused smile crept onto his face. "You had expected to find a monster. I am not a monster."

Philip looked at the old man's face: deeply lined, stained by God knows what memories. For years Philip had believed—a belief implanted by his father—that the Nazis were basically different from other people, creatures who committed horrors of which an American was incapable. But then My Lai wiped out that belief.

"No. I suppose you're not." Philip felt weary. Another failure. Another risk taken for nothing.

"But you are an American." Huberman breathed deeply, "You will expect a logical ending to your story, *nicht whar*?" Something rattled in the old man's throat. A fight for breath? A strangled laugh? "So I give you a logic…" his head sloped sideways, from fatigue or to indicate the past. "What I may have done in the war .. and I did not do much, or your officers would not have made their bargain with Alois Gruber—" Another rattling breath. "—has been repaid by what I have done since." Again, that noise deep in the throat. "A lifetime of healing, Mr. Downz. Made possible by your icon, if you like"

The noise from the throat came back louder. Philip began to wonder if Huberman was going to collapse. Instead, the old man shook his head and his smile became even colder. "A miracle. To satisfy your *American* logic."

CHEVY CHASE, Spring 1990

The symbols of near-success hung in walnut frames on the walls of Philip Downs's den. His B.A. from Yale. The Honorable Discharge from the Army of the United States of First Lieutenant Philip C. Downs. His certificate of appointment as American Consul at Graz. The four outsized, full-color Christmas cards from the White House were a tribute to Leecie's connections. A diploma from a summer session at the

University of Grenoble, sealed with medieval pomp, marked Philip's mastery of the French irregular verb.

All of these stepping stones on the path of glory were canceled by a single black and white photograph, five inches by seven, in a simple black frame. The photograph showed his father having a Bronze Star pinned on his field jacket by Lieutenant General George S. Patton, Jr., somewhere outside Bastogne. The photographer had shot his picture from a low angle so that "Old Blood and Guts" looked nearly as tall as Major Downs. It had been an overcast day. Both men looked weary but fulfilled. The print had turned faintly yellow over the years. But the glow of success was undimmed.

"I hope you're not going to stay up *too* late." Leecie's voice was wry with enticement. A whiff of her bath salts drifted into the room. She was giving Philip good reason to come to bed.

"Not long, Leece. I just need another minute." Philip looked at the notes and papers spread around his open attaché case. He had as much information now as he was ever likely to get. At least, until he tackled one of the men directly. Uneasily, Philip stacked the notes and papers together. Piled them on the copy of Gordon's thesis. Placed the pile back in his attaché case.

What would his father have done, in a fix like this? What was the "Bronze Star" approach? Probably he should talk with Web David again. That thought made Philip feel suddenly dependent. Unsuccessful. Unable to pursue a course of action on his own. What would Web advise, anyway? Philip tried to apply the lawyer's thought process to the case.

But a legal approach could get Philip only a limited distance towards his goal. At some point, he would have to jump off into the unknown. Take a chance. Put method behind him and risk everything—as the old man had once risked everything—on a single action.

"Right." Philip was talking to his father now. But Web's voice crept into Philip's mental conversation. Web's measured tones and considered judgement. Philip smiled, as he imagined Web and his father coming to grips in this argument. Web would be quick to point out that this was a situation already half-a-century old. Nothing would be gained now by precipitous action. The important thing was to resolve every possible certainty before making a move. Philip's father would probably—after spouting a pompous axiom—have agreed.

"No, no, no." Philip spoke aloud to the Web and the father in his head. Philip had had enough uncertainty and suspense. He wanted to end the agony. Win, lose, or draw. Better to get a quick resolution. Get Reid off his back. Beat Murphy to the draw. Charge ahead, as his father had charged in the Ardennes. Accept whatever fate delivered. Philip felt a rush of relief. His mind was made up. The Bronze Star solution.

But then the familiar, sour feeling crept back into his consciousness. Success fading, once again. This was *not* the Ardennes. There were no German tanks to attack. The enemy was 45 years of lost time. Reid's unreasonable expectations. Murphy's clodding across the trails. Web David and Philip's father were correct after all.

Philip stared at the photo of his father and General Patton. Surely it was inherent in Philip's situation that Gordon, Caldwell, Davis would have to be approached. Faced directly. These men were not going to suddenly and on their own decide to return the Mother of God—and in any case, to whom could they return the icon? It was also built in to this equation that Gordon, Caldwell, Davis—one or all three—would have to be persuaded. No force, legal or practical, could be applied against men whose actual possession of the icon was, in the end, entirely conjecture. Success had eluded Philip again. He snapped his attaché case shut and went upstairs.

"I suppose you could do both, couldn't you?" Leecie had sensed his frustration. Pried his worry out. Listened patiently to his whingeing.

"How."

"Well…." Leecie rolled over on her side. She slid her long smooth leg over his. Wrapped her arm warmly around his neck. "That Mr. Davis. He seemed very nice. Perhaps you could talk with him."

Philip slid his hand down her back. He fondled her automatically, his mind working in other directions. If he had to tackle any of the three men, Davis was the best one with whom to start. He was the youngest. Philip at least had a social connection with the Trust Officer. Davis was also the least formidable of the three. There was something vulnerable about the man. Philip sensed in Davis a possible fellow failure. A shared sense of defeat that might make them in some way allies.

"You're right, Leece." Philip felt a new rush of success. A new place to start. The logic of pressing his attack on the most vulnerable point—something D. Webster David, Esquire and Major John Cecil Downs, LL.D.(deceased), would have to approve. "Davis might be approachable. He very well might be." Philip felt the lust of conquest. He squeezed Leecie with relief and pleasure. He ran his hand up the inside of her thigh, to where a great truth was expressed.

∧ ∧ ∧ ∧ ∧ ∧ ∧ ∧

North Atlantic, July, 1948

The *S.S. Volendam*, built before the first World War, was now making her last few voyages. Comfortable, a bit shabby, she steamed mid-way across the Atlantic en route to Rotterdam, loaded with 2,000 American college students headed for a summer in Europe.

The students were bunked in accommodations knocked together for troops during the war. Bunks stacked two and three rows high. Mess halls that fed three sittings at each meal.

Ship's stores now sold the undergraduates Blooker Chocolate for 10 cents a bar, Heineken's beer for 15 cents a bottle. The two-week crossing was one continual beer bust, with scattered lectures, an amateur production of "South Pacific", and more fornication per nautical mile than Lewis Davis had believed possible.

Lewis stood on the C desk, watching the moonlight sparkle on the Atlantic chop. In ten days he would land at Rotterdam. A four or five hour train ride would get him to Nürnberg. Another half hour on the local train would bring him to Altdorf, where it should be possible to a cab to get him to.... Lewis felt again for the ring box in his shirt pocket. The letter from the Provident Tradesman's Trust Department, certifying his income, was safe in his suitcase. Her last letter, written three weeks before, was in his wallet.

∧ ∧ ∧ ∧ ∧ ∧ ∧ ∧

LUBYANKA PRISON, July, 1948

SS Ober Führer Wilhelm Gottfried von Reichenberg heard the food cart make its pre-dawn rattle down the line of cells. The odor of cabbage soup seeped in through the damp air. When the cart failed to stop at his door, he knew. They would hang him this morning. The Russians never wasted food.

This was a moment for which von Reichenberg had been preparing himself for months. Years. He had been surrounded by death for as long as he could remember. Still, the realization that death now stood just outside the door.... his throat felt like frozen iron.

Would there be time for a letter? But he had nothing. No paper. No pencil. All that was left to him was the decision of how he would spend his last few minutes. What he would think of, until the door was opened by death?

Ilse. Would she even hear of his death? Did she believe him already dead? Ilse would be nearly fifty. Old for remarriage. And whom could she marry? There was no one left. Erda was nearly 20. She would have the farm. The horses. Perhaps someone had survived the *Fuhrer's* war and would marry Erda. Maybe an American. She might be married already. Von Reichenberg would never see his grandchildren. If grandchildren there were to be. What would *they* know of him? Their grandfather? Would they ever.... And then the door ground open.

∧   ∧   ∧   ∧   ∧   ∧   ∧   ∧

WASHINGTON, Fall 1990

Philip was no more than half-way through his stack of morning mail when he sensed a presence in the office. A cigarette smell. Looked up to find Reid standing in his doorway.

"Come in." Philip rose to offer Reid a seat. Reid waved the offer away. Both Reid's presence in Philip's office and his refusal of a chair were bad signs. Urgency must have brought him here. That meant danger. Whatever Reid had to say would be delivered on the fly. There would be no chance for Philip to consider or reply.

"We've had some good luck." Reid stepped inside the doorway just enough to make their conversation symbolically private. "The White House called. The President's planning a trip to Europe early next year. He'll include parts of Eastern Europe. The thought is, the President could personally return your religious painting to the Hungarians—the symbolic value of the New World returning hope to the Old World. Bush likes the idea."

Philip felt the words like a cold enema. For an instant he thought Reid was joking. He was about to reply that President Bush might also want to return the Holy Grail to Camelot—but Reid's face was set in an expression of serious satisfaction.

"But...but," Philip felt his mouth open and close with no effect. "They'll put a zillion people on the project, if Bush..." He tried to imagine the circus of White House sycophants, all jockeying to get aboard a job which Bush personally favored. It was madness. There'd be hundreds of blow-dried haircuts chasing around the place. Each idiot eager to take full charge.

"I headed that off." Reid smiled, satisfied.

"You did?" Philip was impressed. His face must have registered awe at Reid's ability to stop a stampede of White house gophers. Reid smiled with satisfaction.

"I told them we had things completely in hand. We'd deliver the painting in plenty of time for the Presidential trip."

In Philip's lower colon the cold enema froze solid.

"Early…early next year? That's three months!"

"Yes. I bought you some time." Reid smiled again. He gave a seigniorial wave of the hand. And then, through some process that didn't seem to involve walking, Reid disappeared from Philip's office. Only the odor of his cigarette remained.

Philip sat down. He stared, unseeing, at the remains of his morning mail. His thoughts raced quickly over his personal finances. At his age, early retirement was not a possibility. He needed to put in five or six more years. He might be able to find a job somewhere in the private sector. But he was not, as Web David was, possessed of a universally marketable skill.

What hurt most of all was to have his career cut short by an absurdity. If he'd made a real mistake—got drunk and lost sensitive papers, punched a foreign ambassador, knocked up his secretary…. But to lose it all because someone at the White house had listened to someone from the Hungarian Embassy about a near-impossible scheme. And because Reid hadn't had the backbone to say no. That seemed wildly unjust. As if spitting on the street had caused a fatal auto accident.

Philip sat thinking, until he reached the bottom of his despair. Then he reached mechanically for the remaining letters. He noted the return address on the top letter. From Zimmerman, in California. Salt into his wounds. He slit open 's envelope. Drew out the letter. It was an announcement of a Stars & Stripes reunion. Zimmerman had stuck a yellow Post-It note to the flyer.

"Your Uncle might be interested in this…Best, Ken."

The Xeroxed announcement of the reunion was on stationery headed with the logos of *The Stars & Stripes* and YANK, the Army weekly. The reunion was scheduled for Friday, October 19, 1990, 6:30 p.m., at the Cosmopolitan Club, 122 East 66th Street, New York City. The reunion committee was listed at the bottom of the sheet. Philip recognized some of the names from newspaper bylines, TV news shows. Andy Rooney. Ralph Martin—Leecie was just now reading his two-volume biography of Churchill's mother, *Jennie*.

Apparently the Stars & Stripes veterans were combining their reunion with the former YANK staffers. Philip considered. That meant that everyone at the reunion would not necessarily know everyone else. He might be able to slip in amongst the group and—but of course, they would all be years older than he was. That would make him instantly obvious as an outsider.

Possibly, if he arrived late…After the dinner. When the drinks and the memories had had a chance to soften everyone's perceptions. When the welling up of good fellowship and good booze made the whole world appear warm and fuzzy. At that point in the evening, there would be less likelihood of his being challenged as an outsider. If he *were* challenged, his "uncle" story would have a better chance of succeeding. And he now had a genuine name that his "uncle" could be seeking: Earl H. Dent, Jr. Dent would *not* be attending.

∧ ∧ ∧ ∧ ∧ ∧ ∧ ∧

"You're probably right." D. Webster David, Esquire expertly jockeyed his dark blue Camry along the Rock Creek Parkway. "After the first hour or two, you could walk in to the party with a brass band and leading an elephant. Nobody would notice." Web swung the car deftly up the slope towards Massachusetts Avenue. As the Camry turned, various impedimenta rattled around the back seat; Web's car always smelled of tennis balls and dried dog food.

"It's about the only hope I have left." Philip watched the tower of the Islamic Mosque rise into view. Perhaps he worshiped the wrong Gods. Or God.

"You've got no guarantee that either of your men will be there, of course."

"Thanks."

"I'm just trying to be realistic."

"Thanks again." Philip studied the spires of the National cathedral as they came into sight. They were still building the fabric. After...how many years? They'd be working on the cathedral long after Philip was out of the Department, after Reid made his retirement, after Bush was history. Maybe if he could take a longer view of life, his personal tragedy would feel less intense.

"But you have got one thing on your side."

"Don't tell me. Let me guess. *Surprise.* Right? I know all about Gordon and Davis and Caldwell. They have no idea that I know. That gives me an edge."

"Yes. You *do* have that. But you also have something more important behind you."

"The Federal Government? You've already told me we can't prove a thing. They could run off to Switzerland. Flog the icon through one of those shady dealers in…"

"True. You can't prove a thing. But what you do have on your side is *right*."

"Right?" Philip felt a bitter laugh rise in his chest like heartburn. "A *lawyer* is telling me that *right* is going to prevail?"

Web honored Philip's irony with a rueful smile.

"In court, no. But you're not in court. You're appealing to a jury of—three, at the most. Possibly one or two. Consider who they are."

"Sure. Old men. In unshakable positions. Who can simply keep their mouths shut and be well beyond the reach of any law."

"*Old* men. Exactly." Web turned up Wisconsin Avenue and headed towards Friendship Heights. "Old men who'll be surrounded by other old men, at their reunion. Men who'll see their own mortality creeping closer."

"You think they'll make a deathbed confession? I've got to get my hands on that damned icon before January."

"But why *do* people make deathbed confessions? Isn't it because they don't want to end their lives without first making restitution? Isn't it because they want to put things *right*?"

"OK."

"And here you'll have men who suddenly see themselves reflected in their peers—they'll be more than usually conscious of their age. Conscious of those who *aren't* at the reunion."

"Like Earl H. Dent."

"Who is Earl H. Dent?"

"One of the veterans who *won't* be at the reunion."

"Ah. The missing faces. The empty chair at the banquet table. Nostalgia can be a powerful emotion."

"Perhaps I should take a violinist with me." Philip wondered to himself. How would "Lili Marlene" sound on the violin? He thought again of his father.

"Just take your common sense with you. Play it by ear. Remember, you can offer them something that few men ever have chance to achieve."

"Spell it out for me."

"All right. Look at it like *this*...." Web David raced the car along Wisconsin Avenue, past the back of the Chevy Chase Club golf course. He hunched forward over the wheel and began to present his case.

∧ ∧ ∧ ∧ ∧ ∧ ∧ ∧

CHEVY CHASE Fall, 1990

The long-haired crafts-sellers outside the Bethesda Farmers' Market were doing a good business in the bright Saturday sunshine. Inside the coolness of the low wooden building the earthy tang of freshly dug vegetables and dried herbs mixed with the noise of suburban housewives. Children scampered along the aisles, their velocity threatening tables of organic baked goods, home-made fruit jams, exotic honeys, and quaintly fashionable *tchatchkas*. Alice Wentworth Downs waited until Tessie paid for a quiche, assembled a dozen gladiolus, and began to hump her purchases towards the double doors

"Philip's in some sort of trouble." Leecie walked Tessie to her Buick station wagon. A golden Labrador greeted them with extravagant waggles.

"Not another—" Tessie half raised an eyebrow.

"No, no. Something deeper."

"There isn't anything deeper." Tessie's voice was rich with experience.

"It's like…" Leecie searched for a word that would help Tessie understand her concern. "…like the time he came home from the Army. Something closed up."

"The Army." Tessie gave her a Bryn Mawr look. "Walter has these…strange friends."

"Old soldiers?" Leecie had been exposed to the professional military. Middle-aged men who lived to re-live names, dates, actions., Army units or Navy ships, reminiscing endlessly with their contemporaries. Most of their wives drank. For that exact reason.

"Not really." Tessie's hand paused on the Labrador's neck. "They're certainly not Postal Service types. They're more like… *Yalies*."

Leecie knew exactly what Tessie meant. Youngish old men. Well mannered. Self-assured. With no discernable vocation but their family's money.

Leecie smiled. "I suppose Walter likes to feel young…"

"He's a dear, really." Tessie slid the boxed quiche where the Lab couldn't reach it. "He tries so hard. It's…" her smile was half contentment, half triumph, "…a relief, really."

"Really and truly?" Leecie remembered all those pained sharings with Tessie, after Tessie had married that abominable Earle Jaspers, when she was a researcher at Time-Life. Tessie had never taken much to the physical side of married life. Leecie could easily imagine her, assuring Walter of the unimportance of his fading potency. Sounding *almost* as if she really meant it. And underneath, really meaning it.

"You must have a wonderful sense of power."

Tessie's chuckle admitted everything. She ran her fingers over the Labrador's head and ears. "So what *is* bothering Philip, then? It's usually something at the office. Something in a size twelve."

"I think he's frightened."

"Money?" Tessie stopped stroking the Labrador and looked serious.

"Not that I know of."

"You'd *know*." Tessie pushed the Labrador's head away as the animal tried to nuzzle the baguette of French bread that poked out of a brown manila bag. "Has he talked in his sleep?"

Leecie shook her head. "He's been…a little too cheerful."

"Oh. *That*." Tessie took a firm hold the of the Labrador's collar and pushed him back from her face. "Leece, are you sure it's not—"

"No. I *could* be wrong. But, no."

Tessie nodded. She had always respected Leecie's judgement. Often turned to Leecie when her own male relationships were foundering. "Something medical? Their prostates start to go around fifty. Maybe earlier. Has he had a physical recently?"

"If he has, he didn't mention it."

"Suggest that you *both* go. For the children's sake. You might smoke him out."

"Perhaps that *is* it."

"I'll ask Walter. He'll know all about prostate trouble." Tessie smiled. "Whatever it is, Leece, it'll pass. Correct?"

"Correct." Leecie patted the Labrador, who was now hanging his head out the station wagon window. "Thanks, Tess."

"We know whereof we speak. Right, Earle honey?" She gave the Labrador a sudden hug. The Buick's engine spun into life. Tessie waved as she backed the car deftly out of the parking slot and swung it onto Wisconsin avenue.

Leecie walked slowly to her Audi. Prostate trouble? Her father hadn't had that until he was nearly seventy.

∧ ∧ ∧ ∧ ∧ ∧ ∧ ∧

WASHINGTON, Fall 1990

Morris Reid watched a rain squall move across the tidal basin and erase his view of the Washington Monument. He lit a Marlboro while he waited for an answer. The number rang only twice before a familiar voice answered.

"Verfaille." The tone was businesslike, the syllables clipped.

"Harry, this is Morris."

"Morry!" The voice came alive. "What's up?"

"Harry, I need someone chaperoned."

"Where's the dance?"

"Not certain, yet. But somewhere in your line of country. May I rely on you?"

"Why not? Who'm I watching?"

"One of my youngsters. A bit headstrong. Inclined to be temperamental. Keep him out of trouble for me?"

"You know me, Morry. Best Nanny in the biz." The voice turned businesslike again. "Name and address?"

"I'll send you a note."

"With a case of Bourbon."

"Don't drink it all at once, Harry."

"Here's mud in your eye, Morry." The voice imitated ice cubes tinkling in a highball glass.

"Much obliged."

"You sure will be." The voice chuckled softly as the phone on the other end was cradled.

∧ ∧ ∧ ∧ ∧ ∧ ∧ ∧

WASHINGTON, Fall 1990

A slight smell of ancient dust never quite left the corridors of the Society of the Cincinnati's neo-classical building. The babble of champagned voices rose towards the lofty ceiling. Hosts and guests drifted among the halls. Lester Lanin rhythms wafted up the stairway. Tessie stopped to admire a Japanese ceremonial sword presented to the Society by Admiral Matthew Galbraith Perry. Walter worked his way towards the bar for more champagne.

"Winslow!"

Walter looked to his left. The smiling face advanced. Walter nodded. "Harry."

"I see your Memsahib over there. With Philip Downs and his missus."

Walter looked back, as if he had only just realized this fact. "Tess and Luzie were at Bryn Mawr together."

"What's he like?"

"The usual. Money somewhere. Trying to live up to his wife's connections." Walter and Harry moved with practiced motions through the jam of thirsties.

"No *particular* interests?"

Walter considered. The existence of Harry's question created Walter's answer. "He pumped me once. About the Occupation of Germany. His brother was there."

"You first." Harry held back to let Walter squeeze up to the bar. Sweating barmen were poured rapidly from a small forest of bottles.

"Thank you—" Walter held out his two glasses for refills. "And a bourbon and ice, please."

"His brother?" Harry moved in behind Walter.

Walter handed the bourbon and ice to Harry. He waited for his own re-fills. "Yes. That's about it."

"Cheers." Harry raised his glass as high as the press of people would permit.

"Cheers." Walter twisted slowly around, careful to keep the champagne from spilling. When he got back to where Tessie and the Downs's stood, Harry was no longer in sight.

∧ ∧ ∧ ∧ ∧ ∧ ∧ ∧

LANGLEY, Virginia Fall, 1990

After midnight the office was almost always empty, except for the odd Duty Officer. The memory of cigarette smoke hung in the air. The ghost of over-boiled coffee. The sharp scent of newly cleaned floors.

Harry left his office fluorescents out. The lone bulb in the student lamp on his desk was sufficient to light the single file folder. The hard copy from the computer looked as cold and precise as a gravestone. Harry's mind turned the sterile alpha-numeric readout into flesh and blood. Places and events. Probabilities.

Downs, Philip Cecil. Born 11/21/46, Potomac, MD. Father, John Cecil Downs, Esquire. Mother, Roberta Elizabeth Wilkinson Downs.

Harry stopped to yawn. The bourbon was catching up with him. Or perhaps he was approaching middle age. He'd have to ask Walter Winslow what to expect.

Harry quickly read down the rest of the page. The report was conclusive. No brother. Not now. Not ever.

Why had Downs used a brother as his excuse? He could as easily have used his father. John Cecil Downs, Esquire, had been a...Harry scanned the page again—a Major, had served in Europe during the Second World War.

Well, the amateurs usually made mistakes like that. That's why they were amateurs. Harry yawned again. He slipped the page back into the folder. Dropped the file into his drawer. Locked the drawer. Harry wrote a note on his calendar to call Simpson. Turned off the desk lamp. Left the office.

∧ ∧ ∧ ∧ ∧ ∧ ∧ ∧

NEW YORK, October 19, 1990

Philip had the taxi stop at Madison and 65th street. He didn't wish to arrive directly at the Cosmopolitan Club. He paid the cabbie. Walked up Madison in the crisp Autumn evening, turned left at 66th. Made his way slowly towards the canopy with the Cosmopolitan Club name. It was almost nine o'clock. The entrance hall, deserted. A hand lettered cardboard sign on an easel announced "S & S/YANK Reunion, second floor." An arrow on the sign indicated the elevators. Philip stepped into the elevator and pushed the button marked "2".

The elevator door opened to an echo of contented laughter from down the hallway. Philip stepped into the hall. Stopped to get his bearings. A long table held an open guest register, a scatter of unclaimed name badges, a sweating pitcher of ice water. Two fold-up chairs sat empty behind the table. The action had all moved into the room at the end of the hall.

More distant laughter. Philip moved carefully towards the entrance to the party room. The room was filled with circular tables, the tables filled with aging men, a few women seated among them. Dinner had obviously been a success. Used glasses and ashtrays were strewn across the linen tablecloths. Cigars and pipes were burning throughout the room, with powerful effect. The air was husky with alcohol and sweat. The ancient and semi-ancient men sat, listening to a speaker who stood at a microphone at the far end of the room. The speaker was too far away to recognize, but his delivery was unmistakable.

"I don't want to die." Andy Rooney's plangent voice cut through the roomful of lubricated companions. "I want to go on living. As long as I can. Because I want to be able to think back, to remember, how great it was, to be on The Stars & Stripes!"

A mixture of laughs, muffled agreements, shouted comment-cum-encouragement swirled around Rooney. He was talking to an audience uniquely his own. Rooney spoke with a depth of feeling that could only be shared here, among these men with whom he must have experienced the most intense emotions of his formative years. These happy few.

Philip forced himself to turn his attention away from Rooney and with his eyes search the room. So many of these old men looked alike. Rounded bellies. Hair thinning or disappeared. Their dress varied: outdated elegant, suburban casual, New York sloppy. Everyone's clothes looked seasons out of fashion. There was a familial similarity in the way the diners leaned back in their chairs, contentedly nursing their drinks. Then Philip spotted Lewis Davis, seated at a table in the left corner of the room. Philip waited for Rooney's words to bring the next burst of laughter. He used the cover of the merriment to edge his way around the dining-room.

There was hectic applause at the end of Rooney's speech. Philip stopped at the now unattended bar, helped himself to a glass of ice and tonic. Protective coloration. The MC brought the ceremonies to a close—Rooney must have been the last speaker. Diners lurched up from the tables to refill their drinks and renew contacts. Small groups formed. Men exchanging phone numbers and greetings. Dropping into earnest conversations.

The table where Lewis Davis sat was reduced to three men. As Philip moved closer he saw that the second man was Professor Gordon. The third man, who looked even older. had a way of moving his eyes so that he took in the whole room. Philip wondered. Was this the former Major Caldwell?

Web's words came back to him. "Play it by ear." Philip paused. Could this be how his father had felt, before he began the action that had led to a Bronze Star? Uncertainty. Desperation. Then Philip felt the sudden lightness that comes from knowing you have cast yourself into the maelstrom, that events would now take control.

"Mr. Davis?" Philip stood at the edge of the table. All three men looked up at him. "Philip Downs. We met at the Radnor Hunt, some months ago."

"Oh...yes. Of course." Davis rose and offered his hand. He was too well bred to ask what in the hell Philip might be doing here. But Davis had a puzzled expression. He paused, as if expecting some explanation. When none came, Davis gestured at the man sitting next him. "This is Professor Gordon...." he indicated the man sitting across the table, " and Major...Mr. Caldwell."

"A pleasure, gentlemen." Philip handed one of his cards to each of them. The improbability of the social gesture was sufficient to forestall comment. Gordon looked up from the card, studying Philip. Caldwell read the card carefully.

"I'm from the Department of State." Philip started with the basics, even though his name and title were spelled out on the cards he had just handed them. "I've been asked to contact you gentlemen."

"Were you in one of my classes?" Gordon sounded half-certain.

"We met at Alumni Weekend. Last spring."

"Ah. *That* was it." Gordon sounded satisfied. Davis appeared surprised that Philip would have met Gordon. Caldwell's lined face still looked alert, unsatisfied.

"I need some help from you gentlemen, if you'd be so kind." Philip moved quickly while he had the leverage of sociability on his side. He pulled out a chair and sat himself facing the three men. "It's about a religious icon. That disappeared in 1945. Just after the Passau murders."

Philip watched the effect of his words on the three men. Gordon raised an eyebrow. Davis became suddenly impassive; a poker player. Only Major Caldwell appeared to take Philip's statement as unexceptional, an appropriate topic of discussion among the four of them. Caldwell's eyes suddenly flicked back forty-odd years. It was the "retro-view effect", done at high speed.. His eyes met Philip's with a look of comprehension.

Philip felt like a man making his first parachute jump. Suddenly, he was out of the plane, dropping through the sky, wondering if and when the static line would jerk his chute open. He swallowed. Took a quick sip of tonic. Continued.

"The Hungarians want… *need* the icon back."

Philip in later months would try to remember in what sequence he had presented his story. All he could ever manage to recall was racing through the details, fearful that some of the other diners might drift back to the table and interrupt his plea. But in those few unnerving moments, he must have spelled it all out for the three men. The Hungarians' forty-five year search. His own efforts to locate each one of them. The chalice, monstrance, vestments from the Church of St. Emeric, showing up in Amsterdam, Zurich, São Paulo. He did not yet mention Bush. It might sound too absurd. And like a comedian playing to an unresponsive house, he had begun to feel the "flop sweat" beading on his forehead. This was all that later reflection brought back to him.

But at the moment, Philip stopped and watched their faces. They were listening with care. They were not reacting. The three men sat there like a court of doom—*doom* in its biblical sense of "final judgement". Philip read his whole future career in their expressions. He was abruptly sunk with a sense of—what? Some intense, unfamiliar pain and humiliation, a terrible urease that he finally recognized: the need to *beg*. He was here without power, without wealth, nakedly vulnerable to the decision of these three faces. No other critical juncture in Philip's life had found him so completely shorn of influence, ability, entitlement. He'd always had *something* on his side in past crises. Family connections. Education. Intelligence. Even some charm. Now, he could only beg.

The atmosphere at the table carried other emotions that Philip only vaguely sensed. He was watching time fade, years roll backwards, as the three old men seemed to shift in their personae. Some internal adjustment was making each of them in some way younger; not just the refocus of eyes that Philip had seen so often now, as men envisioned the events of half a century before. This change was perceptible in the way the three men waited. Body language. Facial set. The balance among them had subtly shifted. Caldwell, who looked very little older than Gordon, was suddenly much senior. Davis, greying, faced lined with years, was clearly very junior. All three men must have unconsciously shifted back to their 1945 roles. Gordon and Davis sat waiting for Caldwell to speak.

"Suppose your…hypothesis, is correct." Caldwell positioned his glass directly between Philip and himself. "Why should we accede to your request?"

Philip realized now the sort of man his father must have been in action. Caldwell had said everything. And nothing. He hadn't wasted time protesting ignorance. Made no attempt to hedge or obfuscate. He hadn't even demanded Philip's credentials. A social connection with Davis was evidently *bono fides* enough. No, Caldwell had gone directly to the key point. Which made him a setup, put him right in the crosshairs of Web David's argument.

"Why, indeed." Philip moved his own glass so it was positioned like Caldwell's. Deep inside his psyche, something in Philip seemed to grab, to start moving. "Because, gentlemen, I can offer you an unique opportunity." He looked at each of the three men in turn, then locked eyes with Caldwell. "I can give you a chance to change history."

After that Philip poured it on. The whole nine yards. Bush. The political effect of the reappearance of the Mother of God of St. Emeric's. The ancient beliefs and miracles. Everything he had learned in months of diligent searching. Then he finished. His adrenalin was still flowing. He took a deep drink of tonic. Waited. His pulse was pounding in his ear.

The silence around the table closed in. The talk and laughter from other parts of the room faded in the distance. Philip looked again at each of the three faces. Gordon was waiting for Caldwell. Davis was waiting for Gordon.

Time shifted again across Major Caldwell's face. Philip watched him make a journey back from fifty years ago. Age once more overtook everything but the Major's eyes. He looked at Philip for one searching moment. The old man's eyes were unreadable. He appeared to fathom Philip right to his core. Slowly the old man's eyes changed from search to decision. The Major turned to Gordon. Gordon nodded to Caldwell's look. Caldwell then turned to Davis. Davis, waiting for orders. When Caldwell nodded agreement, Davis reached inside his jacket and withdrew a billfold.

Davis pulled a small, worn photo from the billfold, wrote briefly on the back and handed the photo to Philip. Philip read a name, an address. A short sentence.

Success had come so quickly, Philip was not prepared to accept it. He turned the photo over several times. Davis must have been carrying the picture in his billfold for years; the surface was rubbed dull, the back stained with age. Then Philip looked up at the three men.

"Thank you." He spoke to the Major. Philip looked at the other two. "Thank you *all*. Very much."

The Major nodded. Gordon smiled. Davis was lost in thought. Philip rose from the table. His offer of a handshake roused Davis from a reverie.

"Thank you, Sir."

Gordon shook with his left hand as Philip rounded the table. Philip stopped before the Major. The old man's bearing triggered a military reflex in Philip. He offered a half-salute. The Major nodded. It was as good as a commendation. Philip now knew what his father might have felt, when Patton pinned on his Bronze Star.

Philip tucked Davis's photo carefully inside his wallet. The elation was so intense, he could now feel almost nothing—like a noise so loud it ceases to be sound and becomes pure pressure. Philip felt an unreality blurring his perceptions. Would he wake to find this a dream of wish-fulfillment? He looked back, just before stepping from the dining-room. The three old men were talking among themselves.

Philip turned into the hallway. Something oddly familiar struck him at once. The figure bending over the long table, reading the open register of attenders. It was Alasdair Murphy. He was carefully running a forefinger down the list of signatures. Murphy was no *doppelganger*. He was all too real.

Philip, already in a state of heightened awareness, moved without thought or hesitation. He strode quickly towards the table. With two hands he seized the pitcher of water, in which the ice cubes had now all but melted. The sides of the pitcher were still sweaty. Philip took a careful grip.

He raised the pitcher. Positioned it over Murphy's back. Dumped the full contents over Murphy's head and shoulders. Strode to the open elevator. Stepped aboard. Pushed the button to descend.

Philip heard Murphy's sputtered half-scream as the elevator doors closed. He got out of the elevator on the ground floor. Set the pitcher on the floor. Walked quickly through the lobby. Out the club's entrance. Turned left towards Madison Avenue. Walking briskly along the lighted street he reached the corner pay phone. When he heard a dial tone he jabbed at the touch-tone buttons. Area code. Number. Credit card number. PIN number.

"Hello." Mrs. Reid's voice was social. It was still well before midnight. "Mrs. Reid, this is Philip Downs. I'm sorry to disturb you at home, but I hoped to have a word with Mr. Reid, if he's available." He struggled to keep the tension out of his voice.

"Of course, Philip." She wouldn't realize he was in New York. It might be a simple social call from his house. He thought quickly while she went to get her husband.

"Evening, Phil. What can I do for you?" There was inquiry, but no surprise, in Reid's voice. The Reids probably didn't have guests.

"I've got it. At least, I know where it is. And I *can* get it."

"Congratulations. I was always sure you would, Phil." But Reid sounded considerably relieved. He could now let his doubts show.

"But there's a problem. You've got to get that FBI clod off the case. Murphy."

"All right. I'll call first thing Monday."

"Not Monday. *Tonight.*"

"Tonight? I don't know if—"

"Morris, he's already come as close as makes no difference to queering the deal." Philip was now in a position to speak to Reid as bluntly as he chose. "By Monday he may have blown the whole deal."

"I see." Reid was playing for time. Hoping to temporize.

"I left him not five minutes ago—headed for the very people who can give me access to the icon. I was able to stall him...." Philip hesitated. Reid didn't need details. He needed marching orders. "Unless Murphy's called off right now, *tonight,* he'll make a mess of things before I can get my hands on the painting."

"Yes. I see." Reid accepted the gravity of Philip's demand. "I'm not sure how quickly...."

"Get on to his boss. Tonight. I'm sure they have lines of communication—Murphy may even be acting on his own. He's sniffed glory."

"Very well." Reid's voice shifted to reluctant acceptance. "I'll do what I can."

"We don't want to lose it, when we're this close."

"I understand. Let me make some calls."

"Right *now*, Morris."

"Right now."

Philip hung up the phone. He stood on the darkened street, wondering. Praying. Then he signaled a passing cab and headed for his hotel.

∧ ∧ ∧ ∧ ∧ ∧ ∧ ∧

"A message for you, Mr. Downs." The Dorset's night clerk handed Philip a telephone slip. *Please call (202) 879-04503.* The number was unfamiliar, the area code DC.

Philip dropped his jacket on the bed. Picked up the phone. Dialed Long Distance and punched in his calling card-number. The phone was answered on the first ring.

"Mr. Downs?" Chieko's voice was tight as a drum head.

"Chieko—where are you?"

"I'm in trouble, Mr. Downs." There were no background sound. Her voice told him there were other people in the room.

"What sort—"

"They'll tell you, Mr. Downs." He heard her speak off the phone, "It's him."

The voice that came on the telephone was precise. Intelligent. Almost pedantic, as the man explained, "Mr. Downs, there will be no serious trouble. We have a small matter of communication. Are you with me?"

"I don't know. Is Chieko—"

"She is quite safe, Mr. Downs. Quite comfortable." He didn't need to add, 'For the moment..'

"What do you want?"

"Very little, Sir. Simply confirmation. We have the name and address Miss Willensky has provided. If you confirm that these are genuine…there will be no further difficulty. Miss Willensky will be dropped at the Watergate in twenty minutes."

"What name? What address?" Whom were they looking for? It took a few seconds for Philip to realize what they were after.

"That is what you must tell us, Sir. If the name and address you give coincides with that provided by Miss Willensky….."

"But…" Philip was still baffled. The man's voice had remained impassive. He sounded too intelligent to make threats which were all too obvious. "…but there are *three* people."

Had he given Chieko away, with his "three people". Maybe she had tried to bluff them.

"Exactly." The man sounded pleased. "Your candor ensures Miss Willensky's comfort, Mr. Downs. And the three names? With addresses, please."

Philip tore open his attaché case. Flipped up the cover of his address book. One by one, Judas-like, he read out the names and addresses of the three men who had just given him the best gift of his life.

∧ ∧ ∧ ∧ ∧ ∧ ∧ ∧

Chapter 6

CHEVY CHASE, October 1990

The phone at Webster David's bedside had to ring four times before he answered. The late hour, Phil's voice, the background noise all signaled trouble.

"Where *are* you? I can hardly hear…"

"At a pay phone on Sixth Avenue. Look, I have to move fast. Can you get over to our place and talk with Leecie *outside* the house?"

"You're concerned about that bug."

"I need my red government passport. Leecie will know where it is. Enough laundry for two days. Right?"

"I'm making notes." Web scribbled on the pad on his night table. His wife was beginning to stir. He gave her a quick "not to worry" gesture.

"Leecie should meet me at Union Station. Three-oh-nine AM. My flight leaves Dulles at 7:25 AM."

"Money?"

"The credit card will do. I can get Deutschmarks at the airport. Could you explain to Kathie, Monday morning?"

"No problem. Anything else?"

"Chieko Willensky. Can you—"

"She called here. Around ten thirty."

"She's OK?"

"You're not her flavor of the month. Otherwise she sounded fine."

"Thank God. Can you think of anything else? I'm punchy…"

"What shall I tell Leecie?"

"I'll fill her in. At the station."

"Call me from Dulles, if you have time. I take it you enjoyed the reunion?"

"Your theory was dead right."

"That'll be reflected in my fee." Web looked at the time on the clock radio. "Don't miss your train."

∧ ∧ ∧ ∧ ∧ ∧ ∧ ∧

WASHINGTON, October 1990

Kathie's first telephone call on Monday morning was from that man whose voice sounded like the operetta she had seen on television—was it *Die Fledermaus* or *The Student Prince*?—Kiri Te Kanewa had been the leading lady.

"I'm sorry, Mr. Szilágyi. Mr. Downs is out of town. He'll be back Wednesday." The Hungarian's voice mesmerized Kathie. His calls made life an adventure.

"You could give him a message, my dear? Sometime today? Yes?"

"His plane won't land until after the office closes, Mr. Szilágyi—"

"He is out of the country?" *The Student Prince* became Dracula. His voice was ice on Kathie's spine. "*Where?*"

"I'm really not permitted to say, Mr. Szilágyi." She wondered what frightened the man so much. She wanted to tell him more. To offer him reassurance. But the rules....

"He never told me he would be out of the country." Tibor was talking to himself.

"I'm sorry, Mr. Szilágyi. As soon as Mr. Downs comes in on Wednesday...."

"Thank you, my dear." *The Student Prince* returned. "Do not trouble yourself, please. I will call again Wednesday. Yes?"

"I'll certainly tell Mr. Downs you called, Sir."

"Ah...yes. If you would be so kind. Yes."

˄ ˄ ˄ ˄ ˄ ˄ ˄ ˄

CHEVY CHASE, October 1990

"Have we met, Mr. Solagee? I don't seem to recall the—" Alicia Wentworth Downs often had to place people with exotic accents. But it was nearly midnight. She was suffering the effects of an evening of bridge with her parents.

"I am a colleague of Philip's, Mrs. Downs. We are engaged in a...diplomatic matter. Yes? Of some urgency. Yes? It is important that I get a message to Philip. You understand, dear lady. Yes?" The unique timbre of the voice, the insistent charm, were unfamiliar to her. She knew the type but could not place the individual.

"Of course, Mr. Solagee. He'll be back Tuesday evening. Is there somewhere he could call you, then?"

"Mrs. Downs, I am...*concerned*. Yes?...concerned that this little matter may not delay until Philip returns." He sounded as if he were trying not to frighten her. Which frightened her.

"I could try to reach him when his flight lands, if you feel it's that important, Mr. Solagee."

"I would be so grateful, Mrs. Downs. Yes?"

"What is your message, Mr. Solagee?" His assumption that she would panic annoyed her.

The man seemed to sense her annoyance. He shifted to a more earnest tone. "Mrs. Downs, Philip was seeking something. Possibly he has told you. Or not. Yes? To seek this object in America was…quite secure. Yes? If Philip is seeking this object *outside* America…."

"I see." Leecie's annoyance died. The fragmentary pause hung between them like a dagger.

"…he should discuss with me, first. Yes? Just a few suggestions I wish to make, Mrs. Downs. Before he proceeds. Yes?"

"Philip knows where to reach you, Mr. Solagee?" She was already leafing through the Yellow Pages.

"I will be waiting for his call, Mrs. Downs."

∧   ∧   ∧   ∧   ∧   ∧   ∧   ∧

FRANKFURT AM MAIN, October 1990

"I am most sorry, Mr. Downts hasn't answered to our paging." The Customer Service agent at the Delta desk ran a ball point down her clipboard. "The Dulles flight 219 landed at 7:34 AM. All persons will have passed through customs at this time. We would be happy to give Mr. Downts your message when he checks in for his return flight, if you wish?"

∧   ∧   ∧   ∧   ∧   ∧   ∧   ∧

NÜRNBERG, October 1990

The air was crisp as an apple. Bavarian blue skies made the tower in the old city, seen from the *Hauptbahnhof*, bright as a travel poster. Philip waited for his rental car to come to the curbside. There was a lingering suggestion of Oktoberfest in the air. The scent of hops and leather. A young woman in a green jacket and loden slacks was playing an accordion, her Tyrolean hat set out on the pavement for contributions. The girl finished playing a polka.

"*Kennen sie 'Lili Marlene'?*" Philip dropped a five mark piece into her upturned hat. The girl smiled, tried a few chords, felt her way into the ancient love/marching song.

Philip watched his car coming up the drive. His vision suddenly blurred. His eyes had begun to tear. The World War II melody brought him with unexpected force into some sort of touch with his father's memory. Might he at last have come to terms with the old man? Philip blinked his eyes, accepted the car keys. Over tipped. He settled in the Audi and started for the exit. The last notes of the accordion followed him, somber as autumn.

The *autobahn* South towards Feucht curved slowly through vast stretches of rolling country, pasture and woodlands now turning to fall's browns and greens. It was a drive through a series of picture postcards. Christmas-tree villages. Onion-domed churches. Winding streams. Rolling hills. The car radio delivered the world-wide *lingua franca* of rock music, interspersed with commercials in German. The Teutonic cadence sounded as if the announcer were ordering a torpedo launch.

At Feucht Philip turned on to Route Six and headed East. At the third exit he left the main highway and turned South again. It was necessary now to get out the small scale map. He checked the position. The schloss was clearly marked, on the forward slope of a large hill. He had about ten kilometers to go.

Philip recognized the schloss when it came into view. Lewis Davis had written the name and address on the back of a wallet-sized photo he had given Philip of the ancient building, the worn picture with a young girl on horseback in the foreground. The iron gates at the driveway stood open. The Audi climbed smoothly towards the house.

18th Century modifications had been made to a house/fortress that must have been Medieval. Windows had been enlarged or added. The arched doorway still suggested fortification. Philip parked on the graveled drive in front. The grounds looked deserted.

Philip got out of the car. Stretched away the stiffness of the drive. Surveyed the land that rolled away from the schloss. Down towards the roadside a horse was grazing. Philip looked along the driveway. Where the gravel ran around behind the house he saw the corners of outbuildings. Probably stables. There was a scent of hay and horse manure in the air. It was time to make himself known.

The bell pull was ornate, discolored, and stiff. He heard the bell echo inside the building. Footsteps. Slow. Regular. The heavy oaken door opened with less noise then he expected.

The woman who faced him was old. Her eyes gave Philip the impression that she was also disengaged. A person who lived in another time. Her look took him in without interest. When she smiled, only courtesy moved her face. She wore a dress expensively made, designed with a look of Nordic, almost Wagnerian, simplicity. She was standing with a cane.

"*Grüss Gott.*" She stepped back, with some effort, to let him enter. "You will be Mr. Duntz, I think?"

"*Grüss Gott.* Yes, Ma'am. I'm Philip Downs. Mr. Davis…"

"Yes. Lewis telephoned." Her vowels had a British roundness. The cadence of her words suggested English, rather than American, instruction.

She led Philip across a bare hall and into a small library. Light fell into the room from three floor-to-ceiling windows, polished the wide-boarded floor. A tea service stood on a small table in front of a leather couch. The aroma of toast and floor wax clung to the room. Toast, dusty books, dried leather. She indicated a chair for Philip. Seated herself on the couch. Positioned her cane with care against the cushions.

"May I offer you some coffee, Herr Duntz?"

"Thank you. I stopped on the way. But I appreciate your kindness."

"Not at all." She raised the silver pot and filled a small blue china cup for herself. She handled the china exactly as she spoke; as if in another time. For a few minutes she appeared content to drink her coffee in silence. To have Philip remain silent. She had the self-contained manner of a woman entirely satisfied with her own company.

"Ms. von Reichenberg—or should I call you Baroness?...."

She smiled again. This smile seemed almost to be in the present. "I think that is...unnecessary. You may call me Erda, if you like." Her use of 'may' instead of 'can' marked the era and origin of her English. It was the way Philip's mother would have spoken.

"Thank you. Erda, did Mr. Davis..." he wondered how much he should clarify. How much she might know already.

"Lewis explained. In his call. You will have to help me, I think, Mr. Downts." She placed her cup and saucer on the low mahogany table. She rose easily from the couch, but needed her cane to walk across the room. The trouble appeared to be with her left leg. Erda von Reichenberg made her way to a large, polished walnut cabinet, with drawers in the lower half. She rested her cane against a lower drawer. The large double doors in the upper part of the cabinet curved at their tops, to follow the line of ogee moulding that crowned the piece. The hinges protested as she drew the doors open. From the darkness within Philip heard a tiny squeal as the woman pulled out a small drawer. Her hand scrabbled for a moment inside the drawer. The knock of metal against the wood.

She shut the drawer. Closed the double doors of the cabinet. Picked up her cane and started across the room towards him. She nodded towards the doorway. "Probably, I should have my coat. If you would be so kind."

Philip saw a row of pegs set in a board at eye-level, to the left of the doorway. A faded loden-cloth garment hung on one peg. That must be the coat she wanted. He picked the coat from its peg. She stood while he draped the coat around her shoulders.

"Thank you. I have begun to feel the cold." She might have been speaking of the day, or of her advancing age. She led Philip back across the hallway, opened the massive oak door, walked out onto the drive.

They walked slowly along the gravel. The afternoon sun was bright but there was still a bite in the October air. Bird song carried over the crunch their shoes made on the gravel. From the distance some large animal—possibly a cow—gave a listless bellow. The dun horse continued to graze down by the roadside.

They strolled like two people out to enjoy the Fall afternoon. Her silence was strangely fluent. He sensed that she was fully aware of him, yet without interest in who or what he was. She did what politeness required, neither reluctantly nor eagerly. It felt to Philip as if they were characters from two entirely different novels, dropped by some literary accident into the same scene. Holden Caulfield, strolling with an Isak Dinesen heroine.

The building they approached was built like the house. Medieval proportions, with Age of Reason trimmings. It could have been a small chapel. It was actually a family tomb. The roof top had the same ogee outline as the mahogany cabinet back in the schloss. Coinstones had been added to the tomb's facade. The doorway had a raised, scalloped edge, painted in the faded yellow of the Austro-Hungarian Empire.

"You must help me, please." She handed him a large wrought-iron key.

Philip slid aside the escutcheon plate that covered the keyhole in the grilled doorway. The key went in easily. Greater effort was needed to turn the key in the lock. He pulled on the fluted iron ring to open the door. Metal groaned. The lower edge of the iron door scraped along a well-worn groove in the marble floor.

She led him inside. A splash of colored light, thrown through the stained glass window at the back of the mausoleum, fell onto the floor and one wall. Dust moats swam in the reds and blues of the probing beams. Chill air touched his face like the breath of mortality. He saw rows of marble shelves, stacked five high, on either side of the room. Marble slabs sealed most of the shelves. Each slab was engraved with letters in faded Fraktur; names difficult to read in the diffused light.

Several shelves stood open, empty. One mid-level shelf held a coffin of black wood, the polished lid dimmed by a layer of dust. Metal handles dulled by years of oxidation. The tarnished silver plate on the coffin had lettering that could still be made out. "Wilhelm Gottfried Freiherr von Reichenberg 1903—1947".

"You must open this for me." Her voice came as a shock. Philip had forgotten she was there. The marble walls resonated her words, hollowed her voice. In the brief instant between hearing her and understanding what she had said, Philip lost his sense of time and place. Friday he had been lunching at the Department cafeteria, among jovial peers. Now he was in the Bavarian foothills. Standing in a mausoleum. Being asked to open a coffin.

"It is quite all right, Mr. Downts." Her voice again rang from the walls, the briefest of echoes, giving added chill to her barren tone. "The Russians did not send back his body."

Philip hesitated. How did one open a coffin? He looked along the length of the moulded lid, trying to see a seam. The coffin had to open somewhere above the metal handles. Philip placed both palms under the double moulding that edged the lid. The smooth surface of the wood chilled his fingers. He pushed upwards. The lid gave slightly. Philip shifted himself closer to the ledge and spread his legs. Braced himself. Pushed up again. The lid rose further. A mustiness of rotted silk struck his nostrils. With a final effort, Philip forced the lid up, until it struck the bottom of the shelf above.

"Can you hold it just so? For only one moment?" She sounded doubtful. "Yes." Philip's word was a grunt. "I can."

"Thank you."

Philip heard a click as she placed her cane against a marble slab. She reached in to the darkness within the coffin. For a moment both her arms groped along the length of the box. Then she straightened up and drew out a small bundle.

"Thank you."

With immense relief, Philip let the lid fall back into place. The coffin closed with a hollow "crump"; a note struck on an enormous bass viol. His arms seemed to leap up, freed from the weight of the coffin lid. Dust swam in the soft red and blue light.

"This will be what you seek." Erda von Reichenberg held out the bundle to him. He reached for it automatically. She took up her cane. She had placed in his hands a coarse canvas bag, marked S S—he had seen such bags in the mailroom at the Department—inside which he could feel a solid rectangular object. The object felt as if it were wrapped or cushioned with something soft.

∧   ∧   ∧   ∧   ∧   ∧   ∧   ∧

The glow of success flowed cheerily through Philip's body. The Audi's motor purred. The Bavarian scenery slid past like a three-D travelogue. Battalions of conifers marched up the hillsides. Baroque puffs of cumulus cloud drifted in a sky of Bavarian blue. A toy-sized church, looking from the distance like a toy beneath a Christmas tree, threw a lengthening shadow across a miniature graveyard. It could have been a *trompe-l'oeil* painting from the 19th century, except for a two-man helicopter that buzzed lazily along the horizon.

Success. The feeling rang through Philip's head like church bells. Each onion-domed church he passed, as the Audi whizzed along the autobahn, seemed to give out peals of jubilant congratulation. Philip had done it. He had the—but what did he have, exactly? Was the icon really lying on the front seat beside him, inside that canvas bag? The dusty smell of the worn canvas filled the car. Was it the smell of success? Or another failure?

Philip let the elation run through him for another moment. He knew that soon the worm of doubt would stir. Right. Called from its lair, the worm went immediately to the weakness in the situation. What, in fact, *was* in the bag? The opera would not be over until the miraculous icon appeared. He could open the bag now. Verify that he had finally recovered the Mother of God of St. Emeric's.

Would he know, even then? The painting—if indeed he found a painting in the bag—might be a fake. Only an expert such as Dr. Burns would really know. If Philip opened the bag now, and later the icon proved to be fake, he might be suspected of—Inside his head Philip suddenly heard his father's voice, mouthing a single word: prudence. The bag was sealed. The bag by all appearances had not been opened for decades. To open it now, here, with no witnesses, simply was not prudent. Philip might find that the icon—if indeed the icon was inside—had become stuck to the cloth over the years. Would need expert handling, to avoid serious damage. If the Mother of God of St. Emeric was to come to light after 45 years or more, it was only prudent that the revelation take place before qualified expert witnesses. If the bag did *not* hold the icon, then it was *especially* important that witnesses be present, to confirm that Philip had delivered the bag unopened, intact. This was the delivered opinion of Major P. C. Downs, Esquire, deceased. Unfortunately for Philip, it made good sense.

Yet to be this *close*. Not to know. Philip looked ahead along the autobahn for a pull-over spot. Nothing in sight. The roadway was cut into the side of a steep incline. Not an easy place to pull over. Still, the highway was nearly empty. Only a fat grey Mercedes drifting in his wake. He would wait and pull into the next rest area. Open the bag. Face the truth. End his doubts.

If the icon wasn't there...he smiled. Grim. Whom the Gods would destroy, they first raise up. Or was it that the Gods made you mad? Whatever. Philip felt himself the focal point of a strange, narrow history. He was in possession—*might* be in possession—of the catalyst for serious political events. The icon he *thought* he had might tip the balance in a Hungarian election. Just as Tibor said.

By returning the Mother of God Philip would close a circle of fifty years or more. He would complete a chain of circumstance that ran back into his father's time. Right through the war his father had fought. Across the very ground his father's foe had inhabited. He smiled, rueful. Philip Downs, man of destiny.

The road was climbing, instead of descending. The drop-off to his right became steeper. In the valley below a stream sparkled through neatly bordered fields and snaked into a woodland. Where would the next rest area be? He reached down at the dusty sack on the passenger side seat. Carefully felt the rough canvas. Turned to glance at the contour of the bag holding—what?

Krackk! *Slapp*! The noise struck in two startling blows. The bullet tore through the side window with a sharp *snick*, instantly followed by the duller blast from the gun muzzle.

In the fraction of a second it took Philip to duck, he glimpsed the body of the grey Mercedes. The massive machine loomed in front, like a shark filling the lens of a face mask. Philip's foot moved instinctively to the brake pedal. The Audi bucked. Shuddered. He swung the car wildly, dodging the Mercedes as it forced him towards the looming valley below.

He released the brake just as the Audi went out of control. He twisted the wheel. Let the car regain balance. Saw the Mercedes ahead, jockeying for another pass at him.

Philip felt himself go out of his body. He watched dispassionately as his corporeal self went through the motions of survival. His mind moved with unnatural speed, presenting him in micro-seconds with information he didn't know he had. His right hand already gripped the lever of the handbrake.

The grey Mercedes was making a slow swing to the left. He knew the Mercedes had enough weight and mass to ram his Audi over the edge. He remembered, crazily, watching a TV game show, where celebrity contestants had guess to which was the real Hollywood stunt driver, who appeared with two impostors. One celebrity had tested the putative stuntmen by asking each how a speeding car is suddenly reversed 180 degrees. The real stuntman explained that they pulled on the handbrake, which skidded the car into an about face.

Philip guided the Audi to the center of the roadway. He jerked the handbrake until his shoulder throbbed. The tires screamed. The car whirled out of control. The valley swam across his windshield, past the snow-flake pattern the bullet had smashed in the shatterproof glass. The road behind careened into view.

Philip squeezed the brake release button. Freed the brake lever. He pressed the accelerator with care, frightened of stalling the engine. The Audi stopped shaking. The road ahead looked clear. He tore around the curve, eyes strained for oncoming traffic.

A glance at the mirror. The grey Mercedes not yet in sight. If he could avoid a head-on crash...Make it off the next "on" ramp. Get within sight of other traffic. A town. Anything. The steering wheel felt slippery in his hands. Sweat had popped out on his face, spread down his back. He was gulping breaths like a long-distance runner.

The first car he met horned madly, then swerved left to avoid him. Did they have a CB radio? Would they call the highway police? He pushed the Audi to top speed. Where was the last on-ramp he had passed? Hadn't there been an on-ramp a kilometer or so earlier?

He didn't know the roads. Would the Mercedes risk running against traffic? Or would they try for the exit ahead? Back track, to catch him? The next vehicle he faced was a truck. The driver's jaw dropped as Philip sped by. The doppler sound of the truck's horn wiped past Philip's ears.

He glanced in the rear view mirror. The truck disappeared around the curve in the autobahn, as the grey Mercedes pulled into view.

How long before they overtook him? Philip strained at the road ahead. Willing an on-ramp to appear. Sweating to think of a move. Any move. To keep them from closing with him. Then the edge of the ramp showed. Just ahead. Possibly the gunmen in the Mercedes hadn't yet seen the ramp. Philip kept the Audi heading straight. He would swerve towards the ramp at the last second.

Another glance. His eyes went to the mirror, drawn by the fascination of fear. The Mercedes was still out of pistol range. He knew they must be natives. They would probably know the on-ramp was coming.

Philip braced himself. Tore the wheel over. Felt the Audi shudder and slide right. As the Audi floated towards the edge of the on-ramp Philip felt a deep resignation. If his car plowed through the guard rail and rolled down the embankment.... Then he felt the tires grip the road surface. The Audi straightened. Leaped forward like a thoroughbred released from the starting gate.

This was the critical moment. The on-ramp was too narrow for cars to pass. If he met someone coming on...Please God, he prayed. The Audi seemed to be moving in slow motion. Then the connecting road came into sight.

No time to pick a direction. Philip kept the Audi turned in the curve started along the on-ramp. Held his speed. He burst onto the secondary roadway. Yanked the wheel. The car flung over to the right lane. Ahead was open road. Behind...the grey Mercedes moved smoothly along in his rear view mirror. Stable. Tenacious. On its own home ground.

The roadway wound ahead. Philip had time to think. There was nothing to think. They were out to kill him. This was not America. Tibor's assurance had no meaning here. Unless...they wanted the icon. To sell? To keep the icon from going back to Hungary? If he could ditch the icon—throw it out the car window...

The Audi charged around a curve in the road. A stand of pine trees shaded the road ahead. The smell of pine needles whipped into the car as Philip sped into the shadow. A bright sunny stretch of road opened. Ahead, the road curved sharply into a cluster of stone farm houses. He turned the Audi. Philip looked at the mirror. The grey Mercedes was out of sight. When he looked back at the roadway his foot jumped reflexively to the brake pedal. A flock of sheep packed the road, where it ran between two large stone barns.

He heard his brakes squeal. There was nowhere to turn. Then from out of the edge of his vision leaped a large Alsatian. The dog charged at the flock. Nipped one of the sheep. Jumped ahead. Nipped another sheep. The flock split. Flowed left and right. The Alsatian raced along the gap. Nipping the flock farther apart. Widening a path for the Audi. The Audi sped through the flock like the Children of Israel.

Philip pushed the car up to speed again. Twisted around the curve. Felt a blow as the Audi struck the edge of a farm wagon, parked half onto the roadway. Saw the Mercedes slide into the right-hand rear-view mirror. Steady, relentless as a dorsal fin cleaving the water. Another thwack! A bullet burst through the rear window of the Audi.

He was out of time. Out of space. Out of luck. The Audi was not responding well to the wheel. Philip's mind was separating himself further from the scene. He watched his hands on the wheel as if someone else controlled them. A farmyard popped up like a film-clip in a newsreel.

The Audi limped and banged across the farmyard. A bucket whanged! out of his path. Another thwack. A farm implement? A bullet? He saw a cattle path, leading between two sheds. Space too narrow for the Mercedes. The Audi might just clear it. The wheel responded almost enough. The Audi bucked and twisted between the sheds. The right hand door mirror flicked off. The car fought along the trail. Slammed through a cattle gate. Banged Philip's left shoulder. Fought against the steering wheel like a roped steer.

The woodlot wasn't far across the pasture. If the pasture weren't too soft.... The Audi took to the turf with a pitch and roll. Bounced past a salt lick. Ground up the slope towards the trees. The Mercedes was not in sight. He had gained a few seconds. If he could ram the Audi into the woods. Abandon the car. Leave the sack. That was what they wanted. The sack. It wasn't likely they would continue to chase him. Not once they had the icon. He could disappear into the woods. Lay low. Creep out under cover of darkness.

Careful! Don't plunge too far into the trees. Leave enough clearance to open the car door. He twisted the Audi's wheel. The car's rear banged against a thick pine trunk. Bounced. Skidded to a halt on the bed of pine needles.

The door stuck. Wedged by the impact with the tree trunk. He flung himself at the passenger door. Crawled over the canvas sack. Felt the sack dragged along with his foot as he gripped the door edge. Pulled himself out. Fell to the forest floor. Through the trees, he could see two figures moving across the pasture on foot. Their shadows stretched along the slope. Their

deliberate walk held his eyes. He tore his look away. Scanned the stand of trees for a path. A break in the pines.

Philip rose from the ground. The Stars & Stripes dispatch bag lay at his feet. Success. Now to be abandoned. To save his skin. All the sweat. The good luck. The twisted trails. The begging. Gone. He heard a chopper pass over the treetops. Christ—if had an M-16 for just thirty seconds!

With his detached view, he watched himself reach down and scoop up the canvas bag. He saw himself run through the stand of pines. Shielding his face from the low hanging branches with an upraised arm. Quick looks. A gap on his left. A sudden slap from a branch. A shower of needles as the branch sprang back. He could taste the rosin.

How deep were these woods? There must be a field on the other side. Now it was a matter of how far he could run. How fit his pursuers might be. Philip slowed. It was important to move through the trees without leaving a trail. No broken twigs. No bent branches. The woods darkened. The tree trunks grew closer together. He had to move with care. Slower. But the cover was deeper.

Philip stopped. Set the dispatch bag down. Fell to his knees. The soil was loose beneath his fingers as he scooped a depression in the earth. He planted the dispatch bag. Covered the bag with soil. Ruffled the surface. Scraped up a fistful of pine needles. Sprinkled the needles carefully to hide the disturbed earth. He mentally marked the position of the buried icon from a twisted pine with one hanging branch. Then he moved swiftly away, into the gathering darkness.

Philip calculated rapidly as he twisted and turned through the trees. If he could elude them until darkness...There must be a village nearby. Later he would retrieve the icon. If they caught him, he could use the hidden icon to bargain for his life.

Two shots sounded from the woods. A third shot. Small caliber. They must be trying to panic him. Flush him like a pheasant. But he could tell from the small arms fire how far back they still were. The shots helped him, more than his pursuers.

At last he stopped again. There was a shallow defile. He could hide from view. Still have a line of retreat. They would have to stalk him cautiously. They would know he had no weapon. But there were only two of them. They might worry about his jumping them from behind. His best chance was to wait for darkness. Finding him in the dark would be harder. Harder still to shoot accurately. And if they split up to stalk him—but that wasn't likely. There was too much chance one of them would accidentally shoot the other. They were too professional to risk that.

Philip's body moved with the reflexes drilled in by the Army. His fingers scraped a pat of the dark soil. Smeared the damp earth across his cheeks. Over his chin. He squirmed down into the detritus of the forest floor. Philip's senses slowly spread out. The pitchy odor of the pine woods. Animal droppings. The slow, regular movement of the treetops. The chatter of birds. His instinct formed a perimeter of sound. Waiting for footsteps. But the ground was soft. By the time he heard anything, they would be almost on him.

A twig snapped. Ahead to his right. A branch whooshed back into place. A crackle as something crushed a dead pine cone. My God, they were careless. Making as much noise as possible. Were they *that* certain of overpowering him?

The last light of day was slipping from the forest. There was just enough luminance to outline the men whose shapes rose slowly into view. Tall. Hatless. Walking easily. The man stopped. Looked around. Raised his arms. Cupped his hands around his mouth.

"Philip…! It's time to come out! Phil—! Can you hear me?"

The man turned to his left. Repeated the call. Turned to his right. "Phil! Don't waste our time! Come on out!"

The voice was almost familiar. The accent middle-class American. Slightly Southern.

"For God's sake, Phil! It's me!" The voice, exasperated-amused, sounded again. "It's Walter. Walter *Winslow*!"

∧ ∧ ∧ ∧ ∧ ∧ ∧ ∧

WASHINGTON, DC November 1990

"Dr. Burns has just arrived, Mr. Downs. Mr. Reid wondered if you could come to his office now, please." Reid's secretary was adept at making an order sound like a request.

"I'll be right there, Sarah. Thanks."

Philip hung up his phone and stretched. He was still jet-lagged. There was an annoying fuzziness in his perceptions as he walked down the hallway to the elevators. He felt quite clearly that he had played it just right. He had sent the bundle, unopened, in the diplomatic pouch from Frankfurt direct to Reid. Philip wanted to watch Reid's face, if the bundle should contain only.... what? A fake? No picture at all? A set of crumbling news dispatches? Filthy postcards? Philip chuckled so loudly that he got a look from a clerk in the elevator. Philip stopped for a moment outside Reid's office. He tried to clear from his head the hysterical notion of Reid, faced with a selection of 50-year-old filthy postcards. It was time for dead seriousness. Philip took a deep breath. Then he stepped into the office.

Dr. Burns was seated in one of Reid's large leather chairs. He recognized Philip. Rose to shake hands.

"This is really Phil's show." Reid moved to the table where the bundle, arrived in the morning's pouch, lay waiting. "We should let him do the honors." Reid couldn't keep his hands off the bundle. The rough canvas bag was stenciled with two large letters: "S S". Probably for Stars & Stripes. The bag carried a smell of aged wood and varnish—a souvenir of 45 years in a coffin. Rope the thickness of clothesline held the bag shut at the top. The rope was cinched by a metal clasp. The lever that opened the clasp was stuck shut with a large blob of dark red sealing wax. Philip was reminded of the seal on a Benedictine bottle. A pine needle was still stuck in a twist of the rope.

Reid set aside his cigarette. Turned the clasp in his fingers. Studied the seal impressed in the dark red wax.

"What d'you suppose that is?" Philip looked closely at the impression in the wax. It was the rampant lion from Lewis Davis's signet ring. "A family coat of arms. Probably Welsh." Philip couldn't resist the urge to flaunt his heraldic knowledge. He was careful not to mention Lewis Davis in front of Dr. Burns.

Reid got a bronze letter opener from his desk and presented it to Philip. "Time to take a look."

"Time, indeed." Philip used the point of the opener to flake away the sealing wax. He pried up the metal catch that held the rope tight. The rope was dried, stiffened, set in the shape in which the clasp had held it for years.

Philip needed to give several strong tugs before he could free the rope from the clasp. Finally, he was able to open the top of the pouch. He reached inside, felt a rough material wrapped around a rectangular object. When he drew the object out the grayish material was easy to unfold, though it held the creases of forty-plus years. What looked like the back of a much varnished, hand-hewn board was facing Philip.

Philip hesitated. Might the other surface, if it did indeed have a painting on it, be stuck to the blanket material? He turned to Dr. Burns.

Burns evidently had seen more in the rough back of the board than Philip or Reid. He was leaning over the darkened wood surface, eyes narrowed with interest. Philip stepped back to let Burns have a closer look at the object. Like a person in a dream, Burns reached out. Took the board with his fingertips. Raised it ever so gently. The blanket material dropped to the table.

Slowly, like a man removing the fuse from a 500 pound bomb, Burns turned the other surface of the board upwards. He caught his breath. His voice was barely audible as he breathed two words.

"*My God….*"

Philip looked at Reid. Reid was intent on Dr. Burns. Burns was now shaking his head in wonder. "Magnificent. Truly magnificent."

His voice came up to full volume as he spoke to Reid and Philip. With reverence in every move, Burns placed the icon upright against the lamp on Reid's table.

"It's a classic, gentlemen." He stood back a pace. His eyes never left the Mother and Child. "You see how the artist has given particular importance to contour. Rather than dimension. The magnificence of the line….." Burns's voice quivered with his passion for the skill of the artist.

Philip was struck by the sensitivity of the Mother's face. Despite the ancient, stylized robe, Her face was as familiar as a woman seen in a news magazine; one of those tragic mothers clutching a dead child in Lebanon, or the shawled face of a trapped miner's wife, waiting at the pithead.

The Child looked up at His Mother with intense communion. He saw Her pain. He saw beyond Her pain. He saw that She would have no escape from Her destiny and He loved Her as an earthly child loves an earthly mother. Though clearly He was the Son of God. These truths the artist revealed. All in a few square inches. On a gessoed piece of hand-hewn wood.

"It's genuine, then?" Reid's question drew Burns out of his concentration.

"Genuine?" Dr. Burns sounded puzzled. He had not understood just how ignorant Reid and Philip were. How little they knew of the characteristics and techniques that would verify an icon by period and type. "It's a Theophanes, almost assuredly."

Philip noticed that Dr. Burns had dropped his usual cautionary hedges. That alone convinced Philip they had found the real icon.

"But is it the picture *we* want?" Reid insisted.

"The one you want?" Dr. Burns was again at a loss. He was used to dealing with the uninitiated. He was not prepared to cope with utter savages. "It's a *Theophanes*. 14th Century. A miracle." He took his eyes from the icon at last. Burns turned to Reid. "Which miracle *did* you want?"

"Philip can tell you better." Reid turned to Philip and waited.

"Yes. Well, actually..." Philip tried to be apologetic, yet not sound as if he were apologizing for Reid. "The Mother of God of St. Emeric. From the Hungarian Church of St. Emeric. At Nádudvar."

Burns nodded. "I see. Well...I'd have to consult my texts.... can't carry everything in my head, of course." He shook his head sadly, a prophet among the heathen. "You've got a treasure here. Probably painted in Novgorod. Late 14th, early 15th century. In the centuries since, this may have been in many different places. An exact idea of the provenance would take time to search out."

"But, it *is* genuine." Reid was grasping for what certainty the Dr. would allow.

"In the sense that you mean, yes. It is genuine." Dr. Burns had turned back to the icon again. He had left the world of the uncultured. He was absorbing the emotions caught by an artist in the age when this image of Mother and Child was worshiped as the very embodiment of those holy figures. "*Sperandarum substantia rerum, argumentum non apparentium.*"

"I'm afraid my Latin's a bit rusty, Dr. Burns." Philip smiled at Reid. Without taking his eyes from the icon, Dr. Burns translated: "Faith gives substance to our hopes, and makes us certain of realities we do not see."

∧ ∧ ∧ ∧ ∧ ∧ ∧ ∧

Professor Gordon stepped off the Metroliner. Shook hands with Philip. Let himself be led through the flow of passengers. Past the rows of shops and newsstands. The vapors of fast food. They made their way to the Department limousine. Philip held the door open. Got in beside the Professor.

"My boss wants to be dead sure. Before we send it to the White House...."

"Hmmn." Gordon chuckled. He was no stranger to organizational politics. The penalties of professional embarrassment.

"If it should be the wrong one..." Philip felt the familiar sag. The imminent departure of success.

"I'll never tell."

"You wouldn't—" But then he saw that Gordon was joking.

"No. I wouldn't lie." Professor Gordon smiled. "Not even for the White House."

∧ ∧ ∧ ∧ ∧ ∧ ∧ ∧

"So you have succeeded. Yes?" Tibor Szilágyi's voice on the telephone was so enthusiastic that Philip had to hold the receiver slightly away from his ear.

"In a manner of speaking. Yes." Philip wondered if the Hungarian understood that Philip was now in the background. That superior forces had taken over. That the project had passed up to higher levels, who never even knew Philip had been involved. Did Tibor realize that Philip could no longer do anything for him? "I'm afraid I'm pretty much out of it now, Tibor."

"The 'Captains and the Kings depart'. Yes?" Tibor's voice smiled. Philip had forgotten how acute the man was. The lessons of survival he must have learnt.

"The 'shouting and the tumult' will come when Bush goes to Europe, Tibor. I'm out of it."

"None the less, you are the 'founder of the feast', I think. Yes?" Tibor's voice twinkled.

"Did you major in English Lit, Tibor?"

"A compliment. Yes?" Then the Hungarian's voice dropped into a different register; another man spoke from Tibor's chest. "At one period in my career, I had much time for reading."

"And they let you have books?" Philip knew there could be only one explanation for Tibor's extensive reading time.

"Only decadent Western writings. It amused them to think they were punishing me." The Tibor voice familiar to Philip returned. "But enough about reading. I have arranged—quite informally, yes?—that you should have a small decoration."

"You never fail to surprise me, Tibor." A Hungarian Order of Merit. Every Yale man's dream.

"There will be no formalities. Yes? Only our gratitude for what you have accomplished."

"Thank you very much."

"A small return. A very *small* return, for what you have done, my friend. But we will leave the big moments to others. Yes?" Tibor's voice had turned conspiratorial. The two of them were small players in the larger drama that would take place, among the presidential visits, the diplomatic receptions, the cavalcade of photo opportunities.

"Yes, Tibor. We'll leave the big moments to others."

∧   ∧   ∧   ∧   ∧   ∧   ∧   ∧

Emeritus Professor Douglas W. Gordon, Ph.D., sat in the Faculty Room idly turning the pages of TIME Magazine, as he waited for his luncheon guest. Several pages into the editorial matter a small headline caught his eye:

> MIRACULOUS ICON RETURNS TO HUNGARY
> The Mother of God of St. Emeric, a 14th century religious icon credited with miracles as diverse as averting plague and turning back Moslem invaders, will be returned to the Church of St. Emeric in Nádudvar, Hungary, when President Bush makes his first trip behind the formerly Iron Curtain early next year.
> The miraculous icon, looted by Nazi forces fleeing the Red Army in 1945, came to light earlier this year from a source that the White House has declined to name. But like many valuable works of art that disappeared at the end of World War II in Europe, the St. Emeric Mother of God was probably in the possession of an American soldier who....."

Gordon wondered. What would Theophanes have thought of such an outcome? Could that gifted visionary of the 14th century have imagined one of his paintings involved in the ending of the cold war? Yes. Gordon decided that Theophanes could all too well have understood the power struggles of the 20th Century. The Greek/Cypriot artist would certainly have known the bitter conflict between the iconoclasts and iconophiles, that had almost split the Eastern church. A man who journeyed from Cyprus to Constantinople and Moscow in the 14th Century would be no stranger to the brutalities of power. Theophanes would not have had the commissions that he did have, without being close to, acutely aware of, the sources of earthly might. Which made it even more remarkable to Gordon that such a sensitive man, working in such a cruel atmosphere, could create delicate images with so much spiritual force. Or was Theophanes simply another gifted monster, like Picasso, George Simenon, or Alfred Speer?

Gordon saw his guest arrive in the lobby. He laid aside the copy of TIME. As he rose to greet his guest, Gordon tucked into the back of his mind a resolve. He would make his own journey. While there was still time and health left to him. He could follow the route taken by Theophanes. Cyprus. Constantinople—where they had recently uncovered some interesting 12th Century mosaics. Moscow would be easy of access now, with the cold war melting. Theophanes had worked there in the Cathedral of the Annunciation. On his way home from Moscow, Gordon thought to himself, he and Janis could come through Hungary. Would the Church re-consecrate the Mother of God when the icon returned to St. Emeric's? An interesting liturgical question. And those extraordinary eyes! Possibly Theophanes had indeed seen that portrait of the Virgin Saint Luke was said to have painted from life. Gordon wished to look, one last time, into those extraordinary eyes he had first seen in the moonlight, along the Donau on Regensburg road, in 1945.

∧ ∧ ∧ ∧ ∧ ∧ ∧ ∧

Lewis Davis moved carefully up the worn steps to the attic. The Davises had added bats of fiber-glass insulation between the rafters, back in the seventies, during the oil shortage. Where the attic floor met the slope of the roof, a few inches of hand-hewn beam still showed. There was enough light from the small square windows at each end of the attic for him to navigate through the collection of hat boxes, trunks, Victorian chairs, electric fans, crib and bassinet.

Davis dragged out the square khaki-painted box with the metal handles. The box had originally held a U. S. Army Signal Corps signal generator. He had picked the box up in Northern France in '45 and used it as a small footlocker. There was dust over the top. He opened the catches, from which the paint had almost entirely faded. Inside the box Davis had saved everything important from his army experience. A handful of *Stars & Stripes* shoulder patches. Some 4 x 5 negatives taken when off duty. A switch cover-plate he'd unscrewed from inside the turret of a Panther tank—the plate was still coated with luminescent paint, designed to glow for a few minutes until the tank crew's vision adapted to the inside of the closed turret. The Krauts had used good materials. The cover-plate still glowed when Davis moved it from the sunlight back into the shadow.

There was a packet of Erda's letters, from 1946 and 1947. He compared them with the letter that had arrived this morning. Her handwriting was unchanged. He opened the letter for the third time. The lines of writing, precise, evenly spaced, might have been written when they both were young. His eyes ran down to the sentences that mattered. "We both have had our own lives and our own experiences, for more than forty years, and I am glad I came through it.

"Now I am glad and happy with this quiet live. I do not want any more. I do not hope, I hurt you with this letter, but this is my opinion.

"Love, Erda"

Lewis refolded her letter. Slipped it in the blue envelope with the German airmail stamps. Struggling with a feeling he neither understood nor chose to endure, Lewis laid her letter with the others. Closed the olive-drab box. Slid his WW II memories back beneath the sloping roof. Climbed slowly down the stairs and closed the attic door.

∧ ∧ ∧ ∧ ∧ ∧ ∧ ∧

Arthur Caldwell had a long-established practice of enjoying a leisurely breakfast on Saturday mornings, before he strolled to the Short Hills Club for a half-hour on the putting green. He had the week's mail in front of him. He divided the letters and catalogues into three piles: junk mail, financial matters, and real mail—those letters addressed by hand or coming from a demonstrably personal return address.

Caldwell read the real mail first. Two letters. One from his grandson, Arthur III, thanking Caldwell for his birthday present, a two-volume biography of George C. Marshall. Young Arthur wrote very clearly for a child of nine. The second letter, postmarked San Diego, was a birth announcement from Betsy's younger daughter—the one he had helped get a scholarship to Wellesley. Mrs. Ursula Johnson was now a grandmother. Betsy, if she had lived, would be a great-grandmother. Warm memories of a cut loaf, stirring in Caldwell's mind, substantially increased the size of the check he decided to send as a baby present.

The letter from the White House was in the second pile. Caldwell had surmised that the envelope would contain a richly flattering appeal for funds from the Republican National Committee. Nothing in the White House letterhead or the letter's form of address contradicted his assumption. The first paragraph thanked him for his vital assistance, which Arthur took to mean the $1,000 contribution made at tax time this year. The second paragraph—where Caldwell confidently expected to find the artful plea for further assistance—gave him pause.

"In a vital matter of international import, the key role you played is recognized and appreciated by me personally, as well as by those at the U.S. Department of State, for whom, I understand, you provided crucial assistance in a sensitive matter.

"As one 'old soldier' to another, I thank you for once again going beyond the call of duty to serve the interests of your nation.

With gratitude,
  George Bush"

The signature looked hand done. Not the machine-inscribed autograph that concluded the usual begging letter. What was Bush talking about? That painting that Gordon and Davis had turned up, back in '45? Most likely. That meant that the youngster from the State Department had been genuine. Good. Caldwell had judged the boy correctly. All's well that ends, Caldwell told himself. Especially if it ends in Republican hands. Caldwell rose from the table. He wanted to start his walk to the club before that old wound in his knee began to predict the weather. Caldwell propped the presidential letter on the mantelpiece where it would remind him, when he got back from the Club, to send the National Committee another check. Bush was doing a good job. The fruits of military experience were paying off in the White House.

∧ ∧ ∧ ∧ ∧ ∧ ∧ ∧

The death notice in *The New York Times* was succinct:

> DIED: Huberman, Uwe, 73, Founder-President of HB Pharmaceuticals, at his home in Princeton, N.J. on December 14th. Survived by two sons, Eric U. and Alois W., both of Princeton, and a daughter, Mrs. Harrison Lauck, of Saddle River, N.J. Interment private. Memorial contributions may be sent to the American Cancer Society.

∧ ∧ ∧ ∧ ∧ ∧ ∧ ∧

WASHINGTON, 1990

Philip left the office a bit early for lunch. He wanted time to think before he had to face a meal with Leecie at the Smithsonian Associates dining room. As he crossed 21st street and turned towards the Mall a half-familiar figure came trundling towards the State Department office building. The man walked like Tibor Szilágyi but the suit was new, well cut.

The sight of Tibor startled Philip—had he forgotten a lunch date with the Hungarian? But the man was carrying flowers. Surely—and then Philip saw Chieko Willensky come out the Department's main doorway. She took Tibor's arm and the pair headed up 21st street.

Philip walked slowly towards the edge of the mall. Winter was here. The clear air pushed coldly against his face. The late morning sun warmed him through the back of his coat. The morning air was almost free of auto exhaust.

"We'll keep a low profile." Reid had said. That meant no public acknowledgment of Philip's part in finding the icon. Credit would go elsewhere. To Reid, probably. Or one of the blow-dried gophers at the White House. "But what you've done won't go unrewarded." The lack of specificity in Reid's promise told Philip just how small the reward was likely to be. Reid had the politician's skill of getting as much as possible for giving the least. Preferably *nothing*.

Philip took the note out of his pocket and read it for the fifth or sixth time.

"Dear Phil:

I wanted you to hear this from me, before the official announcement. The Secretary has decided that Bob Wacker should take over the Austrian Desk, in October. This decision was taken by the Secretary some months ago and communicated to me only yesterday. However I informed him of your good work on the Hungarian matter, and he assures me that your success will be remembered and augurs well for your future in the Department.

The Secretary and I both value your talents and the contributions you have made.

With gratitude,
    Morris"

The note was classic Reid. Even down to the first-name-only signature, meant to suggest intimacy and candor. Philip suddenly understood the sort of man Franklin Roosevelt must have been.

Philip looked across the mall at the red brick towers of the Smithsonian castle. Once again, success had eluded him. He was empty handed. Reid might—doubtless would—short change him again in the future. Why, then, did Philip feel so content? He took a seat on a park bench to consider the question. Settled himself deeper into his overcoat. Continued to ponder.

Looking over the past months, Philip searched for the roots of this unreasonable satisfaction. His mind ran back along the blind trails. The men encountered. The final moment in that chill Bavarian mausoleum, when the old lady had put the icon directly into his hands. All he could summon up was the memory of eyes. Voices. Faces. The way he had watched so many eyes shift from the present back into the past. That "retro-vision" effect He remembered Zimmerman's inward turning look when summoning up a memory of Lewis Davis at the lunch table in the Stars & Stripes billet, using his soup spoon correctly. Philip heard again the time-shift in Davis's voice, as the trust officer became once more a young cameraman on *The Stars & Stripes*. Walter Winslow's wistful recall of the last days of the war, the occupation of Germany. The change in Arthur Caldwell's eyes as they flicked back to 1945 for a few illuminating seconds, then returned to the table at the Stars & Stripes reunion. The Bavarian woman in her ancient schloss, whose eyes showed no change at all, probably because she had never left those years for the present.

Philip realized that in some way he could not yet define he had joined these men, in an event of those years when his father had been leading a company of tanks for Patton. Gordon, Davis, Caldwell and the others had been his father's peers. Possibly even encountered his father. They had all, even the Bavarian woman, shared his father's war.

Philip himself had brought an episode of those dark and distant times to a climax. He had caught an echo of St. Crispin's day. The small black and white photo on the wall in his den was no longer an icon beside which his own accomplishments forever paled. The picture was of flesh and blood with whom in some degree he now had shared an experience. His father had become simply another man. No longer a Deity. Philip was at peace with his father's memory. This serenity, he decided, was worth more to him than the Austrian desk. Far more. Because the feeling would last Philip the rest of his life.

Looking backwards, making his own "retro-vision", it appeared to Philip almost as if the Gods, with an artfulness beyond any psychotherapist, had laid a revealing path for him. Tibor Szilágyi. Dr. Burns. Menelakos. Earl Dent. Huberman. Lewis Davis. Douglas Gordon. Arthur Caldwell. Erda von Reichenberg. Each of them in their way—all of them, together—had led him to the icon. To Her. And then, for Philip, She, the Mother of God of St. Emeric, had worked another miracle.

# # #

About the Author

❀

D. L. Eynon is a writer whose work has appeared regularly in The New York Times, The Atlantic Monthly, LOOK Magazine, Esquire, PUNCH, and on NBC Matinee Theater.